MURDER FOR GOOD

*Further titles by Veronica Heley
from Severn House*

The Ellie Quicke mysteries

MURDER AT THE ALTAR
MURDER BY SUICIDE
MURDER OF INNOCENCE
MURDER BY ACCIDENT
MURDER IN THE GARDEN
MURDER BY COMMITTEE
MURDER BY BICYCLE
MURDER OF IDENTITY
MURDER IN HOUSE
MURDER BY MISTAKE
MURDER MY NEIGHBOUR
MURDER IN MIND
MURDER WITH MERCY
MURDER IN TIME
MURDER BY SUSPICION
MURDER IN STYLE
MURDER FOR NOTHING
MURDER BY SUGGESTION
MURDER FOR GOOD

The Bea Abbot Agency mysteries

FALSE CHARITY
FALSE PICTURE
FALSE STEP
FALSE PRETENCES
FALSE MONEY
FALSE REPORT
FALSE ALARM
FALSE DIAMOND
FALSE IMPRESSION
FALSE WALL
FALSE FIRE
FALSE PRIDE
FALSE ACCOUNT

MURDER FOR GOOD

Veronica Heley

This first world edition published 2019
in Great Britain and the USA by
SEVERN HOUSE PUBLISHERS LTD of
Eardley House, 4 Uxbridge Street, London W8 7SY.
Trade paperback edition first published
in Great Britain and the USA 2020 by
SEVERN HOUSE PUBLISHERS LTD.

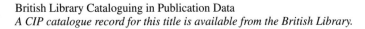

British Library Cataloguing in Publication Data
A CIP catalogue record for this title is available from the British Library.

ISBN-13: 978-0-7278-8902-7 (cased)
ISBN-13: 978-1-78029-638-8 (trade paper)
ISBN-13: 978-1-4483-0337-3 (e-book)

All Severn House titles are printed on acid-free paper.

Severn House Publishers support the Forest Stewardship Council™ [FSC™],
the leading international forest certification organization.
All our titles that are printed on FSC certified paper carry the FSC logo.

MIX
Paper from
responsible sources
FSC
www.fsc.org   FSC® C013056

Typeset by Palimpsest Book Production Ltd.,
Falkirk, Stirlingshire, Scotland.
Printed and bound in Great Britain by
TJ International, Padstow, Cornwall.

ONE

Tuesday noon

E llie heard the post drop through the front door into the letter box and hastened down the corridor to collect it, only to find someone had got there before her.

The woman who was currently occupying the flat at the top of Ellie's big house was ever hopeful that there'd be some post for her and was nearly always disappointed. Now she handed Ellie a wodge of envelopes, saying, 'More good fortune winging its way to you, eh?'

Ellie winced because if what Hetty suggested were true, it wasn't really good news at all.

Ellie discarded the junk mail, set aside a postcard from a friend on holiday in Prague – not many people bother to send cards nowadays, do they? – and was left holding yet another solicitor's letter. Like the others, it had been addressed to Ellie's husband, the Reverend Thomas.

How many solicitors' letters did that make? Four or five? They'd been coming thick and fast. At first they'd been as welcome as flowers that bloom in the spring. Now, not so. In fact, the opposite.

Ellie braced herself to deliver the bad news. Back down the corridor she went and into the library which Thomas used as his study. Although he did take the occasional service since he'd retired from parish work, he still edited a quarterly Christian magazine and made an ever-increasing number of visits to the lonely and sick in the neighbourhood. Ellie sometimes complained that she saw less of him now than ever.

Thomas was on the phone. He held up his hand to Ellie as she entered, warning her he wasn't free to speak at that moment.

'Yes, of course,' he said to his caller, 'I'll see what I can do about it. I'll drop in later this afternoon, shall I? No, no. Please don't bother to make . . . Yes, I know I'm partial to your ginger cake, but . . . No, really. I am supposed to be on a diet, and my wife will kill me if I can't do justice to supper.' He grinned at Ellie, sharing the joke with her and Ellie returned the smile.

This was a second marriage for both of them and a successful one, too. Thomas was a burly, bearded, teddy-bear of a man, a real poppet to his immediate circle, but no pushover when it came to matters of right and wrong. His biggest grief in life was that his married daughter and her children lived in Canada so he wasn't able to see them as often as he would have liked.

Ellie was silver of hair, sweet of temper, and a devoted grandmother. She was also the chair of a charitable trust set up to look after some money that she'd inherited and, although she was inclined to doubt her own judgement at times, she was no wilting angel, either.

Thomas and Ellie lived in harmony and without ostentation in a big old house dating back to the days of Queen Victoria. They loved the place, while being uneasily aware that it cost an arm and a leg to maintain. Over the years they'd been fortunate enough to employ a series of housekeepers. Usually, though not always, these people had become and remained good friends even after they'd moved out and got on with their lives elsewhere. At the moment homeless Hetty was currently occupying the attic flat and making noises about becoming their housekeeper. Which sounded all right, didn't it?

Yes, life should have been a bed of roses for Ellie and Thomas but, as the saying goes, there's always a crumple in the roseleaf, or a letter from a solicitor.

As Thomas brought his phone call to a close, Ellie placed the envelope on his desk.

He blenched. 'Not another one?'

'It might be a bill. Someone might be suing you for something.'

He ripped the envelope open, scanned the contents and passed it back to Ellie. 'I've been left a thousand pounds from the estate of a Mrs Pullin.' He dropped the letter as if it burned him. 'I haven't a clue who she was.'

This was not good news.

Ellie chose her words with care. 'You do so much good in

the community. Obviously it's someone you helped and she wished you well.'

He shook his head. 'Five times. Five people have left me money. Once was a pleasant surprise. Two was a cause for rejoicing. Three was a tad overwhelming, but five! What's going on? No, Ellie. Something's seriously wrong. I can't accept this money.'

Ellie understood that he was uneasy about the situation but she held the view that someone had to be practical in a marriage and in this case, it had to be her. She said, 'Don't be too hasty. This will make up for the rest of the money you lost on the magazine.'

The previous year Thomas had paid a printer in advance for the autumn issue of the magazine only to discover that the manager had scarpered with the loot. Not only had the magazine lost that money, but Thomas had had to find and pay for another printer at short notice. Being Thomas, he hadn't charged the magazine with the loss, but absorbed the shortfall himself.

Normally Thomas and Ellie divided the costs of maintaining their home between them, but since this problem had arisen Thomas had stinted himself of all his little pleasures in life in order to keep paying something – even though not as much as usual – towards the house's upkeep. Being Thomas, he was meticulous about doing so and, as the debt reduced, he'd been looking forward to being solvent once again.

A month ago, the first of a series of letters from a local solicitor had arrived with a cheque from a lady parishioner who had recently died. She'd left Thomas two hundred pounds. It had lifted his spirits no end. 'Bless her! What a nice surprise! How very thoughtful of her!'

A week later there'd been another cheque, this time for five hundred pounds, left to him in the will of an elderly lady whom Thomas had been accustomed to visit occasionally.

'How about that!' said Thomas, flushing with pleasure. 'Remember, I told you about her, Ellie? I was asked to visit her through Age UK. I saw her perhaps once a week last autumn. I thought she'd never forgive me because I beat her at cribbage last time I visited. Poor old soul. She was in chronic pain. It must have been a merciful release! I didn't hear she'd died till some time later, or I'd have gone to the funeral. How very good of her to remember me.'

The following week there'd been two more cheques, totalling fifteen hundred pounds.

They had knocked Thomas for six. There'd been no jubilation in his voice when he'd told Ellie about those two cheques. He'd said how good it was that he'd soon be clear of debt and then he'd gone into his Quiet Room to pray for a while.

Now he'd received yet another inheritance, this time for a thousand pounds.

He said, 'I can't believe I'm complaining because people keep leaving me money, but frankly, I'd rather they didn't. It's my fault I got into debt. I was naive. I made the mistake of trusting a rogue, I lost the money and I should be the one to make up the shortfall.'

He stuffed the letter back in the envelope. 'The first two ladies I knew well. It was good of them to remember me in their wills. Surprising, but most acceptable. The ones I got after that . . . well, that's where I went wrong. I didn't know either of the people concerned. All I could think of was how quickly the cheques would help me out of debt. I rationalized my position, saying these people had heard I was in trouble and wanted to do something to help me. I put the money in the bank and told myself that I was a lucky man to have such good friends. But this latest one is too much. I really don't think I can accept it.'

Ellie told herself that Thomas had an overactive conscience. She knew how much it had cost him not to be able to pay his way with the expenses of the house, and to cancel a projected holiday to visit his daughter and grandchildren in Canada.

'Don't you think you've earned it? You always go the extra mile for people, far beyond the call of duty. You don't just visit the sick but spend time with those who are so unpleasant they've driven away their nearest and dearest. You help housebound people to get carers to look after them and encourage others to socialize. You listen for hours to people who have no one else to talk to. You've earned these windfalls.'

'Not if I can't remember the person concerned.'

Ellie tried reason. 'You remembered the first two. As for the others, well, lots of people leave money to people they don't know personally. This latest woman must have heard that you did a lot of good in the community and decided to leave you something as a sort of reward. Haven't we prayed about the loss and asked for help?'

'Do you honestly think this is God's way of putting my losses right? I know you believe in miracles. Well, so do I. But this doesn't feel right. I wish I could fall on my knees, crying "Alleluia!" But I can't.'

'I don't see what you're worried about. Somebody has got it into their head that you deserve a little more of the world's goods, has mentioned it to his or her friends, and they have all decided to do something about it.'

'Five times over, Ellie. Five times!' He frowned. 'This latest one, for instance. Pullin. It's an unusual name. No, it doesn't ring a bell.' He pulled out the bottom drawer of his desk and rummaged around till he found his bulky day-to-day diary for the previous year.

He did have a smartphone but was not comfortable with it. In the past year he'd lost two in quick succession. In consequence Ellie had bought him a big day-to-day diary into which he was supposed to enter information about meetings, visits and telephone numbers. He'd grumbled about having to enter everything twice: once into his smartphone and once into the diary, but he'd mostly managed to do it. Ellie crossed her fingers that he'd put Mrs Pullin's details into the big diary, too.

Thomas leafed backwards through the months. 'Probate is usually granted six months after someone's death, and it's only after that the money is distributed to people named in a will. So, six months ago . . . probably more . . . sometime last summer . . . September? No. August, possibly? I'm thinking "cats". Why am I thinking about cats? Ah yes, here it is. Request from Bernard to visit a Mrs Pullin.' He drew out the solicitor's letter again. 'Yes, it's the same address.'

'Bernard? That name rings a bell.'

'Minister over Harrow way. I don't think you ever met him but I took over some of his visiting when he fell ill last year. He died in September, and I went to his funeral. Yes, the funeral was on the first of October.' He laid the diary down. 'Pullin. I remember now. I was asked to take communion to her towards the end of August as Bernard couldn't get out that week and there wasn't anyone else available due to school holidays. Mrs Pullin had broken her ankle. He told me to knock in a certain way, and she'd let me in. If I remember correctly, she lived on tinned foods herself but bought cooked chicken to feed her cats with. Three cats? Four? I think she fed them better than she fed herself.'

He laughed. 'That's it! That's what I remember about her. Those cats. Real charmers! She had one cat on her lap and another sitting on the back of her armchair. A third came to sit on my knee, and I had to brush off the hairs afterwards. A long-haired grey that was. What were their names? No, I can't recall. I remember I told her about our cat Midge, how he'd adopted us, not the other way round, and how he terrorizes all the neighbours' cats. Then she gave me the history of each one of hers, which got us off to a good start.'

He leafed forward in his diary, only to shake his head. 'No, I only saw her the once. I saw Bernard almost every week after that. He was going downhill so fast that they brought in a curate to take over his duties until he died.'

'Well, then,' said Ellie. 'Mrs Pullin had met you and liked you and heard you had been unfortunate in a money matter. She remembered you when she came to making her will, and there's nothing wrong in that.'

'Except,' said Thomas, 'that I didn't tell her about my stupidity. Why should I? And who else knew? You and the accountant, that's all. I don't see how she could have got to hear about it. I paid her that one visit, and we talked about cats.'

This was troubling. Ellie said, 'Well, there's no reason why they shouldn't leave you some money. Lots of people leave money for good causes. They met you and liked you and decided to leave you some money. What's wrong with that?'

'In theory, you're right. But it's odd that I have never before, in all my years in the ministry, been left so much as a teaspoon. Now not one but five people have decided all at once that Thomas should be blessed with an inheritance.'

'Not a very large one. The first was only two hundred.'

'True, but now we're into several thousand. I suppose if all these people had known one another, if there'd been some connection between them, one of them might have had the idea of leaving me a little something and told the others, who picked it up and ran with it. Perhaps they all talked to one another on the phone every week or visited one another. I suppose it might have happened that way, but all the same . . .'

He looked out of the window. 'Ellie, if I were of a suspicious frame of mine, I would wonder how it was that five people had popped off after making a will in my favour.'

Ellie felt acid hit the back of her throat. She'd been thinking the same thing, while hoping he hadn't. She tried to reassure him. 'They probably left hundreds of thousands to all sorts of people in their will and the little they left you is small beer.' Ellie's own feelings of unease grew. If she thought of the matter as if it had happened to someone else then she, too, would be wondering that. There'd been one too many serial killers in the papers recently.

No one who knew Thomas could possibly think him guilty of murder, could they?

Yes, of course they could. There'd been plenty of examples of highly regarded people in the community – trusted professionals, doctors and even solicitors – who'd blotted their copybooks recently. Thomas knew it, and so did she.

She forced a smile. 'The first was only for two hundred pounds and the second one for five hundred and you knew both of the people concerned. Nobody would bother killing someone for as little as a few hundred pounds, would they?'

'Murder has been committed for less than that.'

She knew that, too.

Ellie imagined having a conversation about this with her friend in the police force.

Isn't it lovely, Thomas had such a nice surprise today! And one last week, and the week before, too! Yes, he's been left quite a bit of money, several thousand pounds, believe it or not, right out of the blue. He barely knew the people concerned . . .

Her friend Lesley, even though she knew Thomas well, would

say, 'Ellie, pull the other one!' And then, after a moment's
thought, she'd say, 'Ellie? What's going on? What connection
does he have with all these people?'

Ellie would have to admit that she had no idea why these
five people should shower money on Thomas. Lesley would
also think about it and begin to wonder why they'd been so
generous. Lesley knew Thomas well, but she was a member
of the police force and duty-bound to take note of anything
untoward that came to her attention.

So Lesley would have to report what she'd heard to her
superior officer, and that would be very bad news indeed.
Lesley's superior officer was her inferior in the matter of
intelligence but a stickler for exercising the letter of the law.

On an unfortunate occasion many years ago, Ellie had
referred to him as 'Ears' because those appendages of his went
bright red when his blood pressure rose. The nickname had
spread through the force like wildfire and he'd never been able
to get rid of it. In consequence, he'd been heard to threaten all
sorts of action if Ellie transgressed by as little as jaywalking
on their high street. There's nothing he'd have liked better than
to instigate a full-scale police enquiry into the deaths of five
local people who'd all been in contact with Thomas.

Ellie could imagine the headlines. SERIAL KILLER TARGETS
OAPs.

Or perhaps, MURDERING MINISTER PINCHES OAPS'
PENSIONS.

Thomas smoothed out the solicitor's letter. 'I'm not going to
accept this cheque. I've promised to visit someone this afternoon,
but I'll ring the solicitor tomorrow and make an appointment
to see him.'

Ellie temporized. 'You know, we may be blowing this out of
all proportion. If you knew enough about these people to
understand why they'd all decided to leave you something in
their wills, it would be perfectly all right. They were probably
all members of our church here and—'

'No,' said Thomas. 'I don't think so. Well, the first one was,
and the second came through Age UK. I have no idea who the
third and fourth were or how they could have heard of me. I've
just told you about Mrs Pullin, who was definitely not a member

of our church here. I don't know which church the others might have gone to, or even if they went to church at all.'

'There will have been a connection. We just don't know it.'

'A minister has to be above suspicion. I was delighted when I got the first couple of bequests but now . . . Well, I know we'd hoped to fly over to Canada again this year, and that we might have been able to do so if I accept these windfalls and clear my debt, but I won't feel easy if we do. I'm going to pass the word around that, if desired, donations can be made direct to the church but not to me and I'm going to return all the money that's been sent me so far.'

TWO

Tuesday lunchtime

Ellie desperately wanted Thomas to keep the money because it would make so much difference to their lives. Ellie drew a pension from her charitable trust. She had thought it generous when the arrangement had been set up, but it turned out that it didn't really cover major problems such as replacing the boiler or rewiring the house. Or planning another trip to Canada.

The charity had been set up to do good in the world, they entertained applications from many deserving organizations for money, and they tried to invest wisely in housing which could be rented out at affordable prices.

After the unfortunate hole in Thomas's finances appeared, Ellie had thought of asking for more money to defray the expenses of the house, but she was afraid that Thomas would have objected. He had a tender conscience when it came to marrying a wealthy woman, which made his present dilemma all the more difficult to solve.

Finally she said, 'I have an idea. Our young friends Rafael and Susan are coming to supper tonight. You respect Rafael's opinion, don't you? He's a good businessman and he knows lots of people locally, as does our darling Susan. Suppose we ask their opinion about these cheques in confidence?'

'The fewer people who know about this, the better. Ellie, if this gets out, there'll be talk about how you can never trust a man of the cloth.'

'I wouldn't suggest we tell anyone else.'

'Hetty doesn't know, does she?'

Ellie said, 'Certainly not! We won't mention it in front of her but wait till after supper to talk to Rafael and Susan. By the way,' Ellie tried to sound airy, 'Hetty's planning to cook a chicken pie for us for tonight's supper.'

Thomas attempted to smile and failed. Hetty temporarily occupying the top flat after she'd been made homeless was one thing, but Hetty wanting to be their housekeeper and part of their family was quite another.

For one thing their ginger tomcat, Midge, had taken a dislike to the woman and resented her presence in the house. This had led to angry confrontations across the kitchen floor, which meant that Ellie now had to feed him in the conservatory.

The other problem was that although Hetty was a hard-working, cheerful soul, she was also clumsy and gave vent to bouts of loud, inappropriate laughter. Every day Ellie wondered how long it would be before she had to Have a Word.

The necessity for 'having a word' had become more urgent since Hetty had recently started to cook an evening meal for Ellie and Thomas. This was a problem. Ellie liked to cook in the evenings but nowadays it seemed that she could never go into the kitchen without finding Hetty underfoot, preparing some 'special treat' for them. Her helpfulness was misplaced and fast becoming a nuisance, but it was hard to know what to do about it. Worse still, although Hetty was a reasonably good if basic cook, she had a diabolically heavy hand with pastry and this was playing merry hell with Thomas's occasionally delicate digestion.

Ellie knew it was up to her to tell Hetty to get lost but that was easier said than done since it was Thomas who had brought her into their lives. He'd explained to Ellie that Hetty was someone they really ought to help. She was a hard worker who'd had a difficult life. She'd never been trained for anything in particular but after a failed, childless marriage she'd supported herself by taking on a series of part-time jobs, cleaning, working in a shop, shelf-filling in a supermarket. Her aim in life was to buy a little place of her own, but on her wages that could only be a distant dream.

Thomas had first come across Hetty when she'd been unfairly sacked for stealing at an old people's home. He'd helped get her the wages she'd been owed and, as she was about to be made homeless, found her a room in a parishioner's house. Unfortunately that placement hadn't worked out because the elderly house owner died soon after. Thomas had come to the rescue for a second time and found her another place to live, but that good deed, too, ended in disaster, as the lady of that household kept a dog which had taken a dislike to her lodger.

Once more Hetty had appealed to Thomas for help and that was when he'd first involved Ellie, by asking if there was some accommodation available for the woman through the charitable trust fund. Ellie had enquired but found that Hetty couldn't afford even the smallest of their rental properties.

At his wits' end, Thomas had made a mistake.

Susan, their young, red-headed, no-nonsense housekeeper, had left them a while ago to marry her clever, half-Italian fiancé Rafael, leaving her light and airy two-bedroom flat at the top of the house empty. Ellie hadn't re-let the flat because she wanted to renew some of the kitchen equipment and to redecorate . . . all of which had taken far longer than anticipated.

Thomas usually kept out of anything to do with the management of their big house, but at that point he had asked Ellie if Hetty might move into the top floor rooms until she could find something more suitable.

Ellie dithered. It was clear Hetty couldn't afford to pay anything approximating the market price, and Ellie needed that money to help defray the expenses of running the household. But as the painters finally put the finishing touches to the flat, Hetty had been bitten by her landlady's dog, and Thomas persuaded Ellie to offer Hetty the use of the flat as a temporary measure, without rent, until she could get back on her feet.

It had taken Thomas eight long weeks to realize his error.

Some people blend into a household with ease. Susan had

quickly become part of the family and Rafael, her fiancé and latterly husband, had become a good friend despite the disparity of years between them.

Hetty did not blend in.

Since Thomas had introduced Hetty to the household, Ellie hadn't felt that she could speak of her misgivings to him. She could put up with the minor annoyance of having the woman around, couldn't she? And he was so busy that he rarely noticed what went on from day to day in the house.

But, faced with the threat of another leaden chicken pie, Thomas finally managed to broach the subject. 'Ellie, I know it was all due to me that Hetty moved into the top flat. I didn't think it through, did I? After having our lovely Susan around for so long . . . Ah, her pastry and her bread . . . and her choco-late cake! I got carried away trying to be noble and solve everyone's problems. I thought Hetty would volunteer to pay whatever rent she could afford, and that it would only be for a couple of weeks till she found something more suitable. She doesn't see it that way, does she? Only last night she told me how happy she was to be of use to us. As far as I am concerned, she's outstayed her welcome. Do you agree?'

'Well, I asked her the other day what rent you'd suggested she pay, and she said you'd told her she was to consider herself our guest and that she could stay as long as she liked.'

'That's not true. I'm sure I said it was only a temporary measure and that we'd discuss what rent she should pay when she was settled in. I can see I wasn't firm enough.'

Ellie patted his hand. 'It's not your fault. I should have tackled her sooner. As it is, we've never actually asked her to pay rent so in theory she is our guest. As our guest, she ought to have saved enough to rent by now to get somewhere decent, even if she can't afford to buy. I'll have to have it out with her.'

'She's such a poor, well-meaning creature,' said Thomas. 'Where will she go?'

Ellie was conflicted. She felt guilty about leaving the flat empty when there was such a need locally for accommodation, but on the other hand she really could do with the rent money. If only Hetty would stick to her own quarters and pay something for her keep!

Over the years the house had become something of a burden. It had never seemed too big when they'd first moved in since they'd often had friends and relatives to stay. But Ellie and Thomas were not getting any younger, and they had guests to stay less often. She realized she didn't enter some of the rooms for weeks on end.

Ellie said, 'I've told Hetty she's been doing too much for us and that I like to cook in the evenings. She refuses to take the hint. I suppose it makes her feel she's paying her way. I'll talk to her again, and I'll have another go at the next trust meeting to see if they can find somewhere she can afford.'

Thomas rubbed his eyes. 'There's just one thing. I didn't like to mention it, I wasn't absolutely sure till yesterday, but I think Hetty's been going through my papers. It wasn't the cleaners. It was after they'd been. I caught Hetty leaving this room where surely she has no need to be. The only file that had been disturbed was this one where I keep all the papers about the bequests.'

'Oh, dear. I suppose she's so anxious to be part of the family that she wants to know what's happening but no, that's no excuse, I agree. Well, the sooner we can find her somewhere else to go, the better.'

Thomas brightened up. 'Now, about having Susan and Rafael to supper this evening. It's always a pleasure to see them. I do respect young Rafael's judgement. He has an old head on young shoulders. As for Susan, she's a poppet and has an uncommon amount of common sense in her makeup. When she lived at the top of the house it was a pleasure to know she was keeping an eye on you when I was out earning a crust—'

Ellie giggled. 'Who kept an eye on who? Susan did more cooking for us than any other lodger or housekeeper we've ever had—'

'Ah, Susan's pies!' sighed Thomas. 'And her biscuits! I suppose she spoiled us. You'd better warn her that Hetty will be cooking tonight.'

'I will. She'll understand. She'll probably bring some of her own cooking to put in the freezer for us and with any luck Rafael will bring you some beer from a mini-brewery that he's just happened to come across.'

Thomas's expression lightened. He was a beer man and liked
to try the products of the micro-breweries that had sprung up
recently. He looked at his watch. 'Well, I'd better get on and
see what my caller wants. Something to do with making her
will.' He realized what he'd just said and started to laugh. 'Ellie,
what am I going to say to her?'

'Tell her you can't help and she should consult her solicitor.
And, watch the clock. You don't want to be late for supper.'

Tuesday evening

Rafael and Susan drove into the forecourt of the house as
Thomas returned from his errand of mercy.

Rafael's favourite method of transport was a humongous
black brute of a motorbike, but he did have a car for formal
purposes. Susan, his delightful wife, was of slightly less than
medium height and curvaceous. She had never been happy
to ride on the back of his two-wheeled monster and now, being
almost nine months pregnant, she couldn't manage to climb on
to it at all. So they arrived in stately fashion in a family saloon
which had a large boot capable of taking the expected baby's
buggy, et cetera.

Ellie met them in the hall and took their coats. Rafael handed
over a six pack of beer from the micro-brewery he'd recently
discovered, and Susan slipped Ellie a tin of her famous home-
cooked chocolate biscuits.

The formal dining room hadn't been used for its original purpose
for many a long day and, as Rafael and Susan were such old
friends, they all congregated around the table in the kitchen, the
scene of so many good meals and interesting conversations.

Only tonight Hetty made a fifth at table and they got through
the meal to the tune of her merry laughter as she retold the
scrape she'd got into that day. She'd been helping out in one of
the cafes in the Avenue, but had misunderstood the way the
coffee machine would react when she pulled this instead of
pushing that, and the resultant mess had taken ages to clear up.

Everyone smiled in dutiful fashion and tried to eat at least
some of the inedible pie crust so as not to upset the cook. The
ice cream that followed was fine but then Hetty suggested that

as they were all having such a good time they turn on the telly and watch a quiz show together.

Ellie observed a slight shudder run through Thomas and didn't dare look at Rafael or Susan whose faces, she was sure, would be wearing identical polite but blank expressions.

Ellie held on to a slightly rigid smile as she said that of course Hetty must go up to her own rooms to watch her favourite show, after cooking that lovely meal for them. Ellie urged Hetty not to hang about as she, Ellie, was going to clear the table and put everything in the dishwasher. So, despite Hetty's protestations, they managed to ease her out of the kitchen and up the stairs.

Ellie shovelled the uneaten remains of the pie into the bin, Thomas made some good coffee, Susan loaded the dishwasher and Rafael swabbed down the table as to the manner born.

They moved into the sitting room. Rafael settled Susan on the settee, insisting that she put her feet up. Susan, in the final month of her pregnancy, was stunningly and ripely happy about it. Naturally the subject for discussion was names for the baby. Rafael said they both had a list of names but could not agree on any of them. No doubt the baby would decide for herself.

Finally, Thomas felt he could broach the tender subject of the bequests. He laid the papers out for Rafael and Susan to see and asked for their advice.

'I've never in all my years been left any money before. Now I've had five lots in the space of a couple of weeks. Three of the testators I knew slightly, but the others I didn't know at all. If this had happened to one of my friends, I'd be thinking about undue influence and asking to see the death certificates. Tell me I'm not exaggerating.'

Rafael donned the expensive rimless glasses he'd recently taken to wearing and went over the papers himself, passing each one to Susan as he finished reading it.

Finally he said, 'I see what you mean. On the face of it, there's nothing to worry about. Three different solicitors, none of whom are fly-by-night. I've used one of them myself. I don't know any of the people concerned except . . .' He picked one paper out and frowned at it. 'I have come across this one. Thornwell. It's not a common name, but if it's the same one then I'm surprised he left the peel off an orange to anyone in his will. He didn't strike me as the generous type. Perhaps he had a change of heart on his death bed.'

Susan eased her back muscles. 'Thornwell. Haven't I heard you mention that name?'

'Councillor Thornwell. Yes. He was no sweet little old lady. He was a chancer, a man who sailed too close to the wind for my taste. I seem to remember he was overfond of the bottle. Was he had up before the magistrates once for being drunk and disorderly? Something like that. I only met him a couple of times. Business.' He didn't seem to want to say anything more.

Susan persisted. 'Wasn't it in the local papers when he died?'

'It was. There was a lot of talk about . . .' He looked off into space, and what he saw here did not seem to make him happy. At last, he said, 'I suppose I could ask around, see what I can find out. I didn't know him socially, you understand.'

Ellie thought, *Rafael's lying. No, not lying exactly, but he knows something he's not prepared to tell us. What on earth could that be?*

Susan shuffled the papers together. 'I can't see why you're worried, Thomas. It's a lot of coincidences, but that's all they are. I don't see why you shouldn't keep the money.'

Rafael took off his glasses. 'You said you had a slight acquaintance with three of these people, though not with Thornwell or one other. So how come they all knew about you?'

'That's just it,' said Thomas. 'It worries me. Another thing: I've had five cheques so far, in a short space of time. What if I get another tomorrow? You can talk about coincidences, but this lot is going too far.'

Susan protested. 'It must be all above board if it's gone through solicitors.'

Rafael shook his head. 'Reluctantly, I must agree with Thomas. Too many coincidences.'

Ellie held back a sigh. She could see that Thomas meant to return all the cheques. If he felt it was right to do so, then so be it. But if he did it was going to be difficult to replace the boiler and attend to the wiring.

Perhaps there was something she could propose to save the situation?

She said, 'Thomas, couldn't you have a little chat with

the families of these people and find out how they all knew about your money troubles? We know you met three of them through your work. They were all elderly widows whom you befriended. If you don't remember the other two, well, you meet dozens of people in your line of work and it may well be that you've forgotten that you picked one up off the street after a fall or ran an errand for another.'

Thomas said quietly, 'I admit I'd forgotten that I'd been to see Mrs Pullin, but I couldn't forget two more completely. I haven't time to run around asking the families of these people why someone has been sending me money. You know I don't have a minute at this time of the year. Not counting my usual round of visits to people in need, for the next week I'll be working hard to put the magazine to bed.'

Ellie said, 'Well, perhaps I could do it for you?'

Now Ellie was also busy. Apart from the weekly meetings of her charitable trust, she looked after her youngest grandchild one day a week and kept in touch with old friends who had become housebound. She liked to potter around in the garden when the gardener wasn't there, and . . . and . . . but this matter of the wills was more important, wasn't it?

Ellie said, 'There's no harm, is there, in my visiting the relatives to explain that Thomas feels diffident about accepting money from people he hardly knew? I can see how they react. If they all say how they'd heard what a good man you are, Thomas, and what bad luck you'd had financially, then you'd feel all right about it, wouldn't you?'

He rubbed his eyes. 'I would feel happier, I suppose. Though not entirely so. There's something about this which makes me uneasy.'

Susan tried to joke. 'Thomas, don't tell me you smell fire and brimstone?'

He nodded. 'Yes, Susan. I've been trying to convince myself that everything's all right but when it comes down to it, that's exactly what I suspect.'

Susan tried to laugh. 'No one who knows you would think you'd take part in anything untoward.'

Rafael shook his head. 'That's not the point, Susan. Thomas is right. It stinks.'

Ellie's spirits dipped to zero as she realized that Rafael agreed with Thomas that there was something seriously wrong about the situation.

She braced herself. 'Then we're all agreed. I'll go to see the families involved and sort it all out. Now, let's talk about something else. Susan, aren't you tired of living in Rafael's bachelor flat? Haven't you found a house you like yet?'

Rafael said, 'Susan's picky. Wouldn't mind moving into a penthouse overlooking the Thames but won't settle for less.'

Laughing, Susan threw a cushion at him. 'You're just as bad. You want some space, too.'

Ellie said she quite understood. 'We've talked about downsizing eventually but hate the thought of living in a little box somewhere without a garden.'

So the evening passed, with no need to resort to television programmes for entertainment.

As Thomas made his cup of instant coffee before they went upstairs to bed, he said, 'We're lucky in our friends, aren't we?'

And Ellie agreed.

THREE

Wednesday morning

Ellie did not consider herself to be a good businesswoman, but she prepared meticulously for the weekly business sessions of the trust. She had an excellent general manager, and her wizard of a finance director had a brain which acted like a laser on financial problems. She also had a part-time secretary to take notes at the meeting, who kept tabs on what *had* happened, what *was* happening, and what they *planned* to happen in the future. Other people might be asked to attend the meetings now and then, but these three were the ones who made the big decisions and saw that they were carried out.

Her general manager and finance director were so good that Ellie sometimes felt she was only needed to supply coffee and biscuits and to put her signature on things, because they always knew exactly what they were doing. However, she had learned from experience that if she came to a meeting unprepared, the session would last twice as long as it needed to.

So that morning she read the paperwork and pondered this and that. She made a note to ask the trust if they could find somewhere for Hetty to live at a reduced rent. For a start, the trust owned a block of flats down by the river and a number of those were let to groups of friends who had decided to set up house together. Perhaps one of them might have a room for Hetty to rent?

Oh, but would she fit in? Er, probably not.

Ellie reflected that accommodation for single people wishing to live on their own was hard to come by in that area. Ealing was a pleasant neighbourhood, convenient for transport links and shops. The trust tried to keep the rents down but they had to cover their costs and keep a healthy balance against all eventualities. The demand for reasonably priced living space was high, and there were always more applicants than they could accommodate.

She made another note to herself to ask if the trustees had any idea about what she should do about the upstairs flat, which would soon be empty once more. She and Thomas really didn't need any living-in staff now. Years ago they'd inherited their first housekeeper along with the house, and that dear woman had been part of the family for years and been much missed when she eventually died.

After her there'd been this person and that living in the flat, but somehow they'd never quite fitted in until bouncy, red-headed Susan had arrived. Her reign had been a happy one and she'd only left to marry Rafael.

Hetty didn't seem to fit in anywhere. By her own admission she'd never been able to stay long in the rooms she'd rented. Perhaps it was her loud laughter which caused her to outstay her welcome, or the odd hours she worked?

There had always been a problem with the top storey of the house. Several times in the past Ellie had asked the council if she might install an outside staircase so that she could let the rooms out as a self-contained flat, but they'd always refused.

Yet the pressure on the housing market increased year by year. Was it time to try again?

Ellie's thoughts were interrupted by a knock on the door.

It was Hetty, pulling on a jacket. 'Sorry to interrupt, but I'm just off and wondering if you need anything from the shops? I thought I could get some of that fish mix from the Avenue and make a nice big pie for us for tonight.'

Ellie steeled herself. 'No, don't worry about that, Hetty. I've told you before, I like to cook at night.'

'Oh, but it's no trouble, and I know how hard you have to work to keep everything going, and I want to help.' Her eyes were wild, and her lips trembled. Was she going to cry?

Ellie produced a reasonably genuine smile. 'No, Hetty. You must let me use my own kitchen. I don't want to see you cooking in there again. Understand?'

'Oh, but it's the least I can do when you're so good to me. I know I can never repay you for all your kindness, so if I can do anything, but anything—'

'Dear Hetty. Stop right there. You'll have Thomas and I declining into wheelchairs if you coddle us so much. You look after yourself for once, and don't overdo it. Where are you working today?'

'I'm back at the deli, although there's been a spot of bother there because I had to tell the Saturday girl that she was wrapping the ham up wrongly, and she told the boss that I'd been taking home the ends of cheese, which she'd always let me have before and said nothing about it, and what am I supposed to eat, may I ask, when she only pays me the minimum wage?'

Ellie was a frequent customer at the deli and was aware that the boss there had given Hetty a part-time job out of the goodness of her heart, because the rest of her staff were fully trained in such work and Hetty, unfortunately, was not.

The problem was the same one that Ellie and Thomas faced. How could you help someone so helpless, who was working all hours to earn a living, and always falling short?

Ellie's eye fell on the folder for the trust meeting. 'Well, Hetty, I know things have been difficult for you for a long time, but I'm going to see if I can find you a nice place to live at a reasonable rent—'

Tears spurted. 'Oh, no! You know I can't afford anything around here! You're never going to throw me out! You'd never be so hard-hearted!'

Ellie wished she'd never started this. 'Surely you want a place of your own? If you looked for something a bit further out, you'd be able to afford it, wouldn't you?'

Hetty sought for a hankie, in vain. 'I don't want to move far away. I thought you liked me and needed me! I don't get in your way, do I? I'm always trying to do things for you and thinking what you'd like best.'

'Yes, yes,' said Ellie, pushing a box of tissues towards the woman, 'but living in someone else's place is not like having your own home, is it?'

Hetty gulped. 'But I've been so happy here! You and Thomas have been just like a mother and father to me.' A change of tone. 'You've made it all up! You're jealous of the way Thomas has been looking after me. I know *he* wouldn't want to throw me out on to the street! Not Thomas!'

'Both of us,' said Ellie, feeling tired. 'We're agreed. You need a place of your own. I'm going to try to find you something suitable. We've been glad to give you a breathing space, but now it's time for you to think of your own future.'

'No! Oh, no! I can't believe this is happening! Oh! Oh, I can't bear it!' Hetty ran down the corridor and out of the house, slamming the front door behind her.

Ellie sank back in her chair, feeling worn out. 'I should have handled that better. Poor woman. I feel so sorry for her, but . . . Ought I to have gone after her? No, I don't think so. I mean, what could I have said that I haven't?'

Ellie switched off her computer. Now Hetty was out of the kitchen, Ellie felt free to make herself a sandwich for lunch. Of late, she'd found herself putting off making herself a cuppa when she knew Hetty might be pottering around in there, with the radio on full blast.

Hetty loved a noisy environment.

Ellie didn't.

After lunch Ellie checked the diary. Thomas was taking an elderly gentleman to a clinic and wouldn't be back for a couple

of hours, so Ellie was at liberty to start looking into the bequests
he'd received.

She collected Thomas's file of letters and took it into her
study. She turned her chair away from the window, because
if she allowed herself to look out, she knew she'd want to be
out there, mowing the lawn, dead-heading and tidying away
the remains of the spring bulbs.

She told herself that she'd allow herself some time to do
that later when she'd finished work for the day.

She fanned the letters out on her desk. Five people had died
and left Thomas bequests, some little and some large. Ellie
reflected that if there had been just one solicitor involved, that
might have solved the puzzle of why Thomas had been selected
for these bonuses. If someone was trying to think of worthy
causes to leave money to, a solicitor might well have suggested
Thomas.

No, they wouldn't. Solicitors couldn't suggest worthy recipients. Besides, there were three different solicitors involved, none
of them known to Ellie. So she hit that idea on the head.

She considered the bequests in chronological order. Mrs
This and Mrs That. Elsie and Lily. Two hundred pounds here
and five hundred there. One had been a parishioner, and the
other an elderly lady he'd visited now and then for the Age UK
charity. He'd remembered both of them well. Yes, he'd been
surprised when he'd received those two cheques, but had
accepted the good wishes of the testators at face value. Number
three. Ellie scrabbled among the letters to find that one. Thomas
had received numbers three and four in one week. He'd shown
them to her at the time, hadn't he? Or no, that had been the
week that their little granddaughter had been feverish, and it
was quite possible – no, very probable – that Ellie had been so
distracted that she hadn't paid much attention to the details.
She'd been pleased that Thomas had been given some more
money, but she hadn't read the letters herself. She'd had other,
more important things to think about, such as how to bring the
baby's temperature down.

*Dear little soul. Am I looking after her one day this week? I
don't think I am. I must check with Diana.*

Back to the letters. Thomas said that he'd not recognized the name of the third testator. A man. Was this the drunken councillor whom Rafael had referred to? Think, Ellie! Thomas did tell you the name at one point, didn't he? It was something ordinary, like Green. Or Brown. Or Smith. Or, perhaps, Harris?

Ellie had known someone called Harris once upon a time, but it wouldn't have been him. Or rather, her. For it had been the wife whom Ellie had known.

She found the letter. The bequest had been from a Harold Harris of Argyll Road.

Was it . . .? Could it be . . .? Yes, that was the address at which Ellie's old friend Gwen had lived.

Goodness gracious! Harold Harris had left Thomas some money? Really? How extraordinary!

Thomas said he hadn't known the man. Well, why should he? The two men had never met, had they? If Ellie had ever mentioned his name to Thomas – perhaps in connection with a chance encounter she'd had with Gwen – he wouldn't have had any reason to remember it.

Ellie sat back in her chair and sent her mind back down Memory Lane. How easy it was to lose touch with people whom you only saw every now and then.

It must have been some twenty years ago, perhaps more, that she'd first met Gwen. They'd been working in the charity shop in the Avenue at that time. Gwen had been a real asset, patient with customers and always ready to make the tea and provide biscuits.

Ellie had stopped working at the charity shop when her first husband died, and after that had only ever come across Gwen by chance. On those occasions, if they'd had time to have a coffee together, they'd still found plenty to talk about: their families, Ellie's daughter, Gwen's sister who'd been a bit of a pain, what they were doing for their holidays. That sort of conversation.

Over the years Ellie, who had never been tall, had ruefully watched her figure thickening and her hair turning to silver, whereas Gwen had remained the same large and cheerful woman who'd coloured her hair bronze and never seemed to feel the cold.

Nowadays women achieved higher education and managed

to combine work with childcare, but when Gwen and Ellie had got married it was accepted that wives stayed at home and looked after the children while their husbands went out to work. True, opinions about what young married women could and could not do were beginning to change, but rather too late for either of them to have thought of carving out a career for themselves.

Ellie's first husband had held very positive views on this. He hadn't wanted Ellie to have a life outside the home, and his sharp tongue had kept her under his thumb until long after he'd died.

Ellie's only daughter, Diana, was a chip off her father's block. She was a successful businesswoman with a husband and two children under five, but she was still vocal in her amazement that her mother could be responsible for heading up a charitable trust. Diana thought Ellie's place in society should still be that of mother and grandmother.

Gwen Harris had been brought up to regard marriage in the same light, which perhaps accounted for her sticking to a man who hadn't been able to open his mouth without saying something sarcastic or hurtful.

How things had changed! Nowadays if you told a woman that her duty in life was to stay at home and look after her family, and that she must let the man of the house make all the important decisions in life . . . Well, you'd blow a raspberry, wouldn't you?

Ellie remembered when she'd first met Harold. It must have been soon after she'd left the charity shop. The three of them had met by chance in the Avenue on a Saturday morning.

Not as tall as his wife, Harold had had a viper's tongue. The first words he'd said to Ellie were to complain that his wife had stopped in the street to gossip with a friend. 'I understand you've known my wife for some time? She doesn't improve with age, does she?'

Incredibly, Gwen had laughed as if he'd been making a joke. Which he had not.

Ellie had been taken aback by his rudeness and made an excuse not to accept Gwen's invitation to join them for a coffee and a catch-up.

Over the following years there'd been other chance meetings. Ellie remembered an occasion at a school fete when Harold had called Ellie's attention to his wife's size, saying she was eating for two but unfortunately past the age of childbearing! He'd added that he was looking forward to the day that she'd be too fat to get up the stairs.

At which Gwen had smiled and said, 'Oh, you are a one, Harold!'

Another time he'd told Ellie that he was thinking of trading 'this big lump' in for something he could really fancy carting around. As before, Gwen had laughed, and said 'Oh, Harold, give over, do!'

Ellie had concluded that Gwen must be one of those saintly souls who believed in keeping her marriage vows even when the relationship had descended into what most people would consider to be abuse.

Harold had been . . . what? An accountant? Something like that. Gwen had been proud of him, mentioning to Ellie over the years that he'd got a promotion in his job, or moved to another, better firm. They'd bought their large house in West Ealing before the prices had begun to rise and they'd never had any children.

Ellie thought that Gwen must be rattling around in that house now, or perhaps she'd sold it and moved away?

Ellie decided to try the old telephone number she had for Gwen. If her old friend were free, perhaps Ellie could call to see her that afternoon?

The phone rang and rang. Finally, Gwen answered.

Ellie said, 'Gwen, it's Ellie Quicke here. Something made me think of you, and I rang on the off chance you might be in. How are you doing?'

'All right, I suppose. Up and down. You know?' She sounded subdued.

'Of course,' said Ellie, who remembered very well how she'd felt when her first husband had died. It had taken a long time for her to come to terms with her new life. 'It seems ages since we met and I wondered if you were still living in the old house. Tell you what, if you're free this afternoon, I could pop over and we could have a good catch-up.'

'Why not? I'll put the kettle on, though I don't think I've got any biscuits.' Gwen put the phone down without another word.

Oh well. That was short and sharp. Ellie shrugged.

She put the Harris papers aside for a moment to look at the details for the other benefactors.

What about the drunken councillor, Thornwell? Ellie had an uneasy feeling that Rafael had not told everything he knew – or perhaps suspected? – about the man.

What reason would Rafael have for not being open about his dealings with him? Surely, none. However, she ought perhaps to check. Ellie dialled and was lucky enough to find Rafael at liberty to take the call.

She said, 'Rafael, I'm starting to look into the bequests. You mentioned last night that one of the people who'd left Thomas money might have been had up in court for being drunk?'

'Mmhm. Do you need the details? It was in the *Gazette*. I looked them up this morning. He was driving erratically and knocked over a child in the road outside the fish and chip shop in the Avenue. No harm done, and the child didn't have to have hospital treatment. Thornwell was over the limit, which he blamed on some cough medication he'd been taking. The magistrates didn't believe him, he lost his licence and had to do some community work. Not much. Not enough, in my opinion. He remained on the council for years, even after that.'

The information came flowing out without hesitation. Ellie told herself she'd been quite wrong to think that Rafael was withholding information.

A pause, and then he said, 'I suppose I could dig around some more if you like.'

Alarm bells rang. Why would Rafael offer to do that? She said, 'I'd be grateful. And for any other bits of gossip you can turn up.'

'Gossip? Me? Would I!'

He aimed for a comical tone of voice, but something still scratched at the back of Ellie's mind about Rafael's attitude to the disgraced or disgraceful councillor. However, she said, 'Thanks. I need all the help I can get. I knew the wife of one of the other benefactors slightly. I'm going to drop in on her this afternoon. I'm feeling a bit guilty about her, actually. I haven't seen her for ages. I didn't even know her husband had died. Ah well, it will be good to see her again, even under these circumstances.'

'Best of luck,' said Rafael, and switched off.

Yes, indeed. She would need some luck. Did it look like rain? Perhaps she'd better take an umbrella, just in case.

FOUR

Wednesday afternoon

On her way up the hill, Ellie tried to work out when she'd last seen Gwen and Harold. There'd been something odd about Gwen's behaviour that day, hadn't there? If only she could remember what it had been.

She'd been shopping in West Ealing and instead of taking two buses to get home had decided to walk back by way of the Argyll Road.

She'd been thinking about what she'd cook for supper when, entirely without warning, a car had turned off the road and came to rest across the pavement in front of her.

Ellie had pulled up short, her heartbeat going into overdrive.

A cheerful voice had called out, 'Yoo-hoo, Ellie! Watch where you're going!' It had been Gwen, in the driving seat of the car.

Beside her sat Harold, half her size and twice as sharp. In a cracked voice Harold had said, 'Watch what you're doing, you stupid woman! Suppose you concentrate on getting us home safely instead of yakking to all and sundry. Give me strength!'

Gwen had kept her cool as she inched the car backwards and forwards across the pavement, through the gateposts, and finally managed to park in the forecourt of their large, detached house.

Throughout this manoeuvring, Gwen had kept talking to Ellie. 'Don't go away. Hold on a mo till I get this beast safely back home. I've been meaning to ring you for ages, catch up

on all the gossip. No, Harold, I am not making you too late
for your programme. It's the golf, you know, Ellie, from
America. Or is it the cricket from Australia?'

'Gossip, gossip! That's all you're good for.' Harold had
ignored Ellie in order to keep up a running commentary on
Gwen's efforts to park their car. 'Left hand down a bit, woman!
Can't you even remember which is your left and which is your
. . . No, no, no! What idiot of a test driver ever allowed you to
think you could . . .!'

Ellie had thought it a mystery how Gwen managed to keep
a smile on her face.

As soon as the car had come to a halt, Harold had eased
himself out and, leaning on a stick, thumped his way, still
complaining, into the house. His wife opened the boot, revealing
a mountain of supermarket shopping bags. 'I haven't seen you
for ages, Ellie. Have you time for a cuppa?'

A spat of rain helped to make up Ellie's mind. 'I'd love a
cuppa. Let me help you in with those bags.'

'I was all for doing the weekly shop online but Harold
says it costs more, and if it keeps him happy, who am I to
argue?' Gwen ignored the fact that nothing seemed to make
Harold happy.

Ellie had assisted her friend in with the shopping and stayed
for a cup of tea, interrupted by Harold complaining – first that
she'd given him tea instead of the coffee he'd fancied that afternoon, and then that the biscuits she'd given him were stale.

When Ellie had said she really must go, Gwen had accompanied her to the front door. It was only then, in the light of
the bright sun, that Ellie noticed the lines of strain around her
friend's eyes. But what would you do? Living with Harold
must be difficult.

Gwen had put her hand on Ellie's arm as they stood in the
porch. 'Keep in touch, won't you? Perhaps we could meet up
one day next week?'

At the time Ellie hadn't read anything serious into her
friend's words, but in retrospect, she thought that Gwen had
sounded almost desperate.

*Yes, that was it! That was what had been different about that
meeting. Gwen hadn't brushed aside her husband's sarcasm,*

but had shown signs of . . . what? Weakness? Fear? Never before had Gwen suggested making a proper date to meet.

At the time Ellie hadn't found the invitation entirely welcome. Well, she was busy, wasn't she, what with babysitting the new grandchild and the work for the trust? She'd said, 'Yes, of course. We must do that.' And hadn't meant it.

What's more, Gwen had understood that Ellie hadn't meant it. *Oh, the guilt! I should have realized she needed help. There's no excuse.*

Well, Gwen didn't ring her to suggest a date, so it can't have been that important, can it?

You know perfectly well that you declined to make a commitment.

It wasn't Gwen who died.

But maybe Gwen got so beaten down that she helped him to die?

Perish the thought. Anyway, Gwen ought to have suggested a date then and there. Instead, when Harold had shouted for his wife from inside the house, Gwen had waved goodbye and Ellie had departed.

Oh, and I remember that all the way home I amused myself wondering why Gwen had never put weedkiller in her husband's tea.

And then, he died. So perhaps Gwen had really . . .?

No. He hadn't died from weedkiller. Had he?

Ellie realized that she actually had no idea how Harold had died or even when. It wouldn't have been weedkiller, anyway. Ridiculous idea!

Perhaps he'd had a stroke, or been run over in the road, or accidentally taken too many sleeping tablets.

It was a little odd that Gwen hadn't notified Ellie that her husband had died or given her details of the funeral. Ellie would have gone, if she'd known about it.

Not for the first time Ellie regretted that they had ceased to take their local newspaper which had supplied details of local births, marriages and deaths in copious detail. You were supposed to get all that information online nowadays, weren't you? But that had never come naturally to Ellie.

So, where had Thomas come into Harold's affairs? Ellie

couldn't recall a single way in which Thomas might have come into contact with the man. Not through church, or a local committee. On different occasions in the past Ellie might have mentioned to Thomas that she'd met her old friend Gwen that day and had had a coffee and a chat. On such occasions, Ellie might have made some derogatory remark about Gwen's taste in men. Yes. But that was it.

Ellie and Gwen had known one another? Yes. But Thomas? No. So why the legacy?

The big house on Argyll Road looked much as Ellie remembered it. Evidently Gwen was not going to sell, for there was no estate agent's sign outside.

A woman opened the door to Ellie's ring on the bell, but this was not the old, bouncy Gwen. This was a subdued woman who seemed to have lost weight recently. 'Lovely to see you, Ellie. Come on in.'

'It's been too long,' said Ellie. 'My fault.'

'Time flies when you're having fun,' said Gwen, leading the way back down the hall and into the kitchen. She moved lethargically. She'd let her hair grow and the roots showed that she was going gray. A button was missing off her shirt.

The kitchen was clean but there was no sign of food preparation for an evening meal and the house felt chilly. Gwen gestured to Ellie to take a seat and poured boiling water into the teapot, placing it on a mat on the table. She added two mugs, a battered tin containing two broken biscuits, and a half full bottle of milk.

In the old days she'd have got out the bone china and never have dreamed of putting the milk bottle on the table. Also there would have been a good selection of biscuits to offer.

Gwen said, 'I'd left him, you know. Ten days before he died.'

Ellie blinked. She hadn't expected that. 'You'd left Harold?' Well, well. Wonders would never cease. And about time, too.

'Yes,' said Gwen. 'My sister kept on at me to leave him, saying he'd come to his senses if I weren't there twenty-four-seven to look after him. She said he wouldn't starve because he could order food online and he had social services running around after him, and he could get a cleaner to look after the house and neighbours could drop in. I kept telling her it was the pain that made him so short with me. But I'd got a bit rundown, and he said something which upset me, which it shouldn't have done if I hadn't been going down with laryngitis, and I snapped back at him without really meaning it, you know?

'He said I was to get out and I said I would. I packed a small bag and I was going to take the car, but he said it was his car and not mine – although he hadn't been driving for quite some time, it was over a year since he'd stopped. I took a taxi to the station and got to my sister's, and she put me straight to bed and I stayed there all that weekend, mostly asleep.

'I felt better on the Monday and my temperature had come down a bit, so I started to worry about how he was coping without me, but my sister said to leave him to stew in his own juices. Of course I couldn't do that, so I phoned to see how he was getting on, and he said he was fine and he'd got in a cleaner who was looking after him beautifully and he wasn't missing me at all. So I stayed on with my sister all that week, and I did feel much better, almost my old self by the next weekend. Then I remembered he'd got an appointment at the hospital the following day, Monday, and I knew he'd never get there if I didn't take him because he wouldn't waste money on a taxi, would he?'

Ellie backtracked. 'Why wasn't Harold driving? Had he lost his licence?' *He wouldn't have got drunk, would he? Mean old Harold wouldn't have wasted money on booze, would he?*

Gwen was shocked at the idea of Harold losing his licence. 'Oh, no. It was his eyesight. Cataracts, you know? By the time they'd been dealt with, his right hip had gone. The pain was something dreadful. That's why he hadn't taken up driving again. Where was I? Oh yes, so I realized I'd have to get back to him that evening, and I asked my sister to drop me back at the station straight away and she did, and I got a taxi back from Paddington and then . . . and then . . .' Her voice trailed away. Her eyes seemed fixed on the cooker built into the wall, though she probably wasn't seeing it.

Ellie prompted her. 'What happened?'

'I found him. There was a hold-up on the railway, Sunday working, and I didn't get home till about half past ten that night. He's always in bed by then. I opened the front door and called out, "Yoohoo! It's only me." He didn't answer, so I thought he must be asleep. We always left a light on upstairs on the landing in case he wanted to go to the loo in the night, and that was on, which was fine. Then, I'd not been sleeping well and I was so tired, though that's no excuse, of course, but I tripped over my own feet in the hall and crashed into the hall table, and that silly Satsuma vase that Harold had bought in the junk shop, that he was so fond of – the vase, not the shop, I mean – anyway, it crashed to the floor and broke.

'I was so upset, expecting him to wake up and tell me off, which I thoroughly deserved, being so clumsy. Only there wasn't a peep out of him. The house was so quiet. And that's when I realized that something awful had happened because he always sleeps lightly, and he hadn't made a sound.'

'You mean . . .?'

Gwen sniffed and used her hankie. 'He was in bed, in his pyjamas and all. Just as he should be. It looked as if he was asleep, but I couldn't hear him breathing. He snored a bit, you know? Not that he ever admitted it, of course, but he did. He was so terribly quiet. Not like him. I thought at first that if I got the paramedics they'd take him to hospital and bring him round, but they told me when they got here that he'd been gone for hours. He was cold. You know?'

Her voice wobbled, and Ellie patted her hand. 'Don't talk about it if you don't want to.'

'I'd like to. I was fine at first. I didn't cry. I suppose it was the shock. It was like nothing was real and I was on automatic pilot. I told myself it had been a merciful release for him, and that he wouldn't have wanted me to break down and become a nuisance to everyone. So I didn't. He'd left instructions with his solicitor about his funeral, and a will as well. All I had to do was follow what he'd said I was to do. There was to be a small private cremation, nobody to come back to the house after. I had to get the death certificate, write to the utilities and the bank and . . . You know all that, don't you? You've been through it yourself.'

'I have.'

'You know, for quite a while, maybe four or five weeks, I was quite all right. Harold had booked a holiday for us before

I left him. Cruising on the Rhine. He'd thought he'd be able to manage even with his hip being so troublesome. I tried to get a refund but they wouldn't play ball, although my sister says I should have been able to get one, so I decided to go on it all by myself. I had a blast, as my young nephew would say, and I enjoyed it so much, meeting new people and pretending I'd been a widow for ages. When I got back home I was full of good resolutions to lose weight and get a job.

'I wasn't away for long but when I got back I was upset because the house was a tip. The cleaner hadn't come in while I was away, though I thought I'd asked her to. Maybe I'd forgotten to ask. Head like a sieve, me. But I didn't need her, did I? I could keep the house clean myself as I always had done in the past. So I told the agency not to bother, and set about it. Then I made a list of things to do, such as finding myself a part-time job. I kept thinking that Harold would have been so proud of me, pulling myself together like that. I went to three interviews, but apparently I'm too old and more or less unemployable because I'm no good on computers, and I can't stand for long enough to do any shelf filling and that.'

'You poor thing.'

Gwen began to weep. 'To tell the truth, because I can tell someone who's such an old friend, I can't see any point in carrying on. My sister kept ringing me for a while, every night. She said I should go to stay with her for a bit, but she's out all day, she's still working, and her husband and the kids, they're a noisy lot, and I didn't think I could cope with that. Then she was angry with me for not going to stay with her and I don't always pick up the phone when she rings nowadays. She's always been a bossyboots, but I don't have to put up with it any more, do I? She really ought to be more understanding.'

'Dear me,' said Ellie.

'I wasn't too bad really until oh, it must be about three weeks ago. I kept to my old routine, going to the shops even if I didn't buy anything when I got there, and watching daytime television. I got quite interested in the soaps. Then I woke up one morning and started crying and couldn't stop. And I couldn't leave the house. After a bit my neighbour that's on my right side – she's a librarian, so nice, with three small children

– anyway, she came round and told me I had to see the doctor. I didn't want to but she bullied me into ringing for an appointment and she popped me in her car and took me to see him herself. The doctor said I was depressed and I've got these tablets but I can't be bothered to take them. I know that if Harold were here now he'd tell me to snap out of it. He'd say, "Snap out of it, you silly old fool!" But I can't.'

'Understandable,' said Ellie, looking to see if there were any packets of medication in sight.

Gwen said, 'I keep going over and over it. Flashbacks, they call it. I put my key in the front door and call out "Yoohoo!" and then I bump into the table and the vase falls and breaks and I go up the stairs and there he is, lying in bed with his bedside light on, and the house is so quiet I can almost hear it zing in my ears. I reach out to touch him . . . and that's when I come back to myself again. Only it starts up all over again in a minute or two.

'I can't pretend any longer. It was all my fault. He wouldn't have died if I hadn't been so selfish and run away. Or if I'd come back earlier that week, which I had thought of doing. Do you know, when I found him all I could think of was that I'd have to ring the hospital to tell them he wouldn't make his appointment to have his hip replaced? Isn't that awful?'

Ellie patted Gwen's hand. 'You looked after him beautifully all those years, and you weren't at all well.'

'If I hadn't walked out on him, if I hadn't been so silly as to take his comment seriously, he'd still be here.'

'What was it? A heart attack?'

'Paracetamol and sleeping tablets. He'd been given them for the pain in his hip so that he could get some sleep, but he must have taken double or more, and it did for him. If I'd been here . . . but I wasn't. He had his funny little ways, but I should have been more understanding. Instead, I left him when he needed me most.'

Not weedkiller, then. Thank God for that.

Ellie tried to imagine the scene. 'It must have been the most awful shock to find him like that.'

Gwen wasn't listening. 'The house is all paid for, and I get half of Harold's pension. I suppose I should be grateful that I don't have to find a job at my age, but all I can think of is that in his will he said he was leaving nearly everything to his dear wife, and that was after I'd gone and left him!'

'There, there,' said Ellie. 'If you had a little wobble at the end, then I'm sure he knew you'd be back. Because you had forgiven him and returned, hadn't you? His death was an accident and you couldn't have prevented it if you had been here.'

'That's what the doctor says. And my sister.' Gwen reached for a box of tissues and blew her nose. 'Sorry, sorry! I know I'm being a complete drip, but I can't help myself. I hear his voice in my head all the time.' She reached for the teapot and poured into the mug she'd placed for Ellie.

Only, it wasn't tea that came out of the pot. It was clear water. Gwen started to laugh and cry at the same time. 'Silly me! I forgot to put teabags into the pot.'

Ellie stood up and looked around. 'Where are those pills you're supposed to be taking?'

'I threw them away. They didn't do me any good. I hate taking pills, especially when I think how Harold made such a silly mistake and took too many. If he hadn't left them on his bedside table, if he'd put them in the bathroom cabinet like I always did, then he wouldn't have taken double or more, would he? They said he must have been doubling up the dose for days, probably from the moment I left.'

Ellie investigated the contents of the rubbish bin. Near the top she found a pristine pack of pills. She extracted the instructions from the pack and read them through. 'It says you have to keep taking them for a fortnight before they take effect. How many have you taken so far?'

'I don't know. Maybe a couple. Then I stopped. They weren't doing any good.'

Ellie got a glass of water and put that and the pills down in front of Gwen. 'You must accept what happened and move on. I know Harold would say that to you if he were here now. He'd say you were wallowing in your misery.'

A trace of colour came into Gwen's cheeks. 'That's a nasty word, "wallowing"! I'm not "wallowing". I'm grieving.'

'Sure. You're stuck in the mud and need a shove to get you

going again. Come on, now, take your pill. I'll make a proper
pot of tea, and we can talk about where you go from here.'
    Gwen pushed the pills away. 'No, no. You don't understand.'
    'Yes, I do,' said Ellie. 'I went through something like this
when we first met. Frank had died in hospital unexpectedly and
I was distraught. I'd never had to think for myself during all
the years we were married, and it took time for me to discover
that I could manage on my own. As you can. With a bit of help
from your friends. Trust me, you keep on taking those pills and
allow yourself to be pampered for a bit, and soon you'll be able
to cope much better.'
    'I feel so guilty!'
    'You've no need. It was just one of those things. He knew
you loved him and that he could rely on you. His death was
an accident. You have grieved for him and no doubt you will
continue to do so, but sooner or later you will have to take
some decisions about your future.'
    'You talk as if I had a future, but I can't see it.'
    'Well, you could make a start by going back to work part-
time at the charity shop. They always need volunteers, and it
would get you out and about. Have you considered selling the
house and finding somewhere easier to run?'
    Gwen shuddered. 'Of course not. This is our home. We've
lived here all our married life. How could you be so unfeeling?'
    Ellie got up, made a proper pot of tea, sniffed the milk in
the bottle on the table, decided it was just about drinkable, and
poured tea for both of them.
    Gwen still hadn't taken her pill.
    Ellie said, 'Did you make a will at the same time as Harold?'
    'Um? No. I haven't made one. I'm not that old. Anyway,
I've nobody to leave anything to, except my sister, I suppose.
Only, she said that Harold's death was a merciful release for
me as well as for him so I don't think I'll leave it to her. I'm
afraid she never understood him.'
    'Do you know why he made a will? Perhaps a friend
suggested it?'
    'Um, yes. Someone at the golf club, I think. He couldn't
play any longer, but he used to drop in there sometimes for a
drink or a meal. It was almost the only pleasure he had towards

the end. He said someone had been talking about a friend who'd upped and died that week, and Harold said he supposed he'd never get any peace from me till I'd seen him in the grave, which was not at all what I'd said but, well, you know, he did get hold of the wrong end of the stick sometimes.'

'I expect he discussed the terms with you before he made his will?'

'Oh, no. He knows – that is, he knew – that I've no head for business. No, he told me afterwards that he'd done it. While I was staying with my sister, in fact. The week before he died. He said he'd made some bequests to old friends, that sort of thing. He tried to explain what he meant when he said I was the residuary legatee, and I think I understood. The solicitor was the executor because Harold knew I'd be no good at all that stuff, taxes and bequests, and form-filling. The executor was wonderful and made it so easy for me to understand what I had to do.'

'It was good of him to leave my husband something. I didn't know they were close.'

Gwen shrugged. 'Was he? His friends were a closed book to me. He knew lots of people I didn't. Men are like that, aren't they?'

'Did you know any of the other people he left bequests to?'

'Mm? No, I don't think so. The executor did read the list out to me, but I wasn't up to dealing with them, so he did it for me.'

'I was surprised you didn't tell me about the funeral. I'd have come if I'd known.'

'Harold left instructions that it was all to be very quiet. He'd no kith or kin left alive and, as you know, he'd never got on with my sister, so there were just a few of us at the crematorium. From his work, mostly. I did think his friends from the golf club might have come but there . . . I don't suppose anyone told them, and I wasn't really up to ringing round, especially when Harold had said he wanted it nice and quiet.'

Ellie pushed the pills further towards Gwen. This time, Gwen took one. Success!

Ellie said, 'I'm glad he recognized how much he meant to

you at the end, Gwen. You were a good wife to him. It was
right and proper that he called you his "dear wife" in his will.
I expect you look at your copy now and then, to remind you? I'd
love to see it, if I may.'

'I've put it away somewhere. I can't look at it at the moment.
Seeing his signature . . . oh dear.' She mopped tears again.
'He remembered all sorts of people, you know; some charities,
the British Heart Foundation, that sort of thing. And the rest he
left to "my dear wife." He did love me, you see. He just wasn't
very good at showing it.'

Ellie wasn't entirely sure that Harold had meant to use those
words of endearment. The solicitor might have put them in as
a matter of routine. But they comforted Gwen and that was all
to the good.

Ellie said, 'He relied on you for everything, Gwen.'

'I keep telling myself that. My sister keeps saying he didn't
love me, but felt he owned me like a slave. She's completely
wrong, and I've told her so.'

'Of course. You knew him far better than she did. Now some
time has passed, perhaps you could ring her up and perhaps
arrange to visit her for a few days? She was good to you when
you were poorly. Perhaps you could arrange to give her a treat,
instead? What about taking her away with you for a weekend
at a spa, or giving yourselves both a course at the beauticians?
Perhaps she could go with you on a spree to buy some new
clothes?'

'Oh, I don't think I could go so far as that.' Gwen tugged at
her hair, which was showing grey at the roots. 'Do I really look
so awful?'

'I'm sure Harold would tell you to look after yourself, and
not let yourself go.'

Gwen bit her lip. 'You think I look terrible.'

'I think it will make you feel better if you smarten yourself
up a bit. Then perhaps you could offer to put in a couple of
hours a week at the charity shop, where we met all those years
ago? You know how short-handed they get, and you are so good
with customers. Do you remember when I made such a mess
of working the till? And you were so quick with it. I felt quite
ashamed of myself.'

'Oh, you!' said Gwen, but she actually managed a smile. She also drank her tea. 'It's going to take time. I know that, and I suppose you are right about doing something to my hair. I haven't coloured it for a while. But I'm so tired . . .'

'The pills will kick in soon.'

'I suppose. As for ringing my sister, well, she does keep ringing me, every now and then. I usually put the phone down when I know it's her, but I suppose she means well.'

Gwen went on talking, gently moving herself on with her life. Ellie listened, and made the appropriate comments when necessary.

The phone rang. Gwen picked it up and said, 'Oh, it's you!' And to Ellie, 'It's my sister!' Then back to the phone: 'I'm glad you rang. At least, I think I am. I've been so down lately. I went to see the doctor and he said . . .'

Ellie washed up the tea things while Gwen talked through her state of mind with her sister, and finally agreed that yes, she would continue with the pills and that they would speak again the following day.

Gwen put the phone down and said, 'You haven't any sisters, have you? So you probably don't understand. I do love my sister. Of course I do. But at a distance. We can talk on the phone, and everything's lovely till she starts criticizing me and then I put the phone down. Harold taught me to do that. He used to say, "If she upsets you, just put the phone down." That's what I do. But when we're together, face-to-face, I can't just walk away, especially if I'm staying with her. Besides, I like to be quiet in my own home.' She looked around her. 'Well, I suppose I'd better see what I can cook myself for supper. I haven't felt like eating much lately.'

Ellie thought that it was too soon for the pills to have kicked in and that probably all that Gwen had needed was someone to talk to for a bit. Whatever the reason, Gwen was on the mend. So Ellie arranged to have a coffee in the Avenue with her friend very soon, and left.

FIVE

On her way home, Ellie realized she was no nearer finding out why Harold had left Thomas any money or to unravelling the mystery of his death, if indeed there was a mystery. It might just have been accident. The coroner had apparently thought so. Harold had been left alone with his pills, he'd been in pain, he'd overdosed. Yes, it had been an accident.

Except . . . except that the Harold Ellie knew would have been meticulous about taking his pills at the right time every day. He would have set alarms on his watch, to remind him when to take them. He would have been careful to take them before or after meals, whichever was indicated.

He hadn't been in agony. Or had he? If the pain in his hip had been so bad that he took double the painkillers to give him a night's sleep, then he might well have risked it. Or, if he'd been fuddled with sleep and woken up, he might have forgotten he'd already taken the recommended dose and dipped into the packet again.

Either way, nobody had seemed to think the manner of his death extraordinary at the time. Thomas ought to be content with that. If only Ellie could find out why Harold had been so generous to him, then all would be well.

Probably.

Ellie arrived home to find Hetty banging pans around in the kitchen, with the radio and the television competing against one another at full blast.

Ellie braced herself. Hadn't she told Hetty not to bother cooking that evening? Oh dear, was Hetty going to stage another scene? Something had to be said.

'No, no, Hetty. Really! I told you I was going to cook tonight.'

Hetty was flushed but determined. 'Oh, go on! Let me! It's so little I can do to repay you for all your kindness to me. I'd be sleeping on the streets if it weren't for you and Thomas.'

Was she trying to pretend that Ellie hadn't asked her to move on?

'Oh, surely not!' said Ellie, trying to put her foot down while aware that she wasn't going to be anywhere near firm enough. 'Now, please! No arguments. I'm cooking tonight, so off you go and put your feet up in peace and quiet.'

'Oh, but I've such a lovely surprise for you tonight! I saw a whacking big bacon joint in the supermarket. It was reduced to a real snip, and I'm cooking it for you with my special dumplings and cabbage. I know Thomas will want at least two helpings!'

'I thought you were going to buy some fish . . . Oh, never mind. That's very good of you, Hetty. But please, I really don't like you going to so much trouble for us.'

Ellie knew she was being weak, but she couldn't bear to see the woman weep, which she seemed likely to do at any moment. So instead of sticking to her guns, she said, 'I'll tell Thomas what to expect.'

She went down the corridor to the library to find Thomas standing at the window and looking out over the garden even though his computer was still on . . . which meant he hadn't finished work yet. The second desk was empty, which meant his secretary had already left for the day.

On hearing Ellie's step, Thomas held his hand out to her. She went to stand close at his side, and he circled her shoulders with his arm. The gardener hadn't been that week, and the lawn was looking shaggy. She really must find time to mow it before the weekend. For a moment she wished Thomas would offer to mow the lawn but dismissed that idea as ridiculous. He really was no gardener. He probably hadn't even noticed that the lawn needed a cut.

Instead, Ellie broke the bad news in a bright voice. 'Hetty's cooking again tonight. I asked her not to, but she'd already started. She thinks it will be a real treat for us.'

He sighed. 'She means well. I think I have some indigestion tablets left.'

Ellie said, 'I have spoken to her about finding her another place to go to. She didn't take it well and now she's pretending I haven't said anything. I'll ask the trust again if we can find somewhere within her price range but I don't think there is anything.'

'She could move further out and find something cheaper.'

'I've suggested that. She doesn't want to. Some day soon we'll have the house to ourselves, I promise. And no more lodgers. I suppose then we'll be complaining the house is too much for us. We're both so busy that I suppose we'll always have to have someone come in from outside to help.'

'We won't always have to work as hard as we do now. Most people are fully retired by this time. I keep going because I enjoy it but for how long will that last? You're amazing, Ellie. You never seem to get tired and you always find time to help people in trouble. Will you ever learn to say "no" to people?'

She grinned. 'Isn't that the pot calling the kettle black? Who's out morning, noon and night, looking after other people? Not to mention the hours you spend on the computer editing the magazine.'

She relaxed, leaning against him. Then remembered that she still had to report what she'd discovered that afternoon. 'I went to see Gwen, whose husband Harold was the third person to leave you some money. He made a will without consulting her as to the details and signed it when she was away for a few days. She says he left bits of money here and there, to charities and so on and so forth. His solicitor was also his executor and seems to have done a decent job of steering Gwen through the worst of the paperwork. Harold died because he'd taken too many painkillers and sleeping tablets. There must have been an autopsy but nobody is screaming "foul play". According to his own wishes, he was cremated in a small private ceremony.'

'I don't remember him at all. Or her.'

'I dare say. I've known Gwen for donkeys' years. I've probably mentioned her to you now and then, but there's no reason why you should remember her. She says that it was someone at the golf club who'd reminded Harold about making a will.'

Ellie's son-in-law, Evan, was a long-time member of the golf club. He and Diana were often there in the evenings. 'Diana and her husband must have come across Harold there. I expect they told him you were a worthy cause.'

Thomas said, 'Humph!' which was as far as he would go in criticism of his stepdaughter and son-in-law, neither of whom had approved of his marriage to the widowed Ellie and who continued to be vocal about it.

Ellie said, 'Gwen's very down at the moment. She's promised me she'll take her tablets for depression. They should kick in soon. Also, her sister's in touch with her. Harold didn't treat her well but she certainly didn't wish for his death.'

'It would have made more sense if he'd left money to you than to me.'

Which was true, except that Ellie didn't think Harold had ever liked her much, either.

Thomas said, 'I've been trying to recall what happened when I went to see Mrs Pullin, the one who's left me a thousand pounds. You remember I said she had several cats? I wonder what happened to them after she died? I suppose they were found another home somewhere. What I do remember now is that, after she'd had communion, she asked me to stay while she served me some really good coffee. She knew her coffee, ordered it from some specialist place somewhere.'

Thomas was a coffee addict. He smiled, remembering how good Mrs Pullin's coffee had been. 'She had a slight accent. She wasn't British by birth, but she'd been living here for many years. Perhaps she was naturalized by marriage? She didn't say. Was she Austrian? No; Polish, I think. Her husband had died a few years before. It was a second marriage and child-less. He had two children and a grandchild by his first wife, but his second wife – that's the Mrs Pullin I knew – said they'd never liked her and only visited when they wanted a handout. It seemed to me that she was lonely but doing her best to cope under difficult circumstances.'

Ellie said, 'Shall I try to visit her people tomorrow?'

A yodelling cry came echoing down the corridor. 'Come and get it! Oranges and Lemons are all on the table! The last one up is a cissy!'

Ellie disentangled herself from Thomas's arm and ran her

fingers back through her short, silvery hair. Was she presentable for supper? Well, she was who she was and Thomas didn't care.

Thomas turned his computer off and patted his pockets to make sure he had his indigestion tables with him. 'It's coming up to one of my busiest times of the year or I'd go to see the Pullin family myself. You shouldn't have to do it for me, but I'm rather glad you are. I've a feeling we're up against time in this matter. The moment one person starts asking questions about the money I've inherited, everyone will know.'

'I'm on to it. Come on, we mustn't keep Hetty waiting.'

Thomas followed Ellie down the corridor, humming, 'Onward, Christian soldiers'.

Thursday morning

Thursday mornings were always devoted to a meeting of the trust. Because Ellie's finance director was such a busy woman, they started promptly at nine thirty. Sometimes the reports needed talking through, and sometimes they could be passed without comment. Today they got through scheduled business early.

True to her word, Ellie once more put in a plea for suitable housing for Hetty. She was, said Ellie, the sort of person whom they had set up the trust to help. She was unskilled but hard-working. Through no fault of her own she had descended into a life in which she rushed from one low-paying job to another, living in rented rooms but never managing to save enough to buy a place of her own. Ellie's request was greeted with frowns.

Stewart, her general manager, said, 'You mentioned her before. We simply don't have anything she could afford. I did wonder if she'd agree to share. We've got a two-bed flat which will become vacant at the end of the month but there's three couples after it already, people who've been on the waiting list for some time. Supposing we let her have it, could she find someone to share with her and how would they split the rent? They'd have to pay equal amounts. We can't have Hetty paying less than her flatmate.'

'I understand,' said Ellie, because she really did. 'It's frustrating. What about that house we're doing up near the university for students?'

He consulted paperwork. 'Already oversubscribed and it's not ready for occupancy yet. The decorators have only just moved in. You remember we had to have the place rewired? That took a little longer than we'd hoped. And would this woman . . . how old is she? Would she fit into student accommodation?'

Ellie knew the answer to that one. 'No, she wouldn't. Well, perhaps there might be something at the end of the month? Could you keep looking?'

Her finance director said, 'Ellie, you know as well as I do that our remit is to provide affordable housing, but overheads such as council tax and maintenance bills still have to be paid, and we have to cover our costs. We are not in the business of providing free accommodation for the homeless.'

'Perhaps we ought to consider doing just that,' said Ellie, thinking aloud.

Her general manager threw up his hands. 'If you want to run a hostel for the homeless, then that's a totally different matter. We would have to locate and buy a suitable house and turn it into very basic accommodation that can withstand wear and tear, not to mention abuse. On top of that, you'd also have to employ staff to live in and manage it for you.'

Ellie sighed. 'Yes, I know, I know.'

Their finance director said, 'Your protégée should find some-where she can afford, further out of London.'

Ellie sighed again. 'I've tried suggesting that. She's not listening.'

The finance director's smartphone vibrated. It turned out to be an urgent call, which led to her making her apologies and leaving for another meeting. The general manager said he'd keep an eye out for something for Hetty, though he wasn't hopeful. He'd bring the matter up again at their next meeting.

As Ellie saw them off, she told herself it was a good thing they'd been interrupted as she really had no right to ask for favours for herself. That was not what the trust was about.

She took the coffee things out to the kitchen, wondering if it were time for her to put another matter on the agenda for the trust, which was the future of this big house. The mainten-ance costs rose every year and Ellie couldn't help worrying about them. Also it seemed absurd for her and Thomas to rattle

about in such a big place. On the other hand, she couldn't
imagine them moving into a tiny flat somewhere, and she really
did need a garden.

Oh well, she'd solve the maintenance problem somehow.
They'd probably still be wondering about a move in ten years'
time.

The doorbell rang, strong and steady.

Oh dear! Ellie knew that ring. Her daughter Diana always
rang the bell as if the Hounds of Hell were on her heels. Ellie
hastened to open the front door, and yes, it was Diana.

For one awful moment Ellie wondered if she'd forgotten she
was supposed to babysit her granddaughter that day. But no,
for Diana – in full business black and white and complete with
briefcase – strode into the house without a baby in tow.

Diana was a businesswoman who was more or less running
her husband's estate agency nowadays. Their firstborn, little
Evan, was at nursery full-time and their baby daughter was in
the care of a nanny for all but one day a week, when Ellie
usually looked after her.

This was not a day on which Ellie was supposed to be
babysitting, so why was Diana here in the middle of a work
day?

Diana didn't waste time going on the attack. 'Mother! It
comes to something when I have to hear of your good fortune
from people at the golf club. When were you going to tell
me? That's what I'd like to know!'

Ellie felt a trickle of apprehension. So Diana had heard
that Thomas had been left some money? The news had got out
already? 'Well, it's not exactly a fortune.'

'We need to talk about this.' Diana brushed past her mother
into the sitting room and took a seat. She opened her briefcase,
extracted a laptop and gestured for Ellie to sit opposite. 'Now,
how much exactly is it, in total? My informant guesses it's over
fifty thousand but admits it may well be more. I am shocked
that you haven't seen fit to put me in the picture. We both know
you've a bad head for business, and it's up to me to stop you
throwing it all away. You haven't got rid of it yet, have you?'

Tap, tap, went her fingers on her keyboard.

Ellie realized that Thomas was right. The bequests couldn't

be kept under wraps. If Diana and her husband knew today, then the world would know tomorrow. Then the police would start to ask questions, and who knew where it would all end!

'Diana, I don't know what you've heard or from whom. It's true that Thomas has received several small bequests—'

'Is it over a hundred thousand, that's what I need to know? If it's less . . . But I rather hope for more, which is the amount I'm thinking of for—'

'Stop! Diana, listen to me. Thomas received two hundred pounds from one, five hundred from another, fifteen hundred from two more, and Tuesday he got a thousand. And that's it.'

'What! But I was told . . .! And it was Thomas who received . . .? Not you? But why on earth would anyone want to give Thomas fifty, let alone fifty thousand pounds?'

'He's received a total of three thousand, two hundred pounds. He's not happy about it, and he wants to return it to the solicitors.'

'What! He can't do that! Why . . .' Her eyes switched to and fro. 'It can't be as little as that. No way! He's telling you porkies, that's what it is. I've never trusted him. Believe me, he's concealing the real extent from you so that he can spend it himself. He's had at least forty thousand pounds, maybe more.'

'I assure you, no. I've seen the paperwork.'

Diana wasn't listening. She crashed down the lid of her laptop, thinking hard. 'How ridiculous, him thinking he can pull the wool over our eyes. You'll have to face up to it, Mother. He's no good. He's probably planning to do a runner with the money, back off to Canada or wherever it is the rest of his family has taken refuge, leaving you with this big house and no money to run it with. I've told you over and over, it's about time you cashed in on this white elephant of a place, downsize to something small, and release the money for the benefit of the family, who need it more than you do.'

Ellie wondered if she could get out of this argument without going off into a faint. Of course Diana had got her facts wrong. Thomas would no more think of cheating her than he would of taking up lap dancing. As for running off to Canada, he preferred a warmer climate and couldn't ski. Visits, yes. Staying there, no.

Ellie told herself to take a deep breath and start again. 'Diana, you've been misinformed and I can prove it. Shall I show you the file of letters from the solicitors?'

Diana's shoulders were tight with tension. 'Don't be ridiculous. It's a hundred thousand, not a penny less. We need that money.'

Ellie braced herself. 'You're in trouble, financially?'

'My beloved husband is such a fool. He's cracking up. He fell over a toy engine which little Evan had left in the hall, which my darling little boy is perfectly entitled to do . . . leave it there, I mean. It's his house too, isn't it? Now Evan's back in his wheelchair and drinking more than ever. He had this scheme, get rich quick, it's not the first time he's let himself into such a stupid . . .! I told him! I said! And it's true we did make a killing on that scheme for the town centre, but then he put everything we got from that, and I mean everything, into an option to develop a site down by the river. We thought we'd get permission to develop and it hasn't happened and now the vendor is asking us to complete the sale and if we don't they'll go elsewhere and we'll lose all the money we've invested so far. It's infuriating!'

Angry tears spurted. Diana dabbed at her eyes with a tissue.

'I'm so sorry.' What else could Ellie say?

Diana narrowed her eyes. 'I'm not having the business go under just because my husband's losing the plot. You'll have to help us. If the cash from the wills isn't sufficient, you'd better take out a mortgage on this house. Yes, that's what you must do. Or, better still, put it up for sale. Any developer worth his salt would redevelop the site, put up a block of flats, and have no difficulty selling them. Yes, I'll put out some feelers today. I know who might well be interested.' She opened her laptop again.

Ellie told herself to be brave. 'Thank you for your advice, Diana, but I am not prepared to bail you out of whatever fix you've got yourself into now. Before you go, I'd like the name of whoever gave you this false information, as it needs to be corrected straight away.'

'How should I know? One of Evan's friends.'

'Then you'd better ask Evan who it was and get him to

contradict the rumour. Now, if you don't mind, I'm due elsewhere.'

Diana snapped her laptop shut, stowed it in her briefcase and looked round her. 'Yes, yes. I dare say you will quibble, but selling this place is the only answer. It's getting to look shabby, but that doesn't matter when it's going to be pulled down. I'll see you get an offer that you can't refuse. Now I must go. I have to get Evan to a doctor's appointment. I can't trust him to go by himself. For one thing, he's not fit to drive any longer. I'll be in touch.'

Ellie told herself to hold her tongue as she saw her daughter off the premises. It was no good indulging in hysterics or having a slanging match.

Diana's car spurted gravel as it left the drive.

Ellie closed the front door, leaned against it and fought off a desire to have a good weep.

Dear Lord, what can I say except, 'Help! Please, tell me what to do?' Our whole way of life, Thomas's reputation is under threat. If the police get hold of this, or the papers . . .

She thought of going along to the study and unloading this latest problem on to Thomas. But no; he would be working hard today on the magazine. She wouldn't interrupt him. He'd learn about it soon enough.

Why spread the worry? A worry shared is a worry doubled.

With some hesitation, she decided that she might as well carry on with her plan to speak to the Pullin family, if she could. They didn't seem to be on the telephone, but if she went along in person she might find an estate agent's board or a neighbour who could give her a contact number.

She looked up the location of the house. It wasn't far away, though perhaps a little farther than she was prepared to walk in her house shoes. She changed into some comfortable sandals, telling herself that it was good for her to walk for at least twenty minutes, twice a day. All the medics said so. The medics also said she was supposed to cut down on fats and alcohol, but there were limits to the amount of advice which Ellie was prepared to take on that subject.

She found her jacket and her keys and set off, thinking that though she didn't go in much for alcohol, there was nothing like real butter, and as for cream . . . What bliss to have a home-baked scone, lathered with butter, surcharged with jam and topped off with clotted cream! Or were you supposed to put the cream on before the jam, and miss off the butter? She wasn't sure which was correct. Personally, she liked to put the cream on last, but everyone had their own ideas about such things.

Not that she intended to have a scone of any sort for her tea. It would be good to lose a bit of weight. She didn't want to go in for proper dieting. Yes, it would be good to go down a dress size but she believed in moderation in all things. Well, most things, anyway. And if she wanted to binge on a chocolate orange every now and then, well, that was her concern and no one else needed to know about it.

She scolded herself. She was rambling. Trying not to think about the unthinkable.

She came to a standstill outside a substantial red-brick, semi-detached house with a small, neglected garden in front. The privet hedges on either side had not been cut in months. Was this the house?

SIX

Thursday, noon

Yes, it was the right address.
Ellie surmised that the rooms would be large with high ceilings and tall sash windows. She could hear the rumble of the Underground railway nearby. Did the District Line run behind these houses? The path to the front door and inside the porch had been finished with matching red tiles, and there was an original piece of stained glass in the window of the front door. Such touches always added to the value of a house.

This was a desirable property with good transport links. A solidly built family house, three storeys high. Worth perhaps around a million?

There was a For Sale sign attached to the brick-built gatepost which said, 'viewing by appointment only'. Ellie made a note of the contact number for the estate agent then, ignoring the injunction that viewing was by appointment only, rang the doorbell just in case someone still lived there.

The door cracked open, and a long, sour face topped with tight peroxided curls appeared. 'Can't you read? "Viewing by appointment only". I said this would happen if we put up a board outside, and what happens? The board goes up and people start knocking on the door, wanting to be shown around.'

'I'm not here about that.'

The woman's expression did not relax. 'Jehovah's Witnesses? No.' She answered her own question. 'No, there's only one of you, unless your partner is hiding in the bushes. You're selling something? I never buy at the door. No, you haven't a backpack. You're collecting for a charity? In my book, charity begins at home. Go away. I'm busy.' She swung the door to.

Ellie had heard about men putting their foot in a door to stop it closing but she wasn't quick enough to do so now. Anyway, she was wearing sandals, which wouldn't be any protection if that heavy door had closed on her foot. So, she rang the bell again.

And again.

And kept her finger on the buzzer till the woman opened the door the same few inches.

Ellie said, 'My name is Ellie Quicke, and I'm from the church. I came to thank you.'

'What for?'

'I assume you are a relative of Mrs Pullin's? She left some money to my husband, the Reverend Thomas, which is most welcome. I wanted to say how grateful we are to your . . . stepmother, was it?'

'Just like her. Wouldn't you know!' The door opened a fraction more, revealing a bony woman in her fifties. She was wearing a plastic apron over a T-shirt and jeans, and her hands were encased in yellow household cleaning gloves. 'Well, don't just stand there. Come on in. You'll forgive me not offering you a cuppa, but I've a lot to do. The For Sale board went up yesterday against my wishes for the place is not fit to be seen, but would my brother listen? Not he! My niece and her boyfriend have been staying here and did they do diddly-squat to keep the place clean and tidy, never mind getting the house ready to show? Not they!'

She led the way into a high-ceilinged sitting room which was filled with an old-fashioned three-piece suite, footstools, coffee tables, a glass-fronted cabinet and a small television set. All pre-Second World War, except for the television set. Pictures with dark, heavy frames had been taken off the wall and stacked in a corner, while posters of gigs had been Sellotaped on to the wallpaper in their place. Ornaments of the Toby Jug variety had been crammed into the cabinet, and there were three – no, four – small clocks, now mercifully silent. Thin, unlined curtains had been drawn halfway across the window and the room seemed dark. It smelled of stale beer and something else, less pleasant. There was a fine layer of dust over everything.

Did the place smell of cats? No. Not cats. Stale food? An empty drink can rolled under Ellie's foot and she nearly fell.

The woman pounced on the can and threw it in a rubbish bin on wheels which she'd stationed in the middle of the room. The bin was already overflowing with newspapers, plastic food trays and pizza boxes.

'You see what comes of letting youngsters look after the house?' The woman continued on her way round the room, collecting trash as she went. 'You don't mind if I carry on, do you? I need to get this room and the next done before I leave. I have to get back before *EastEnders*, don't I? Who did you say you were?'

'My name is Ellie Quicke. It was my husband, a minister in the local circuit, who inherited some money from your stepmother. Can I help at all? I could do the dusting if you tidy.'

'I'm Dawn Pullin, her stepdaughter. Your husband's a minister? Hah! I don't believe in all that stuff. I know Mum did, more fool her, though Dad wasn't that bothered. I don't hold with bells and smells. They give me hay fever.'

'It's not that kind of church,' said Ellie, dumping her jacket and handbag to pick up a duster and a can of polish. 'My husband is a retired minister who brought her communion one day after she'd broken her ankle and her own minister was poorly. He got talking to Mrs Pullin about this and that. He liked your stepmother. He was surprised to hear she'd left him some money, but also grateful.'

The woman looked at her watch and stripped off her gloves. 'I've been at it since ten and hardly touched the surface. Time for a cuppa. You won't mind the mess in the kitchen, will you? They left a mountain of washing-up to do, and I daren't think what the sheets are like in the bedrooms.'

Ellie picked up her cue. 'I could wash up for you, if you like?' It was definitely the right thing to say.

'I'll admit I could do with a hand.'

Ellie blanched when she saw how dated the kitchen equipment was, and how much washing-up needed doing, but there seemed to be plenty of hot water so she got down to it. Meanwhile Dawn sought out some clean mugs and boiled a kettle, complaining that everything was broken, including the immersion heater, and what the plumber was going to charge to look at the damp patch on the landing she couldn't imagine. There was hot water only because she'd turned the central heating on since the house felt damp and for some reason that had triggered the hot water system into life.

Finally, they sat at the table to sip a cuppa each. Dawn said, 'I shoulda brought a sandwich, but I didn't think.' She opened a tin which had contained biscuits and upended it to shower crumbs on the table. 'See? No biscuits. Locusts, that's what they were. Never thought of replacing anything. Not so much as a toilet roll, so I don't advise your using the loo while you're here.'

'Understood. The family let your niece stay here for a while?'

'Fact is we didn't know what to do with the house until probate was granted. Neither my brother nor I could afford to buy one another out so we knew we'd have to sell. To leave it empty was asking for trouble, what with squatters and a dripping tap in the bathroom and a spot of what I swear is wet rot on the landing and all. We argued about it something chronic. I've my own little council flat, Lewisham way, and that's nigh on a day's journey, what with two buses and a stint on the Underground. I work mornings at the school as a dinner lady, and then in the cleaners down the road in the afternoons. I wasn't going to give up my jobs to look after this place for six

months, now, was I? Then my brother – him that works for the
town hall, though what with the cuts I don't know how long
that's going to last – he said he couldn't get to his job if he
moved over here, and his wife that's a fair cow, pardon my
language, but she is, she said she was blowed if she'd put her
job at the hairdresser's at risk. And she didn't say "blowed", if
you know what I mean.'

Ellie knew. 'So you let your niece move in and look after
the house till probate was granted and you could sell it?'

'I insisted she sign a month to month lease, no rent but paying
for the repairs. My brother didn't think it was necessary, but
he's a fool where she's concerned, and luckily the solicitor
agreed with me. We had her sign everything, right and tight,
but did she look after the house? Did she, heck! She got that
no-good boyfriend of hers to patch up this and that, like putting
a plaster on a fatal wound, if you ask me, but finally we got
her out and I agreed I'd come over when I could and make a
start getting the place ready to sell.

'So I got a day off and here I am. And did I have a shock
when I walked in here this morning! It's clear that the job's
more than I can cope with in one day, not to mention it needs
a plumber and a carpenter too, I dare say. I rang my brother
just before you came to put him in the picture. I said we should
sue my niece for damages and he said, "Oh, come on!" I said,
"You should see the mess the place is in. It's going to knock
thousands off the price to put it on the market like this."'

Ellie nodded. 'At least. Have you had a survey done?'

'My brother said it wasn't necessary and that the house should
sell like hot cakes, being in this nice neighbourhood. I told him
that was pie in the sky. Then I said I shouldn't be out of pocket
because his daughter has let things slip and that if he didn't
stir his stumps and do something about it, I was going to go to
the police and charge her with damaging my property.'

'Really?' Ellie admired someone who could stand up to the
next generation.

Dawn nodded. 'Well, I probably wouldn't have, but
the moment I threatened to bring the police in, he said he'd
come round and see what could be done. After all, we really
don't want the police poking their noses in again, do we?'

Ellie choked on her tea. 'Oh? The police were here before? Why?'

Dawn gave a long, heavy sigh. 'There was this awful palaver over our stepmother's death. To hear them talk, you'd have thought she'd been murdered in her bed. The questions they asked! It went on for days. I lost a day and a half's work and when I asked the police who was going to make that time up for me, they were quite rude. In the end they agreed it was just what we'd all thought in the beginning.'

Ellie felt the hairs rise on the back of her neck. 'There was cause to suspect something not quite right about your stepmother's death?'

'No, of course not. It was an accident, but Her Next Door had to poke her nose in, didn't she? She used to come round to complain every time one of the kitties strayed into her beloved garden and did a whoopsie, which you can't stop cats doing, now can you? They always covered it over neatly, as cats do.'

Ellie said, 'Your neighbour had a grudge against your stepmother's cats? Well, it's true, they do go over the garden wall and pay a call wherever they wish to do so, and I suppose it can be annoying if they scratch up the earth where you've sowed some seeds. But what has that got to do with her death?'

'Oh, she was just making trouble, like she always did. She said she heard shouting in the kitchen the night of the accident. She said it must have been one of us, seeing as we were always on at our stepmother to sell up and downsize. What she heard was our stepmother's radio that she played far too loudly. But there you are, you can't tell some people, can you?'

Ellie looked around and, sure enough, there was a big, old-fashioned Bakelite wireless on a wooden cabinet set against the interior wall. Noise from that might well penetrate next door.

'I think I can understand the situation,' said Ellie, with care. 'I'm in a somewhat similar position myself. This is a big old house, and valuable. Your stepmother was getting on in years and you felt she would be happier in a small flat somewhere, while you and your brother could do with the money from the sale of the house. Is that right? Did you argue about it?'

'Of course we argued about it. It was only common sense. She wouldn't budge, not she. She liked her independence, she

said, though she was getting slow on her pins and then she
broke her ankle and it was extremely inconvenient for me or
my brother to come over and do her shopping for her, and my
sister-in-law never lifted a finger which is par for the course,
if you get me. We did our best to look after her, and if it wasn't
enough then she had her savings to get some help in, didn't
she? But no, she wouldn't have a cleaner more than once
a week, and the doctor got social services involved and they
were running in and out at all times of the day, nasty prying
busybodies that they are. It was only common sense for her to
downsize, but she was that obstinate!'

'And she had the cats to look after.' There was no evidence
of cat dishes or cat litter to be seen. 'What happened to them?'

'We asked the Cat Protection people to take them to be
rehomed. I couldn't have them, not with my allergy, and my
sister-in-law wouldn't demean herself to look after anyone but
herself. We knew the oldest cat probably wouldn't be found
another home, but there . . . It is what it is.'

Ellie said, 'It must have been hard for you when the police
took your neighbour's story about a quarrel seriously?'

'It was. Fortunately I'd collected my friend from her place
that evening and we went to the pub together. It was quiz night,
see, and we were there till closing time. We came second,
which was a scandal, because we ought to have won by rights,
but it's men as run these things, isn't it? My brother and his
wife had a barbecue, with friends round. Not that they invited
me and I don't bear a grudge, not at my age. And my darling
niece that's trying to make it as a model – can you believe?
– she and her boyfriend went to some party miles away and
didn't come back till morning.

'No, we was lucky there. We'd all got alibis. What it was,
our stepmother was cutting up some chicken for the kitties
and, well, we don't know what happened for sure, but I reckon
one of them tripped her up and she fell on the knife. They
say she wouldn't have felt much, that it would have been all
over in a minute or two. It depends where the knife goes in,
you see. If you get an artery, it's quick. I'm glad it was quick.
She wouldn't have liked going into a home, not really.'

Ellie said, 'It must have been horrid, having the police around when you're trying come to terms with your stepmother's death. Had you seen her recently?'

'N-no. Not really.' A shrugging of shoulders. 'Not after we'd had words about us wanting her to be sensible and sell up, and her saying we only wanted to feather our own nests, which was probably spot on for my brother, trying to satisfy my sister-in-law's ambitions to move up the housing market, though she probably wouldn't have been satisfied if he'd given her a house in Mayfair, knowing her.'

Ellie noted that Dawn had avoided answering the question about her own needs. Ellie suspected the woman could have done with a windfall herself. Ellie said, 'They do say that a son is a son till he gets him a wife. So your brother wasn't on good terms with your stepmother? How did you get on with her?'

Dawn shifted in her chair. 'Our real mum died when we was small. Complications from a still birth. They did their best but everything went wrong. We was on our own with help from an auntie, but she had her own brood. Dad met this woman at the pub one night; she was serving behind the bar, quite a gadabout as they say. After a while she moved in to look after us and they got married. You know she came from someplace in Europe? Looking for a better life, wasn't she? And found it. Don't get me wrong, she did all right for us according to her lights, though it wasn't the same. Couldn't be, could it? Yes, it was all right when I was growing up, but then I had my spot of bother and Dad took against me.'

'What happened?'

'I was being courted by this lad. He thought I'd come into money, and I kept telling him my dad was as mean as a tick, but Alan was sure we'd be given a nice handout when we married, which we did down the registry. Only, Dad told him to get a job and pay his own gambling debts and our step-mother wouldn't go against Dad, and there was me with a month-old baby and no money coming in. So Alan left me, didn't he? In a rented room, which the landlord didn't like my having a baby there. Give her her due, our stepmother slipped me the odd tenner, but Dad said he didn't see why he should scrimp and save when he was coming up to retirement and I should go on the social, which is what I had to do. And then the baby died that winter. Asthma, they said. Because of the damp in the walls of our room.'

'I am sorry,' said Ellie. 'That must have been very hard.'

'Tell the truth, I never got over it. Not really. Alan leaving, and then the baby following after. I could have married again. That's what our stepmother said. I had one or two offers, but I didn't fancy it, somehow. You can be let down once too often.'

'I understand. But you couldn't help dreaming that things might improve when your stepmother died. Not that you wanted her to, but you could see that one day you'd come into some money, enough to buy yourself somewhere decent. You did know she'd made a will in your favour?'

'Sure. She made it the first time when Dad died. She had this leech, some friend who advised her on her investments and such. Probably made a fortune for himself out of her if the truth were but known. She called him her "gentleman friend", which tells you all you need to know about him and her, right? He got her to update her will every year, would you believe? That way he pocketed a fee each time, didn't he?'

'Did she change the conditions each time?'

'To be fair; no, not much. She left some money for a couple of old friends and some to the church, and someone she used to play bridge with, and yes, her cleaner. Some of the names changed every year as her old friends died off and she thought of leaving a bit to someone different. But yes, my brother and I knew we'd get the rest and yes, it was something to look forward to.' Dawn looked around her. 'Not that it's much, when you come to look at it. It's going to take for ever to clean the place up ready to go on the market.'

'She left money to my husband, Thomas, too.'

Dawn wasn't interested. 'Well, that's the way it was. It was her right to give someone a bit here and a bit there. I didn't know some of the people at all, but we didn't know everyone that came into the house looking for a handout, did we?'

That all sounded reasonable to Ellie. If Thomas had been one among many who'd benefited from the will, no one could point the finger at him or talk about undue influence.

Ellie probed one last time. 'I expect she had friends who were also making their wills at that time of life, and they all talked about who they'd leave their money to and decided that some should go to the church.'

'I suppose.' Dawn was dubious. 'She didn't discuss that with us. I rang her once a week to see how her ankle was doing and that. I told her I was going to come over the next Saturday to see if she wanted some shopping done, but she said not to put myself out if it was going to be that much trouble, so I didn't. Truth to tell, I hadn't seen her for over a couple of weeks when she died. If it hadn't been for her leaving the wireless on, and Her Next Door being a nosy whatsit, she might not have been found for days. Unless the social had been round, which I suppose they might, seeing as they was supposed to see she was stocked up with food.'

'You mean the neighbour realized something was wrong because the wireless was on all night?'

'Yep. She come round, banging on the door and no one answered, so she rang the police. Can you believe she did that without telling us? Though to be fair, she didn't have our phone numbers. The police were going to break in, which would have played merry hell with that old front door and we'd have had the devil of a job to get it repaired, but anyway, along came the social, as should have come the previous day but hadn't, and she had a key and let them in.

'Our stepmother was . . .' Dawn gestured to the back door. 'Huddled up over there. They called the ambulance, but . . .' A shrug. 'The blood was everywhere, all under her and, well, you know. There was some lino there – my niece got her boyfriend to take it out back and burn it, which he did, and what a stink that was, giving Her Next Door something else to shout about.'

'Who was her doctor? There was a post-mortem?'

'She went to the surgery just off the Lane, never saw the same doctor twice. Every time they gave her pills. More pills. Pills for this and for that, and when I opened the cabinet they all tumbled out, gave me such a fright. I don't think she took half of those she was supposed to, but it all ended in tears anyway, didn't it?'

'Yes, it did. I'm so sorry. What a shock for you.'

'In a way it was expected but yes, it was a shock. And another shock when the police started with their questions, and if we hadn't had alibis I don't know what might have happened. But she was all by herself, cutting up food for the kitties. One of them tripped her up and she fell, cutting an artery. It would all have been over in five minutes, they said. My brother and I were the residuary legatees but it turns out there wasn't much money in the bank, and what there was went in bequests to old friends and the solicitors who are executors and bank charges and funeral expenses and that. We'll get some money when the house is sold and not before.'

'Isn't there even enough in the bank to pay someone to clear the house for you?'

Dawn shook her head. 'Wanna see the rest of the house? Our stepmother didn't do any decorating and precious little maintenance since my dad died, which was ten years ago come December. My darling niece had her friends in for parties and wouldn't have moved out but that my brother refused to pay the water bill so she had to go. No water for the loo, you understand? Once she'd gone, he paid the water bill and the gas, and I forked up for the electricity but not for the landline phone. We had to let that one go.'

Dawn beckoned Ellie to follow her, and in silence they went up the stairs, up and up, two flights to the attic, which was cobwebbed and gurgled with old-fashioned pipes from a huge water tank. There were also mountains of junk interspersed with bits and pieces of furniture and old suitcases.

Dawn said, 'My grandparents' stuff. They died when I was little. My dad didn't like to throw anything away.' She tapped a dust-covered round table. 'Woodworm, I shouldn't wonder.'

Ellie said, 'There might be something here worth sending to auction. It wouldn't cost you anything to get someone round to see if there's anything of value.'

'You think? It's all rubbish. I wouldn't give it house room.' She led the way down to the bedroom floor. 'My Lady Muck and her boyfriend took the big room at the front, and goodness knows who slept in the other rooms, but the best thing for the bedding would be to send it to the dump.'

Ellie was forced to agree. What a mess! There were blankets and tatty eiderdowns instead of modern duvets on the beds. The sheets and pillowcases were all soiled, and probably the mattresses, too. Ugh.

The fittings in the bathroom were ancient. Somewhere a tap dripped. There was a nasty smell of something in the back bedroom, and mould on the landing wall.

The house shouldn't have been put on the market before a plumber had dealt with those problems. Likewise, the house ought to have been cleared of furniture, and a team of cleaners brought in to make the place look decent. A report on the structure of the house from a surveyor would also have been a good idea.

One thing was clear: Dawn was not going to be able to wave a wand and transform the house into a saleable proposition without some expenditure of money and, if the house was sold as it was, then it would go for a fraction of its potential.

It occurred to Ellie to wonder if the trust might be interested in buying it. The rooms were all of a fair size and if money were to be spent on it, the house could become an attractive proposition.

'Seen enough?' Dawn led the way downstairs, looking at her watch. 'Time flies when you're having fun, eh? I ought to be on my way if I want to miss the rush hour on the Underground. Now where did I leave my bag?' She led the way back to the kitchen.

Ellie had been thinking that she liked Dawn's guts, and that it would be good to help her if she could think of a way to do so. She said, 'Look, my husband wasn't happy about being left money by someone who was all but a stranger to him. Suppose I ask him to lend you something towards clearing the house and getting a plumber in?'

Dawn's face lit up with hope for a moment, and then she shook her head. 'No. Why would he do that for me? I don't know the people who came from the church.'

Ellie crossed her fingers. 'I think my husband would regard it as only fair to help you out. He got a thousand pounds. What do you say?'

Tears stood out in Dawn's eyes. 'Would he? Why would he do that?'

'Because he's a good man.'

Dawn sniffed. 'There's not many of those around.'

'True. I'll talk to him about it, shall I? Meanwhile, would you like to let me have your address and telephone number?'

Someone fumbled a key into the front door and threw it open. A voice bellowed, 'Dawn? You still here?'

Dawn said, 'That's my brother!' She called out, 'Bob? We're in the kitchen. You've come to see how bad it is, have you? Your Bryony should be shot for leaving it in such a state!'

SEVEN

Thursday, noon

Bob Pullin was a lanky man in a cheap grey suit and a poor complexion. His breathing was noisy. 'You leave off our Bryony,' he said. And then, 'What's that smell? Haven't you had the plumber in to fix it yet?' And, on seeing Ellie, 'Who's this? Some friend of yours that's come to see if there's any pickings for her, eh?'

Ellie recognized a bully when she saw one.

His appearance on the scene caused the voluble Dawn to become nervous, plucking at her tightly permed hair. 'No, no. This is Mrs Quicke, from the church. One of those that got left some money.'

'Is she, now?' He assessed Ellie for her rateable value and managed to produce a smile for someone who didn't buy her clothes in a charity shop.

'Yes,' said Ellie. 'I came to say how much we appreciated the windfall.'

Dawn fidgeted. 'She helped me with the washing-up—'

'Which I'm afraid I didn't quite finish,' said Ellie.

'And she offered to give us some of the money back,' said Dawn. Was she hoping to soften her brother's mood?

'Did you, now?' The smile widened and became unctuous. 'Well, now, that's decent of you. Our stepmother gave the church money every week, regular as clockwork, so it's only right some should come back to her. How much, did you say?'

Ellie didn't like the man. He was not, in her estimation, someone you would trust with other people's money. Or rather, you could trust it to disappear as quickly as a pickpocket could whip away your wallet. Ellie had had no qualms in offering to help Dawn without putting paperwork through a solicitor, but this man was a different kettle of fish. She rephrased her offer.

'I understand you are temporarily embarrassed pending the sale of the house. I can see that putting it on the market as it is, the price will be way below what you could get if you had it cleaned up and the plumbing attended to. I might be able to organize a firm of cleaners to come in and—'

'Dawn's doing the cleaning up,' said Bob.

Dawn looked ready to cry. 'You know I can't. They gave me time off today, but I can't expect more. I'd lose my jobs and—'

'Well, if I can have the afternoon off to look after our affairs, then so can you. What sort of jobs have you got, anyway? They pay tuppence. Not like my job. You can't expect me or Mamie to stop work to clear up here, when—'

'It's your Bryony's fault that the house is in such a mess!'

'She had to live somewhere, didn't she?'

'We'd have done better to go to a lettings agent!'

Ellie hastened to intervene in what was clearly an ongoing quarrel. 'I do understand the difficulty. The sooner you get the house in better nick, the better the price you'll get for it. I know a plumber and a firm of cleaners who could start work here within days. I could advance you money to pay for them – up to a certain limit – on the understanding that you repay me when the house is sold. Agreed?'

Dawn got the message. She didn't like it, but she understood that Ellie's offer would have strings attached. In subdued tones, she said, 'Oh, would you? That would be—'

'Dawn!' Bob was not going to let her take over negotiations. 'I think you'd better leave business matters to me. Mrs, er, Quicke, is it? It's only right and proper that you should wish to help us out. You pay the bill to put the house in order, and we'll be forever grateful. No need for paperwork. A "gentleman's agreement," right?'

Ellie thought Bob would think 'gentlemen's agreements' were for suckers. Bob Pullin was too sharp for his own good.

Yes, Ellie liked to help those who deserved it, but in her estimation Bob Pullin did not come into that category. She said, 'Your stepmother very kindly left some money to my husband, who brought her communion when she couldn't get out herself . . .'

No need to say it had only been the once that Thomas had seen Mrs Pullin.

'And I think Thomas would like to do something for Mrs Pullin's family in return for her kindness to him. On a business footing, of course.'

Bob's eyes narrowed as he realized Ellie was not going to be a pushover, as he'd first thought. He said, 'She left money to all sorts. People we don't know from Adam. If she hadn't done that we'd have been quids in and there'd be no need for us to ask for charity. We appreciate you kindly giving the money back to us.'

Ellie produced what she hoped was a steely look. 'It wouldn't be charity. It would be a loan, properly signed and witnessed. If you agree that it would help you to get a better price for the house then I'm prepared to organize it for you. I'll pay for a plumber and house cleaners. You'll get someone from the auction house to take what furniture is of value and have house clearers to do the rest. There'll be a cap of a thousand pounds on how much I spend, right?'

Sotto voce, Dawn mumbled, 'It wouldn't be necessary if Bryony had only looked after the place better.'

'You keep out of this, Dawn.' Bob's colour rose, but he wasn't going to admit his daughter was at fault. 'She did her best. She's busy, going to interviews and doing her photo shoots—'

'Chance would be a fine thing,' muttered Dawn, but quietly enough that Bob could ignore her interjection if he wished. And he did wish.

'So,' he said, turning on Ellie. 'Your card, if you please. Now, when can you get the cleaners and your plumber started?'

Ellie saw the trap and neatly avoided it. 'Not till we've got a loan agreement signed by all three of us. I won't spend more than one thousand pounds, to be repaid when you get the money from the sale of the house. That might take months, as you know. Shall we add five per cent interest to the loan?'

He yelped. 'Five per cent?'

Ellie raised her eyebrows. 'You think six or seven would be more usual?'

He almost gobbled. 'Five per cent. Of course. I'll get our solicitor to draw something up, next week. Yes, sometime next week. I can't keep taking time off to attend to these details. You can start your people tomorrow, right?'

'I'll get *my* solicitor to draw an agreement up,' said Ellie. 'I'll contact you as soon as it's ready and bring it round for you both to sign. At that point you can let me have a key, and I'll start the plumber and the cleaners off. Meanwhile, you'll tell the estate agents that you've temporarily taken the house off the market to have some work done on it, because you'll only get rubbish offers the way it looks now. Next, you'll get the auction people in to look at the best of the furniture and organize a house clearance firm to take away the rest. Agreed?'

Bob looked sour, so Dawn intervened. 'Oh, come on, Bob. You know she's right.'

'And if,' said Ellie, smiling sweetly, 'you don't repay me when the money comes in, I shall have no compunction about involving the police. Understood?'

Bob shuddered. 'We've had enough of them. I still don't understand how she came to stab herself like that, but I don't suppose we'll ever know.'

Thursday afternoon

Ellie trudged home, trying to make sense of what she'd learned. She hadn't found any connection between Thomas and the people who'd left money to him. She hadn't found any connection between these two deaths, either. Both had been followed by an autopsy, and both had been declared accidental.

The only difference was that in Mrs Pullin's case there'd been some police involvement. But it hadn't resulted in further investigation, so . . .?

Ellie decided that none of this was in the least alarming,

unless she found that any of the other deaths had been subject
to an autopsy. And if that happened . . .?

She didn't want to think about that.

It was past her usual lunchtime and she was hungry, so she
went straight to the kitchen when she got in. Thomas didn't
seem to have been in to make himself a sandwich. She'd left
some of her homemade soup on the stove for him to heat up
but that hadn't been touched, either. Perhaps he'd had to go out
somewhere? But when it got this close to putting the magazine
to bed, he usually stuck to his computer till it was done.

Ellie went down the corridor to the study. Thomas wasn't
there, but his part-time secretary was and she wasn't looking
as serene as usual.

'You want Thomas? I don't know what's the matter. We were
getting on famously this morning until he went to fetch the
post. He came back looking quite ill and I said, "Shall I get
you something?" He said, "No, I'm perfectly all right," when
it was clear to me that he wasn't. Not all right, I mean. He
said he'd go and sit in his Quiet Room for a few minutes
and he hasn't come back and there's I don't know how many
pages he's got to sign off today.'

The Quiet Room overlooked the drive at the front of the
house. It was a space set aside for sitting and thinking. Diana's
little boy, young Evan, liked to have his afternoon nap there,
and Ellie also spent time in it when she had to think through
a particular problem. Thomas used it every day to say the daily
office.

He was sitting there now, holding an envelope in one hand,
and a letter in the other. He looked as if he'd lost weight since
that morning.

Ellie felt a pang of fear. Was he ill? Was he dying of some
deadly disease? How could she ever manage without him?
She said, 'Are you all right?'

He closed his eyes. Shook his head. Didn't speak.

She sat down beside him. 'I saw the Pullin family. The house
is in a mess and they haven't the money to clean it up, so I
said you'd lend them some of your inheritance to get the
cleaners in. It's a loan not a gift, to be repaid when they eventually manage to sell the house. Mrs Pullin accidentally cut herself

and died of blood loss. The police were satisfied that it was an accident.' And then she said, 'Something's happened?'

He held a letter out to Ellie. It was a solicitor's letter from a firm in the north of England, enclosing a cheque.

The cheque was for twenty thousand pounds.

Ellie couldn't believe it. Was this the money that Diana had referred to? The inheritance that someone at the golf club had been rattling on about?

Thomas cleared his throat. 'This is the sixth cheque. At least I did know this man. He was an old school friend. We used to meet up in town for a meal two or three times a year. I don't think you ever met him. He ended up as dean of a theological college in the north. We used to argue something chronic about forgiveness, and how some people can and others can't, and whether it's all a question of faith or grace, or of letting time do its work.

'What else can I tell you about him? He never married. His father manufactured soap. The family sold the business after the war. He used to make jokes about coming clean. After he retired he spent the winter months in New Zealand, visiting cousins. He stopped over in several places, Hong Kong and so on, on his way back, caught some bug or other and died on arrival. I went to his funeral. It was well attended. I didn't go to the reception afterwards because I had to get back here for a meeting of some sort. He was a good man.'

Ellie felt considerable relief. At least Thomas knew the reason why this cheque had come his way. She said, 'Diana came this morning. She'd heard through someone at the golf club that you'd received a large inheritance.'

'Had she?' A long, long sigh. 'If it's got round the golf club then it'll be everywhere tomorrow. Well, that's torn it. We thought we had time to investigate these windfalls while we could keep the matter to ourselves, but if they're common knowledge then there's no time to waste. I'm not waiting for the police to start asking questions. I have to go to them myself.'

'No, Thomas. That's not right. You know where this last cheque came from and the circumstances surrounding it. Whatever you do about the other cheques, this one is genuine and you can keep it.'

He managed a smile which was more like a grimace. 'So you agree with me that the others aren't genuine?'

Ellie was silent, because that was exactly the conclusion she'd been coming to herself.

Thomas's secretary appeared in the doorway. 'Sorry to interrupt, but Diana's on the landline asking if anyone's at home. She's rung the front doorbell but can't get any answer.'

Ellie groaned. 'The wiring to the bell must have come apart again. I'd better see her. Thomas, don't do anything till we've spoken again, will you?'

He lumbered to his feet, holding on to the arms of his chair. He'd been sitting in one position for too long. 'Look at the time! I should have been . . . There's still a lot to do today. Ellie, we have to talk about this. Seriously.'

'I agree. We'll talk as soon as I've got rid of Diana.'

She saw him off down the corridor and hurried back to the hall. Opening the front door, she found her daughter there, fuming at being kept waiting. And yes, the wiring leading from the doorbell to the battery inside was hanging loose. Again. Thomas had tried to fix it. And so had the last handyman who'd been in to look at a sash window that was sticking.

Ellie decided she'd have to get an electrician in to deal with the wiring in the porch. The man they'd always used in the past had retired. She would have to ask around to find someone who could be trusted with a screwdriver, and who didn't inflate his bill. Perhaps she could use one of the men employed for such jobs by the trust?

Diana stalked in. 'About time! Didn't you hear me?'

'Sorry, no. The wiring has—'

'Old houses need a lot of attention. I've told you till I'm blue in the face, it's about time you realized that and downsized.' She marched straight through to the sitting room. 'We need to talk.'

Ellie sighed. 'A cup of tea?'

'No. This is serious. Sit down.'

Ellie followed her in and sat.

Diana said, 'I have never made any secret of my feelings about your marrying a penniless man—'

True, thought Ellie.

'But I never thought he was quite such a low-life as he has turned out to be. You do realize he's been cheating on you, right? Or are you the last to hear about it?'

Ellie subdued an impulse to have hysterics. Or to hit Diana. Or both. Perhaps she could hit her first, and then lie on the floor and scream? 'Don't talk nonsense, Diana.'

'Oh, it's true. I don't know what else he's been concealing from you all these months, but once a man starts lying to you, you need to look into what else they've been doing. I suspect that what we're seeing now is only the tip of the iceberg. The awful truth is that he only married you for your money and now he's going to take you for what he can get.'

Ellie told herself to relax. She put her hands on the arms of her winged, high-back chair and hooked a stool into position. She put one foot up, and then the other. She breathed deeply. In and out. In and out. Only then did she say, 'Rubbish.'

Diana flushed. 'How can you be so blind! Everyone knows—'

'Everyone knows what?'

'You denied it this morning so I went back to my informant and it is perfectly true. Thomas has been left a large sum of money from a former friend of his. Twenty thousand pounds! What do you say to that?'

'That's true,' said Ellie. 'I didn't know about it this morning, but he received a cheque in the post at midday. Twenty thousand pounds from an old friend. He doesn't want to keep it. He plans to return it to sender, or rather, to the solicitor, so that it can be redistributed to the other heirs.'

Diana did a tee-hee laugh. 'If you believe that, you're even more stupid than I thought! That man has you so bamboozled you'd believe him if he said he was penniless. He's got you right where he wants, hasn't he?'

Ellie suddenly felt very tired. 'Diana, Thomas has not deceived me in any way. Now, you really must tell me how you came to know about this bequest before we did. Somebody has been indiscreet, somewhere along the line. Solicitors are not supposed to talk about such things, are they?'

'Of course they ought to be discreet but the information is available to everybody once probate has been granted and the will is in the public domain.'

'So who told you about the twenty thousand? And when?'

'My own solicitor, who'd heard about it from a friend who knew the link to you. He chanced to hint at it when he was advising me about, well, this and that.'

'About the unwise investments your husband has been making? You asked your solicitor where you might find some more money and he told you that there was money coming my way? He shouldn't have done that.'

'There's no harm in it. He's friendly with lots of professional people who go to the golf club.'

'They drink too much, and then they talk too much. Is that it? What other nuggets of information have you been gathering? Don't some of our town councillors foregather at the golf club, too? Don't you hear what building applications are likely to be passed before they come up? Doesn't this give rise to the possibility of corruption on a grand scale?'

Diana gasped. 'Are you accusing Evan of corruption?' She flushed and dabbed at her throat.

'No. But your reaction shows me there's something in what I said. Diana, I can't help you out here. The cheque arrived after we spoke this morning. Thomas doesn't want it and is going to return it. I have no money to lend you, and neither has Thomas. And no, for the umpteenth time, I am not going to ask the trustees to pay your debts, which they wouldn't agree to doing, anyway.'

'As I've already said, you can downsize. You can put this white elephant of a house on the market and let me have half the value.'

'No. We like living here. It suits us very well.' Ellie crossed the fingers of one hand under her skirt so that Diana should not see what she'd done. Yes, the house did need a lot of maintaining. Yes, there were rooms she didn't enter for weeks at a time. And yet . . . and yet . . . the garden, the space . . . they liked it. They were accustomed to high ceilings and large rooms. They were comfortable in them.

Diana wasn't giving up. 'That twenty thousand. You say Thomas doesn't want it. Well, let me have it, then.'

'Why would he do that, when you have just accused him of theft and corruption?'

'He doesn't need to know that. I tell you, I'm desperate.'

'Sort it out with your husband.'

'He's . . . not well.'

'You told me he'd twisted his ankle or something. He's back in his wheelchair for a while? So what!'

'I said, he's not well.'

Ellie narrowed her eyes. 'Drinking too much? Not going in to work? Making bad decisions, work-wise?'

'I . . . yes.' Her voice sounded strangled. 'His temper is . . . He's forgetful. I want to get him to the doctor's but he's refusing. He says there's nothing wrong with him, but there is. I tell him there's tests that he should take to rule out . . . But he's not being reasonable about this.'

'You suspect something major?'

Diana's hands twisted one around the other. 'No, of course not. But if there is, then the sooner we know the better. He's unliveable with at the moment. I suspect . . . No, I don't know what to think, I really don't. What I do know is that he can't seem to walk any more and he's incapable of making decisions at work. He hasn't been to the office for some weeks.'

That sounded serious. Ellie sank back in her chair, thinking that Diana did have bad luck, with two children under five years of age, and a husband no longer capable of running the business.

Diana said, 'You see why I need the money.'

Ellie tried to think clearly. 'You must take steps to protect yourself and the children. Get Evan to give you power of attorney.'

'I tried. He won't do it. He says there's nothing wrong with him and he's not going to submit to any tests. I don't know what to do.'

Was he that far gone? If so, Diana did indeed have a problem. Ah, a thought. 'Why don't you go to see Monique? She's a good businesswoman, runs her own group of estate agencies. Even though she's Evan's first wife, she's still fond of him, and he respects her. She might help you out by investing in Evan's estate agency.'

Diana gulped. 'What! How dare you! You really are the limit!'

'What? What's the matter? What have I said?'

'But you knew! Evan rang and told you!'

'Told me what?'

'Monique. She had a fall, broke her thigh, went into hospital and died within a few days. Surely you knew!'

Ellie felt as if she'd been punched in the stomach. She'd liked Monique. They hadn't met often, but Ellie respected and admired the woman and believed that her feelings had been reciprocated. 'I didn't know. When is the funeral? I'd like to go, unless . . . Has it been held already?'

'I suppose Evan forgot to tell you.' Diana was coldly furious. 'He does that a lot nowadays. I can't rely on him for anything. The funeral's tomorrow, some church up in North London. I don't know the name but it's on her road, at noon. I suppose you have her address somewhere. Afterwards we're invited back to her house for the reading of the will. That is, you and Evan are invited, but I'll have to go with him, or he might well wander off and . . . Anyway, he can't be trusted to drive nowadays, so I'll have to take him.'

Her frown eased. 'I'm hoping, well, he's hoping, that Monique will have left him something substantial, which would be only right and proper considering that they've always been on such good terms in spite of his marrying again.'

Ellie hid a smile.

Evan had been married four times, and Diana thinks Monique didn't mind?

Diana bit her lip, calculating the odds. 'At the very least, she'll have left him the freehold of our house, won't she? She's leased it to us for so long. Yes, I'm sure she'll have done that. Then, she's more or less adopted Evan's daughter, the one he had by his second wife. Monique took the girl straight from university into her business so she'll be well provided for as well. Yes, I'm sure she'll have left us something. It's all a question of how much, and how soon we can get it. I believe it takes about six months to lay your hands on the money, and we need it now, not then. The only thing is, we'll have to borrow against expectations. Mother, you'd back me up on a loan, won't you?'

EIGHT

Ellie was only half listening to Diana.

Monique was dead? Ellie struggled with conflicting feelings of grief – yes, she really did feel sorrow at Monique's departure – and amazement that the woman had died so young. Yes, Monique had been suffering from back pain and had been walking with a stick. Yes, her last operation had not gone well, but she'd still had all her marbles and if she'd only lived longer then Monique and Ellie might well have become good friends.

Ellie mourned what might have been.

'Mother, you're not listening!'

Ellie said, 'I'm truly sorry to hear Monique's dead. I liked her and I thought she was very fair in her dealings with Evan. Even if they were only married for a short period of time, they did have a child together. I wonder how the boy has taken the news of her death.'

'Him? The mental case? Forget him. He's in a secure unit, and not likely to be released. She wouldn't have left him anything.' Diana's lips curved into a secret smile. 'I'm thinking, hoping, she'll have left the bulk of her fortune to Evan. That's what he thinks, too.'

Ellie tried to make sense of what she'd been told. Poor Monique! She hadn't had much of a life, had she?

Diana frowned. 'The problem is that Evan's stopped listening to anything I say. He's making grand plans to buy up more brown sites for redevelopment and frankly, his judgement's gone. I've argued him with him till I'm blue in the face. He can't face the fact that we haven't the money to conclude the sale for the river site. He says I don't think like a successful property developer, that we ought to borrow money to invest in more properties, and that way we keep ahead of the game.

He won't listen when I say we're short of money to pay the gas bill this quarter, and he's bought a new car and there's the bill for the nursery and, well, everything. That's why I came to you. I need you to tide me over. Give me the cheque Thomas received today. That would help.'

Ellie was still thinking about Monique. She'd had a difficult life. She'd not been a pretty woman, but she had had a good head for business. Her one-night stand with young Evan, the up-and-coming estate agent in her father's firm, had resulted in pregnancy and marriage, followed by a divorce and long years of watching their only son deteriorate.

Ellie mused aloud, 'Monique was a fighter. She made the best of a bad job. Thank you for telling me about the funeral. I'd like to go.'

'You're not listening to me, Mother. I'm desperate. Whatever Monique has left to Evan, he won't be able to lay his hands on it till probate is granted, and I need money now to pay the household bills. Otherwise we'll be having the bailiffs in, and how will you like that! You have to help us out or at the least, guarantee us a loan.'

Ellie took a deep breath. 'Diana, how many times have I said that I can't access the trust fund to pay your debts? Even if I wanted to, the other trustees would veto it. Thomas and I manage well enough if we're not extravagant about holidays and the like, but I personally don't have spare cash to lend you. I'm probably going to put off changing the boiler this year, which I had meant to do, and . . . Look, you aren't really so badly off, are you? The agency must be bringing in some money so—'

'The property downturn has meant I can hardly pay myself anything.'

'I gave you our old house outright. You could have rented it out to give you an income. You sold it and what you've done with the money I do not know.'

'I invested it. It's not my fault that—'

'It's never your fault!'

Diana shouted, 'You're sitting on a pot of gold, and you won't help your only daughter when she's facing disaster!'

Ellie felt as if her head were going to explode. She tried to keep calm. 'Diana, be reasonable.'

Diana's eyes switched to and fro. Some thought grew in the back of her mind. She nodded once, sharply. 'I've got it. Your trust has money to burn. Get them to buy the site down by the river for us. They could easily get the land re-zoned for development. We'll go halves on the profit.'

'You told me yourself it was an unwise investment because the council will never permit building on a flood plain.'

'You've never had a business mind, Mother. You don't understand how these things work.'

'Do you mean that you think you can bribe some of the council to give you permission—'

'Did I say that? Would I ever say such a thing?'

Ellie thought, No, you wouldn't say it. But you might well connive at it happening. She stood up, slowly, stiffly. 'Diana, your best bet would be to get your doctor to set power of attorney in motion. It takes time, but it can be done. Then you'd be able to control your husband's affairs.'

Diana also stood. She was very pale. 'Is that your last word?'

'I can't help you.'

Diana spat, 'You silly, stupid, old woman!'

'Diana, that is more than enough!' Thomas, looking bleak, was standing in the doorway.

Diana turned on him. 'You keep out of this, you . . . you creep!'

Thomas didn't reply but turned sideways and stepped back so that she had a clear run to the hall. She swept past him, her head held high.

The front door opened and then clonked shut.

Ellie sank back on to her chair and held out her hand to Thomas. He took it, drew up a chair nearby and sat beside her. He stroked her hand, or she stroked his. They took comfort from one another.

Ellie thought of saying that Diana didn't mean it. But Diana had meant it. Ellie knew it, and so did Thomas.

He said, 'Are you listening? Rafael rang. He's got a bit of gossip for us about one of my many benefactors. He said he'd collect Susan from work and drop in on us later. He said he'd bring some food with him. I said he didn't need to do that, but he insisted.'

Ellie struggled to concentrate. 'It must be something important. We only saw them the other night.'

Rafael had married Susan as soon as she'd finished her training as a chef. Originally they'd planned she would work full-time in a local restaurant, gaining experience as she did so, but her pregnancy had put paid to that. Nowadays she liked to work the odd shift and was currently learning what she could from the pastry chef at a good local restaurant. If Susan brought them supper, they'd be one happy family sitting round the kitchen table. Slobbing out.

Oh, but Hetty had insisted on cooking that night, and she'd planned something indigestible. Poor Thomas had been suffering so much from his stomach of late! Ellie told herself she must take back control of the household, no matter how difficult that might be. Oh, the tyranny of the weak!

Thomas continued to stroke Ellie's hand. 'I told Rafael about the latest dollop of money. He asked me to hold off taking it to the police for the time being. I said I would, but only till tomorrow. This business of the cheques is not going to go away. We have to deal with it.'

Ellie thought Thomas was probably right. She was exhausted. She must tell Hetty that there would be guests again tonight. Hetty wouldn't like that, especially since Rafael and Susan had been here earlier in the week. Worse, Hetty must know that Susan had been a great success as her predecessor. And Susan was younger, prettier and newlywed.

How did Ellie deal with that?

And how could Diana say such things?

Thomas said, 'Do you want to talk about it? Diana's frightened, isn't she? Is she really in such a bad way?'

'Yes, probably. There's a pattern. She and Evan are two peas in a pod. They make a pot of gold and invest it, but it's fairy gold and melts away in the sunshine. They like to take risks with their investments but are not clever enough to tell brass from gold.'

'Poor creatures. They used to call it fool's gold, didn't they?' He patted her hand. 'We'll manage, Ellie. We always do.'

It was good to share their troubles. She said, 'Evan is sinking into an irascible old age. He's becoming forgetful. She thinks he's losing his judgement.'

He nodded. Didn't comment. They both knew how hard it was for the elderly to accept the gradual loss of what they had once been. Perhaps it was even worse for those who loved them and had to watch their deterioration.

Ellie stirred. 'Diana says Monique died a while back. The funeral's tomorrow, and she's going to make sure Evan gets there. I'd rather like to go, too. Are you free to come with me, or shall I take a cab? Don't worry if you can't. I know you must be tied up with the magazine.'

'Do you mind going by yourself? I'm just about on schedule. Two more days and I can put the magazine to bed and turn my attention to other matters.'

'You want to get the magazine out before you go to the police?'

His lips twitched. 'Yes, I must do that, before they arrest me for murder and screwing money out of my friends.'

'You're not going to be arrested for anything. Look, over the weekend I'll see if I can find out some more about the people who've sent you money. When we go to the police, it will be a point in our favour that we've tried to work out what's been happening.'

He held her hand to his bearded cheek. 'Ellie, my love.'

That's all he said. It was enough.

Thursday evening

Ellie switched off her computer for the day and, prompt on cue, her phone rang.

It was Rafael on the line. 'Are you in? I've rung the doorbell several times, but it doesn't seem to be working. We're outside in the driveway and Susan's struggling with a mountain of food for you.'

Bother! Ellie realized she hadn't yet told Hetty that there were guests for supper and that they were bringing food. Hetty would take umbrage, there would be a scene, and it would be all Ellie's fault.

She hastened down the corridor to the hall, calling out to Thomas that food was up. She opened the front door, and yes, saw that the wires in the porch were not just hanging loose but trailing on the ground. Oh dear.

Rafael called out to Susan to wait for him to help her, as she was struggling to get out of the car while holding on to a number of foil boxes.

Predictably, Hetty appeared at Ellie's shoulder. 'Was that someone at the door?'

'Afraid so,' said Ellie, bracing herself. 'We really must get someone to deal with the wiring for the bell. Now, I forgot to tell you, but—'

Hetty peered around Ellie. 'The nerve of them. They were only here the other night. You'll have to tell them to go away, because I've made you a lovely dish of roasted ham and dumplings and there's nowhere near enough for five.'

'It's perfectly all right,' said Ellie, trying to be firm. 'It's all very last minute and I didn't know till just now, but they're bringing in food for us four to eat tonight.'

'But I'm just dishing up and—'

'Nothing will go to waste. Look, you take what you want for yourself up to your flat, and we'll freeze any leftovers. You work so hard that I'm sure you'll be pleased to have an evening to yourself.'

Hetty looked as if she were going to cry. 'Oh, but if they've brought food, we could all sit down together and—'

'You've done enough for us this week,' said Ellie. 'Now you take your meal upstairs and enjoy yourself for once.'

Hetty sobbed, 'Thomas wouldn't want me to be cast aside like this! I'm going to ask him what he thinks of your being so nasty to me!'

'Thomas leaves the running of the household to me. Now, off you go.' Ellie actually gave Hetty a little push to see her on her way.

Hetty sobbed aloud as she fled back to the kitchen.

Ellie felt guilty. Poor Hetty! She was so alone in the world, and so anxious to please. But lines had to be drawn.

She turned back to welcome Rafael and Susan. 'Come in, come in! Hetty's just dishing up her own meal in the kitchen, and the dining room is too big for a cosy meal for four. Suppose I fetch the hostess trolley from the kitchen with some plates and cutlery, and we can eat on our knees in the sitting room?

Oh, we'll also need some glasses. Beer for the men, and soft drinks for me and Susan, right?'

A glance was exchanged between Rafael and Susan. 'Sounds good,' said Rafael.

Susan picked her words with care. 'Hetty's occupying the kitchen at the moment?'

Ellie nodded. Thank goodness, neither Rafael nor Susan was going to make a fuss about it.

Thomas, however, was not the sort of person who ate on his knees. He said, 'There's a gateleg table in the window in the sitting room. Why don't we use that? It's got a plot plant on it at the moment, but we can put that on the floor for the time being. I'll bring in a couple of chairs from the dining room and we can eat in comfort.'

'Splendid,' said Rafael. 'Home from home. Susan doesn't have a lap at the moment. A ledge, but not a lap!'

Susan, still holding the foil dishes, aimed her elbow at him. 'Who's responsible for that, pray?'

Thomas and Rafael had only just started to rearrange the furniture when Hetty appeared, sniffling. She reached out to touch Thomas but didn't quite make it. 'Thomas, could I have a word? Please?'

'Yes, of course.' Thomas sent an 'Oh dear!' glance to Ellie, put down the chair he was carrying and disappeared with Hetty in the direction of the kitchen.

Susan and Rafael looked questions at Ellie, who shrugged. 'Hetty hasn't fitted in. I've asked her to find somewhere else to go to. She's upset. I hate to cause her distress, but . . . well, it just hasn't worked out.'

Susan nodded. She'd seen enough to understand what was wrong with having Hetty in the household. Rafael checked with Susan that Ellie was doing the right thing and made no comment as he fetched another couple of chairs from the dining room.

Thomas did not return for ten long minutes, during which the others chatted about when Susan's next appointment at the hospital was to be and when she should stop even trying to work.

At long last Thomas returned, trundling the hostess trolley

with him. He'd brought plates, cutlery, glasses, some beer and
a jug of water. 'Sorry to have held you up. Hetty was upset. I
told her to leave everything in the kitchen as it was and take
herself off up to the flat. Now, what good things have you two
wonderful people brought with you tonight?'

He didn't seem to want to say any more about Hetty, so
they investigated the contents of the foil dishes Susan had
brought for their meal. An excellent beef stew with vegetables
was polished off in short order, followed by one of Susan's
specialities, an apple crumble infused with spices and topped
with proper clotted cream.

Only when they had finished everything in sight and the
women were clearing the table, did Thomas bring up the subject
of the latest cheque to land on his doorstep, and handed it over
to Rafael.

Rafael put on his rimless glasses to inspect the latest solicitor's
letter and cheque. 'A reputable firm, and you knew the man. I
don't see why you shouldn't accept this.'

Ellie, stacking dirty plates on to the trolley, said, 'I agree.'

Thomas nodded. 'Yes. I've thought it over, and I believe that
money was given me in good faith. I don't feel the same about
the others. If this had been the only cheque I received, I would
have accepted it with gratitude. But it isn't. It's the sixth, and
I'm turning it in, along with the others. Now, don't argue, please.
The news is out that I've inherited a small fortune, and I'm
taking the problem to the police before they come knocking on
my door.'

Susan said, 'Well, I think it's all a storm in a teacup, myself.'
Then she covered her mouth and burped.

Rafael reached over to rub her back. 'Can't take her anywhere.'

Susan shifted in her chair. 'Baby's active tonight. According
to the hospital, she's not due for another week, but I think she's
anxious to get going.'

Rafael informed Thomas and Ellie, 'Sometimes she tries to
push me out of bed, and I have to speak to her severely.'

Thomas and Ellie laughed, as they were supposed to do.
Rafael passed Thomas a second bottle of beer, which was duly
uncapped and poured out.

Susan nudged Rafael. He gave her a 'not now' look.

Thomas picked up the hint. 'So Rafael, you have some news for us? Was it about your drunken councillor? Ellie went to see the widow of another of my benefactors this afternoon, but her husband was neither a councillor nor a drunk.'

Rafael seemed reluctant to talk about this, but when Susan nodded at him, he sighed and got on with it. 'Councillor Thornwell. He was a councillor for twenty years or so, in a wealthy part of Acton. I got to know him when I was arguing with the planning officer at the council about putting in a fire escape at the back of my block of flats. He wanted it at one end, and I wanted it in the middle. I contacted the councillor for advice, we met briefly when I explained why my plan ought to be adopted, he spoke up for me in the council meeting, and we got it through. I'd forgotten it was he who'd been had up for driving when under the influence and knocking over a child in the Avenue. I just remembered he wasn't a very likeable man. But someone must have liked him, because he managed to remain on the council afterwards.

'I'm amazed he lived as long as he did. He was no advert for a healthy way of life, being short, fat and breathy. I didn't take to him, but I believe he was kind to dogs. He had a Labrador with him when we met. The dog died of old age, his wife left him, and he drank. His replacement on the council is an old school friend of mine and was happy to give me the latest gossip about the late and unlamented Mr Thornwell.'

Thomas drank his beer. 'I never met him. Why would he have left me any money?'

Rafael moved his beer glass around in circles. 'He left lots of small amounts to all sorts of charities. Samaritans, Cancer Research – you name it, and they all got a mention in his will. I think it was conscience money, myself. Perhaps he was hoping to leave a good impression in people's minds, even if he hadn't managed it in real life? I can't think there's anything untoward about his gift to you. I believe you can accept the money and be thankful.'

'He didn't leave any to his wife?'

'There'd been an amicable divorce, and she wasn't contesting his will. I can understand why, if he had no other family to leave his money to, he'd parcel it out to charities.'

'That makes sense,' said Thomas. 'If I knew why he'd picked on me, I'd be content.'

'He had all sorts of people buzzing around him towards the end, paid and unpaid carers, Age UK, anyone who was willing to give up their time to care for him. He had carers three times a day, people bringing in food, doing his shopping and cleaning. He was well looked after. Someone must have mentioned how much good you do in the community and he remembered it when he made his will.'

Thomas sighed. 'So, we're back to the beginning again.'

Susan nudged Rafael again. 'Go on. Tell him the rest of it.'

Rafael flushed from chin to forehead. 'Maybe it's not appropriate. Not now.'

Susan put her hands on her ample hips. 'If you won't, I will.'

Rafael kept his eyes down, concentrating on his beer. 'Go on, then.'

Susan said, 'Ellie and Thomas, they say that leopards don't change their spots, don't they? I'm here to tell you that sometimes they do, even if it does take time and effort. When I first met him, Rafael thought of nothing but how much money he could make. Oh yes, and how he could get me into bed without commitment. Then he met you two, he got to know me better and somehow we managed to reactivate his sense of right and wrong.'

'Somehow!' said Rafael, but he smiled as he said it. 'You'll be telling them next that I was rescued by the love of a good woman.'

'And don't you ever forget it!' said Susan. 'So yes, he's learned to think more about people and less about money. But in the past . . . Well, what he didn't tell you is that Councillor Thornwell had suggested Rafael grease his palm in order to get his planning permission through and Rafael paid up.'

Rafael defended himself. 'Everyone was doing it at the time. It was all disguised as paying for specialist services. Yes, I paid Thornwell off. Look, he was well known for taking bribes to get various dodgy planning permissions through. He'd been on the council for ever. He knew everyone and everyone knew him, which is what saved him from being shot out of office when he blotted his copybook.' He stopped abruptly.

Susan said, 'Rafael thinks that Councillor Thornwell was not the only one who thought it was perfectly all right to help his friends get planning permission.'

Ellie looked at Rafael's downcast eyes. A nasty suspicion wriggled through to the front of her mind. Diana and Evan, plus the development down by the river, plus Councillor Thornwell's early death . . . equals debt. She put her hands to her mouth. 'Oh, what a mess!'

Thomas was puzzled. 'Ellie? Explain!'

Ellie said, 'Some time ago Evan bought an option on a piece of land down by the river for housing. It had been designated as a flood plain years ago. There hasn't been any flooding there since they dredged the river upstream, but in theory you can't build on a flood plain. So my question is, why did they think the development would ever be permitted? I'm wondering now if they were assured by Councillor Thornwell that he could get the land rezoned at a price? They have to complete the purchase now or lose what they've spent on the option. Most inconsiderately Councillor Thornwell – if it was indeed he – died before planning permission could be granted and now they have to complete the sale, for which they haven't the money, and the permission to build is nowhere to be seen. Evan and Diana haven't the money for that or for their ordinary household bills, so they're up the creek without a paddle.'

Rafael nodded. 'I asked a few questions today, and yes, that seems to be exactly what's going on. Councillor Thornwell did have a finger in that particular pie. Evan's advocate on the council for planning permission is six feet under, and there's another group ready to move in and take over the project. If Evan can't complete the purchase price he loses what he's spent on the option. The item is coming up on the agenda next Thursday.'

'Wait a minute,' said Ellie. 'This other group, whoever they may be . . . what makes them think they can get planning permission through now?'

Rafael shrugged. 'What do you think? My information is that there is someone else on that committee who is prepared to help push it through, but that his terms for rezoning are too high for Evan to meet.' He spread his hands in apology. 'I'm sorry to bring this up, what with Evan being your son-in-law and all. I didn't know whether you knew what Evan was up to or not.'

Thomas looked from one concerned face to another. 'Evan bribed a councillor to get planning permission through for a dodgy development, but the money's gone and he can't afford a second expensive bribe? Also he stands to lose the money he's put into the project if he can't complete the sale? Hmm. How big a loss is he going to sustain?'

Ellie said, 'It's serious enough for Diana to ask me to mortgage or sell this house in order to tide her over.'

Susan and Rafael exchanged quick glances.

'You don't want to do that, do you?' asked Rafael, rather quickly.

Ellie said, 'No. We love this old place. Inconvenient it may be, but we love it.'

Rafael exchanged another look with Susan. Ellie wondered if she were missing some subtext but couldn't think what it might be.

Thomas shook his head. 'I'm sorry for anyone who loses money in a bad deal, but in this case—'

Ellie said, 'Evan planned to cheat the system, and lost. I've been bailing Diana out in small ways and big all these years. She says they're on the breadline and may not be able to meet the utility bills this quarter. She thinks me very hard-hearted for not helping her now but, even if I had the money, I don't think I'd give it to her. Or would I? The consequences of their being unable to meet their day-to-day bills don't bear thinking about.'

Thomas said, 'You mean Evan and Diana could lose their home?'

'No,' said Ellie. 'They don't own it. It was owned by Evan's first wife, Monique, and they pay her rent for it. By the way, it's Monique's funeral tomorrow. Diana says Evan was supposed to tell me about it but didn't. I only heard about it today. I liked Monique. Diana's hoping she'd left them the house at the very least. She might have done, I suppose. She must know that Diana and Evan have an extravagant way of life and two small children to bring up.'

'There's a fine line between ethical practice and bribery,' said Thomas. 'I understand that in some countries it's normal practice to allow a certain amount for bribes or "extra services". I hope we never get like that here.' Then, he listened to what he'd said, and sighed. 'All right, I know it does exist here, too. Every now and then there's a case comes up in the papers and someone gets sent to jail. But I'd hoped it was the exception.'

Ellie looked into the future and saw Diana in tears, Evan confined to a wheelchair, and two young children put out on to the street. She followed this up to see what might happen next, which was the whole family descending upon Ellie and Thomas to demand housing and support. Ellie had the room in this big house, of course. But. Ellie cringed at the thought of the disruption, the chaos, the shouting, the wails of the children.

Enough! She would not let that happen. She might have to find them somewhere to live in one of the trust properties, which would mean she herself would have to foot the bill. But no, she simply didn't have that sort of money at her disposal.

Thomas put his hand over hers. Warm and comforting. 'We'll manage. We always have done.'

She tried to smile. She couldn't see how they were going to manage, but it was good to know he was behind her.

Rafael got to his feet. 'I think that's enough bad news for one night. I can see Susan is drooping. She's usually asleep by ten, and it's five past already. I'll help you clear up and then I'll take her back home.'

Susan started awake. She rubbed eyes. 'Where . . .? Oh dear. Sorry, all. Rafael, did you ask them about—?'

'No, not now, Susan.' Rafael scooped empty glasses on to the trolley. 'Ellie, have you a lift to the funeral tomorrow? Monique made a strong impression on me when we met and I'd like to attend her funeral, too. Why don't I take you, and you can scold me all the way there and back about not giving bribes in the way of business.'

NINE

W hen they'd seen their friends off, Ellie and Thomas
took the remains of their meal through to the kitchen.
Hetty had left the lights, the radio and the television
on before she left and the meal she had been preparing for them
was still on the table. The food had not been covered and flies
were gathering around it.

Thomas was annoyed with himself. 'This is my fault. She
was in such a state I told her to leave everything. but I didn't
think she'd walk away and abandon the food, uncovered. And
the oven's still on! I'm sorry, Ellie.' He set about sweeping the
spoilt food into the bin.

Ellie reached for her apron. 'I'm sorry she's upset, and I'm
sorry you had to deal with her, but this is the outside of enough.'

Thomas said, 'Poor woman. I feel sorry for her in a way.
No family, no place of her own. I kept telling her that if you've
promised to find her somewhere to live, then that's what would
happen. She wanted me to persuade you to let her stay on here.
I said that wasn't an option, that we had both decided she
ought to move on. I don't think I handled it well. She said . . .
Well, people say lots of things they don't mean when they're
upset.'

'Did she turn on you? How could she, when it was you who
brought her here in the first place!'

'I should have known better. She says I got her hopes up
about staying here for good, but I'm pretty sure I didn't say
anything of the kind.'

'The sooner she goes, the better. Oh dear. I do feel guilty
about taking tomorrow off for the funeral, when I ought to be
chasing up somewhere for Hetty to live and visiting the families
of those who have left you some money.'

'No, you must go to the funeral. Make my apologies to

whoever is arranging everything. Is it Evan? Can that be right? He and Monique were hardly on those sort of terms, were they?'

He put the last of the plates in the dishwasher and switched the kettle on for his late-night coffee.

'I don't know who's arranging things. Diana didn't say. I'll find out tomorrow.'

Thomas made his coffee, they switched off the lights and went upstairs to bed.

Friday morning

Rafael collected Ellie in good time. By mutual consent they talked of unimportant things till they were approaching the road in which Monique had lived. Rafael slowed down, looking for a parking place.

'Nice houses,' he said. 'Worth a bit. Much like yours.'

'I suppose so. We've got a drive at the front, which these haven't. But still, it's a good neighbourhood.'

'Yes.' He seemed distracted. He found a parking space and backed into it but didn't get out straight away. 'There's something Susan and I want to say to you. This isn't the right time, but I don't know when it would be the right time. The thing is, if you ever want to downsize, would you let us know before you talk to anyone else about it?'

Ellie stared at him. Where had this come from? Did he mean that he wanted to buy them out? Surely not. Didn't he have enough on his plate, managing the block of flats that he'd renovated? And what would he and Susan want with such a big house? 'I don't understand.'

Rafael washed his face with his hands. 'It's just that we had an idea. We thought about what might happen if you ever decided the house was getting too much for you. You're fine now, but some day you might find yourselves thinking otherwise. I'm not asking for an option to buy. Nothing like that. But if push ever comes to shove, we did have an idea of something that might work.'

'You mean, if Diana and Co were to descend on us and we were driven so mad by their shenanigans that we went in for wholesale murder?'

He twitched a smile. 'Precisely. Just store the idea in the back of your head, will you? It may be years before you need to look at it.' He got out of the car. 'In the meantime, we have a funeral to go to.'

Ellie gave him an old-fashioned look. 'I haven't a clue what you're talking about. As you say, we're not thinking of a move in the foreseeable future.'

He helped her out of the car and she looked around.

She said, 'I wonder who'll attend the service? I don't think Monique had any brothers or sisters. She was a successful businesswoman but her marriage to Evan was a bit of a farce, and her health deteriorated after she gave birth to their only son. He's in Broadmoor and not likely to come out. Some people would say she hadn't had much luck in her life, but she never went on about it. I admired her.'

'Somebody must have arranged the funeral and phoned around with the details. A cousin, perhaps?'

'Or her solicitor? There is one other option. Evan had a daughter called Freya, whom he neglected disgracefully. Freya was a nice child and bright, heading off to university when I knew her. She was no blood relation of Monique's, being from Evan's second disastrous marriage, but Monique told me she was going to offer the girl a job when she graduated. I suppose it appealed to Monique to forward the career of a daughter Evan had never appreciated. I hope that's what happened. I liked Freya. She was very down to earth, rather like Monique herself, in fact.'

Rafael gave her his arm. 'Let's get to the church. If you feel you should go back to the house afterwards, I'll find myself a sandwich nearby. Ring me on your mobile when you want to leave. You have got your mobile with you, haven't you?'

He was right to ask. Ellie often forgot it, but this time she could produce it with a smile. 'I know you think I don't know how to work this thing, but I'm sure I can remember how to call you. I press this and this. I wait for your name to come up and then I press this button here. Right?'

'Excellent. I suggest you switch it off now, and switch it on again when you leave the church? Then I can contact you if I need to do so.'

*   *   *

The church was early Victorian and probably on the high side as there was a whiff of incense in the air. Ellie picked up an order of service and discovered that Monique had been cremated earlier that day, and that the service in church at noon would be a celebration for her life. The organ was being played, softly, by someone who knew what they were doing. Ellie smiled, thinking that anything connected to Monique would be properly done.

The church was fairly full, indicating that a respectable number of people had wanted to remember Monique. There was no coffin, but a plethora of flowers.

Ellie found a seat towards the back, and Rafael slipped in beside her.

There was a disturbance at the entrance. Evan arrived in a wheelchair, trundled in by Diana. They didn't see Ellie but went straight down to the front of the church, exuding importance. Ellie supposed it was only right that Evan should sit at the front, as he was the only man Monique had ever married. Diana settled her husband in the aisle and slipped into the pew beside him.

Did Evan really think that Monique had left him something in her will? Evan had left Monique for another woman, Freya's mother. Ellie saw no reason why Monique should have left him anything, even though Diana thought otherwise.

Both Evan and Diana were wearing black. Diana wore black nearly all the time, but Evan didn't usually do so. It looked to Ellie as if he'd lost weight since he'd last worn that suit. It gave him the look of a man in decline. Possibly because that was in fact the case?

The organ music changed and a young woman, flanked by two substantial grey-haired men, walked down the aisle to the front. The men had a professional look to them. Were they old friends of Monique? Or relatives? Solicitors, doctors or bank managers?

The young woman was Freya, whom Ellie hadn't seen for a while. She was now in her early twenties. In the old days she'd worn her thick fair hair in a plait down her back, but now it was in a stylish bob. She was wearing a simple black coat dress and no jewellery. She didn't need jewellery to shine any more than Monique had done.

As the trio reached the front pews, Evan beckoned his

daughter over. She stopped to listen to what he had to say. He seemed to be asking – no, demanding – something. Whatever it was, she shook her head in response. One of the grey men touched her on her shoulder, indicating they should move into the front pew on the left, and she did so. Evan waved his arms about in frustration. The second grey man said something short and sharp to Evan and turned away to join Freya.

Diana soothed her husband.

What had Evan wanted? Whatever it was, Freya and the grey man had vetoed it.

The minister arrived, and the service began. Ellie was pleased to hear many tributes to Monique as a good friend, as a canny businesswoman and as someone who'd borne her afflictions lightly.

One of the grey men announced himself as a distant cousin of the deceased and read a poem which he said had been a favourite of Monique's. The other said they'd been friends from childhood and retailed an anecdote which spoke of her humanity and wisdom.

Freya did not speak and neither did she weep, but she bowed her head when the second grey men said how much joy her adopted daughter had brought to Monique in the last few years of her life.

Just before the final hymn, Evan spoke up, loudly announcing that he, too, wanted to pay a tribute to his first wife. Perhaps this had been anticipated and discussed by the grey men beforehand? For, while Freya kept her eyes to the front, one of the men with her slipped across the aisle to have a short word with Evan, who subsided into his chair, mumbling angrily to himself.

After the service, Freya spoke a few words to her father, and then walked back down the aisle, flanked by the two grey men.

They stopped here and there to speak to people they knew. Freya looked tired and unhappy. She was, after all, still a young woman and Monique had been a surrogate parent for her.

Freya spotted Ellie and came over to speak to her. 'I'm so glad you could make it, Mrs Quicke. I remember you well, and Monique always spoke highly of you. My father promised he'd get you here. You know which house it is? We'll expect you there.'

'Freya!' That was Evan, trying to manoeuvre his chair through the press of people leaving the church. Either the girl didn't hear him or didn't choose to linger, for she continued on her way out. Frustrated, Evan cursed everyone who got in his way, earning himself many a startled look.

Rafael and Ellie exchanged glances. Rafael said, 'She invited you specifically to go back to the house. Do you want to drop in for a while? As I said, I'll find something to eat locally and take it back to the car. Give me a ring when you're ready to go.'

Ellie said, 'I've got a nasty feeling Evan's going to make a scene.'

'Swearing in church? Yes. I didn't think I was shockable, but it seems that I am. On the other hand, wasn't he within his rights to want to speak about his wife at her funeral?'

'That depends,' said Ellie, 'on how he behaved to her then, and thereafter. Which wasn't well. He may convince himself that he meant a great deal to her, but I really don't think he did.'

Rafael split off down the road while Ellie followed Evan, Diana and a few other mourners into a solid, three-storey Edwardian house nearby. A hired caterer took their coats and ushered them into the drawing room, furnished with solid, practical, modern furniture. Apart from Evan and Diana, it appeared that two other women and a youngish man had been invited to attend the wake.

'Would you care for a drink?' said one of the grey men – the childhood friend? – standing beside a table equipped with tea, coffee and a variety of soft drinks. No alcohol, but some plates had been piled high with sandwiches. Ellie was hungry and helped herself to food and a mineral water.

Freya moved a small table out of the way, to allow space for her father's wheelchair to be placed near the food. She seemed very much at home.

Ellie hoped Monique had made sure Freya would keep her job at her estate agency. The girl had earned it.

The second grey man – the cousin? – produced a sheaf of papers from a briefcase, cleared his throat and asked if they were all sitting comfortably. One or two people smiled at the slight joke, but not as if they meant it.

The grey man introduced himself as a solicitor as well as

being Monique's cousin. He said that she had made her will a while ago when it was clear the last operation on her back had failed. He himself was not only her solicitor but also her executor, and would be submitting her will for probate. Her aim in making this will had been twofold: to reward those close to her and to ensure that her only son would be well looked after if he were ever to be released from Broadmoor prison.

Evan folded his hands and nodded approval. 'Monique always did the right thing.'

The grey man who was reading out the contents of the will produced a thin smile. He seemed to be enjoying this. He said, 'We'll come to that in a minute. First there are bequests to a number of charities.' And he named them. The usual suspects. Cancer. Lifeboats. Donkeys.

'Then,' the grey man continued, 'there is a legacy of a thousand pounds to each of the carers who did so much to make Monique's life easier over the last couple of years.'

The two women who were strangers to Ellie smiled and dabbed at their eyes. 'I was dead fond of her,' said one.

'Ah,' said the other. 'She was wise-cracking to the last. I thought I'd die laughing when I visited her in the hospital. Next day, she was gone.'

The grey man nodded. 'There is also five thousand to the manager of her group of estate agencies, who had become a personal friend. She was godmother to his son, and she suggested' – and here he turned to the single man – 'that you put the money in trust for the little boy until he's eighteen.'

The youngish man blinked hard. And nodded. 'Will do. She was a good 'un.'

The grey man glanced around to make sure everyone was following his every word – which they were. 'As you probably know, Monique ran a busy estate agency in Kensington. She had expanded the original business considerably, and over the years had opened two more branches. These were recently sold to a reputable chain which has promised to keep the personnel on.'

'That is so,' said the youngish man. 'We're all very happy under the new regime.'

'The money from the sale,' said the grey man, 'is to be thrown into her estate and—'

Evan said, 'Get to the point, man! How much has she left me?'

'Nothing.'

Evan's colour rose. 'What? That's not possible! As her husband, I—'

'Ex-husband.'

'Nevertheless. She owes me something for—'

The grey man lost none of his professional cool. 'She owes you nothing. I've read the divorce papers. You played around—'

'She was too sick in her pregnancy to have sex, and too ill afterwards. She failed as a wife.'

'She left you in possession of her house, for which you've never paid a proper rent. You have married three times since she divorced you, and you have never paid a penny for the upkeep of your son—'

'Well, he's out of the picture. They'll never let him out of Broadmoor.'

'They might. When I visited him last and spoke—'

'You've visited him in hospital? What on earth for?'

'He's my second cousin. And your son. I understand that you have never visited him, but I used to take Monique once a month. She never missed a date, in spite of living in constant pain. The doctors say there's been some improvement in the boy's condition and it is possible that one day he may be released on licence.'

'Great Jehovah! Who would ever think to unleash him on the general populace!'

'Monique wanted to make provision for his possible release.'

Evan thumped the arm of his chair. 'So that's it, is it? You're going to feather your nest, take all the old girl's money under the pretence of looking after that idiot? You do that, and I'll sue the pants off you.'

A thin smile. 'No, I declined the responsibility but the money has to be looked after. It can be used for charitable purposes in the meantime, but in the event of the boy ever being released, suitable housing must be found for him and an allowance made for his daily living expenses.'

'That's it, then! I'll take the money and look after it for him.'

'Monique noted that you have never visited your son. She

did not feel you cared enough about the boy to be responsible for his future, if he is ever released.'

Evan swung round on Freya, who had seated herself a little to one side and taken no part in the conversation. 'You? My daughter? You are going to look after the money for him? Well, well.' A painful smile. 'Perhaps that is not such a bad idea, after all. You are so young, you have no idea how best to safeguard a windfall. You will take advice on how to handle it, no doubt. You can't be expected to know how to deal with large sums of money, and will allow other, wiser heads to help you with it.'

Freya shook her head. 'Monique didn't leave that money to me. She took me in and gave me a job in one of her branches to see if I'd like the work, which I did and which I will continue to do. She helped me to rent a small place nearby. She didn't want to give it to me outright, but suggested I find a flatmate and pay her rent money, so that I could learn how to budget. And that I have done. She has also set up a trust fund to provide me with the wherewithal to get on the housing ladder, but I can't access that till I'm twenty-five. She wanted me to stand on my own two feet, and that is what I will do.'

Evan swung round. 'Who gets the money, then?'

Ellie nearly dropped her empty plate. 'Oh, no! She didn't, did she?'

'You're ahead of me, Mrs Quicke,' said the grey man. 'Yes. Your trust fund is the residuary legatee, on condition that you provide Monique's son with suitable living conditions and a reasonable amount to live on if he is ever released.'

TEN

Friday lunchtime

Ellie blinked. She couldn't possibly have heard correctly. Monique wouldn't have left her the bulk of the estate. No! Ridiculous!

Evan didn't think so, either. 'What! Ellie gets . . .? No way!'

'Correct,' said the grey man.

As if at a tennis match, the heads of the other occupants of the room turned first one way and then the other.

Evan looked as if he'd been hit on the head. 'But . . . what about me?'

'You are not mentioned in the will.'

'But to give it to Ellie? No! Monique should have given it to a member of the family.' Evan's eyes narrowed. 'If she didn't leave it to me, why didn't she give it all to Freya?'

'Monique decided not to burden a young and inexperienced woman with this legacy. She discussed it with Freya and with me. We all three agreed that this was the best thing to do.'

'But . . . Ellie? Why on earth—?'

The grey man almost smiled. 'Monique had the greatest respect for Mrs Quicke and everything that she does. Her trust fund alleviates hardship in the community, and that is what Monique wanted to do herself. Monique had observed Mrs Quicke in action from time to time, and she believed that if circumstances arose, Mrs Quicke could be trusted to safeguard her son's future.'

Evan had turned a nasty colour. 'How much does she get?'

The grey man steepled his fingers. 'There is a portfolio of stocks and shares, the money from the sale of the three branches of her agency, and some housing stock including this house and the one which you, Evan, currently occupy.' He went on to estimate a sum which caused jaws to drop all round.

Ellie felt dizzy. So much? It was a king's ransom. No, an emperor's. Except we didn't have emperors nowadays, did we? Let's say it was the amount a corrupt president might have filched from his subjects before he fled, one step ahead of the police, into luxurious exile.

'What!' from Evan. 'As much as that? She can't be trusted to look after all that! No, you can't mean that my house is now owned by Ellie! That's ridiculous!'

Diana gasped. 'Mother? You own our house?'

Evan said, 'She wouldn't dare to turn us out! No, not even she would dare do that!'

Ellie put a hand to her head. She couldn't take in what Monique had done. It was so unexpected. Except that, knowing Monique, Ellie could see how the woman had been thinking. It did make sense, in a horrid sort of way. But . . . so much money? She said, 'I never expected . . .! No, I don't want . . .!'

'No, I don't suppose you do,' said the grey man, understanding how she felt. 'It's a huge responsibility but Monique thought you were up to it.' He turned to the other recipients of money under Monique's will and handed out some cards. 'Feel free to contact me at any time, if you have any queries. Freya will see you out.'

Picking up her cue, Freya rose from her seat and ushered the three other legatees out of the door, saying she was so pleased they could come and that she was delighted that Monique had left them a token of her regard.

There was silence in the room until the front door was heard to shut and Freya returned to the room.

This interruption in the proceedings had given Ellie a chance to think. If she took this money, she could do so much to help people who couldn't get on the housing ladder. The trust had recently been offered a terrace of rundown houses in Southall. Developers had not been keen on the site as they would not be able to sell housing stock in that area for their usual inflated prices.

However, if the trust could afford to purchase them and bring them up to scratch with renewed wiring, plumbing, new kitchens and bathrooms . . . it would cost a huge amount, but then the houses could be sold as starter homes or rented out at affordable prices. They could house young families or, if some were turned into flats, they could provide single people with a home.

People like Hetty?

And, what about the Pullin house? They could buy it, put it to rights and let it out. It would help the Pullin family out of a hole. It was near enough the university to make good student accommodation for which there was always a need. Or, it could be turned into three flats and rented out for those who, like Hetty, were saving to buy something for themselves.

Yes! I see now why Monique chose to leave her money to me. But, the complications! People will assume, Diana will assume, that I can be tapped for funds. It's true the trust has a brilliant finance director and general manager, and that they really carry the day-to-day burden, but am I personally up to dealing with such a huge responsibility? Dear Lord, grant me the wisdom to decide how to handle this. Oh, and the strength to stick to my decisions.

Evan reached across to grab Ellie's arm. He shook it. 'Wakey, wakey! I asked you a question!'

Ellie tried to free her arm, but he clung on. She decided not to make a scene by trying to free herself. She needed time to think. What did Evan want? He wanted to know he was safe in the house he'd been renting all these years. Monique had allowed Evan to live on in that big house ever since she'd walked out of the marriage. It had been his home and she'd left him to enjoy it. He'd brought up his family there. He'd gone through three wives before he married Diana. Monique hadn't had a high opinion of Diana, thinking her to be something of a gold-digger, but she had come to realize that Diana was a good mother to her children.

At no time had Monique ever threatened to reclaim the house. Evan had maintained it well enough. Monique had not been a cruel woman, and she had not left instructions for Evan's house to be sold and the money thrown into the trust fund.

Ellie said, 'If I've understood Monique's intentions correctly, she wouldn't have wanted to turn you out or she would have said so, but—'

Evan's grasp on her arm didn't relax. 'You'll help us out with a loan, won't you?'

'That's different. I have to think about that. At first sight, I can't see how that would be possible. Monique didn't leave her estate to me; she left it to the trust fund. It's not up to me to decide what will happen to your house and to grant or withhold loans. I can't make promises to you for, well, anything. It's not what I want, but what the trust wants. Yes, I'm the chair, but the other trustees will have to take everything into consideration.' She tugged her arm free, and Evan let her go.

Diana joined in the fight. 'Shame on you! How could you even think of turning your own grandchildren out into the street?'

'I didn't say—'

'No, not even you could be so hard-hearted. No, of course not. You'll help us out. Of course you will.'

Ellie felt helpless. Part of her wanted to reassure Diana that everything was going to be all right, but the other part told her that she must not be rushed into making decisions which might prove unwise. She looked for help to the grey man.

He was smiling. He was now off the hook. It looked to Ellie as if he were enjoying the sight of someone else having to deal with the complications arising from Monique's will.

Ellie said, 'A thought. Who administers the trust fund that's been set up for Freya?'

The grey man said, 'It's a separate trust fund, set up over a year ago. The bank is the administrator. Nobody can get round them.'

'Good,' said Ellie, and smiled at Freya, who twitched a smile back. Freya was in a difficult situation, wasn't she? It was her father who was in financial trouble . . . not that he'd ever been a good father to her. Freya might have thought it incumbent on her to help her father out, so Monique had left her enough to live on, but not enough to make her the target of her father's greed.

Diana said, 'I see what it is, Mother. Monique gave the rest of the money to you so that you could keep us going.'

Ellie shook her head. 'No, no! I haven't read the exact wording of the will. I need time to understand her wishes, but I don't believe she wanted me to bail you out of trouble.'

The grey man stowed paperwork in his briefcase. 'Correct, Mrs Quicke. The money is for charitable purposes. I will let you have a copy of the will soonest.'

Diana pounced. 'Mother, I can see this is all going to be too much for you to handle. You don't want all the aggro at your age. You can decline the legacy and allow other people to handle it.'

The grey man was smooth. 'In the event that Mrs Quicke's trust declines the legacy, Monique has made it clear that everything will go into a separate trust fund run by the bank, to cover her son's future needs.'

Diana thought that over. 'Is the money an outright gift to my mother, or are there strings attached to it?'

'It is an outright gift, not to your mother, but to her trust fund, with the proviso that her son will be looked after if he is ever released from Broadmoor. It will, of course, take time for probate to be granted and the money to be handed over.'

'My mother can borrow against it now?'

Raised eyebrows. 'If the trust were to apply for a loan, I suppose the banks might agree.'

Diana rounded on Ellie. 'Then that's all right. You can borrow against expectations and save us all. If that isn't charity, I don't know what is.'

Ellie shook her head. 'Don't push me, Diana. I can't promise anything until I've had time to consider exactly what Monique wanted, and then I have to consult the trustees and . . . don't push me!'

'You are not going to refuse to help us. Not even you could be that evil.'

'First, I have to consult Stewart and the other trustees.'

Ellie stared at Diana, and Diana stared back, realizing what her mother meant.

The trust's highly capable general manager was Diana's first husband, Stewart, from whom she had parted on bad terms. Stewart was an honest, straightforward man and an excellent general manager of the housing side of the trust. He had not been up to Diana's weight . . . but then, who would be?

Well, Evan had been up to Diana's weight in most ways. But Evan was an alpha male of the first order, while Stewart had been too much of a 'gentleman' – in old-fashioned terms – to be able to deal with Diana.

Stewart liked to see the best in everyone but in the trust this was balanced by their finance director's more worldly point of view. They made a good team.

Diana's expression showed some of the dismay that must be eating into her as she thought that any plea to the trust fund must be run past her despised first husband. She flushed. 'I suppose you mean Stewart would automatically turn down any request from me.'

In this – as in many other areas – Ellie thought Diana was wrong. Stewart was always very fair.

Diana judged others by herself. If she'd been in Stewart's

shoes, she would have decided against everything he suggested just because, as a husband, he'd not measured up to her expectations.

There was something else to be taken into consideration. Diana had taken as little notice of her and Stewart's first son as Evan had done of his first, the young man who had ended up in Broadmoor.

Stewart and Diana's son had gone to live with his father, who had married a lovely woman second time round, and completed their happy family with a pair of delightful small girls. The boy had grown up much loved. He was doing well at school, was a useful football player and, though he had his father's peace-loving temperament, he had sufficient backbone to stand up to local bullies.

Ellie wondered whether Monique had known all this, and concluded that yes, she had. Monique would have made it her business to find out exactly how Ellie's trust fund was administered, who the trustees were and what their strengths and weaknesses might be. Therefore, Monique had known that Diana would not get everything her own way if she tried to bully members of the trust.

Ellie could see that Diana was building these inconvenient facts into the equation. Her tone was almost pleading as she said, 'Mother, you know how to manage the trust. You can sway them any way you want. I know you can.'

Diana was right in thinking that Ellie could probably push through a measure of which Stewart would disapprove. But she would not be able to get it through their finance director . . . or could she, if she tried hard enough? Well, she might.

And there was the rub. Would Ellie even want to try?

No, she wouldn't. Which meant there were going to be fireworks in the near future.

'No,' said Ellie. 'I don't think that bailing you out is what Monique intended. She could have left money to Evan, but she didn't. She could have left the deeds of the house to him, but she didn't do that, either. Her purpose in leaving her estate to me was to use it for the common good. She relied on me to carry out her wishes, and that is what I am going to do. So, with reluctance, Diana, I will not be asking the trust to bail you out.'

Diana paled and then flushed an even darker red. 'Perhaps I haven't made myself clear. We need that money, or we go under.'

This was going to be difficult. Ellie cleared her throat. 'I have heard how you've been spending your money. You can't have expected me to approve, and I don't. The answer is the same. No.'

Diana flamed into fury. 'You . . .! You wicked, wicked woman! I can't think of words bad enough! You sit there and smile at the thought of your family being thrown out on to the street! I'm told some people admire you. Well, I don't! And I'm going to make sure everyone knows what you are! You are nothing but a leech on society! Oh, sugar wouldn't melt, would it! But when this gets out . . .! You and that creep you've married, you're two of a kind. I hear he's been killing off his parishioners for a few hundred here and there. Do you really think I'm going to sit down and let you both get away with murder? Well, I'm not! If you won't behave like a mother should, I see no reason why I should keep silent about his career in crime and, if you force my hand, I will have to do so. Help us out, or I inform the police that dear Thomas has been knocking off his old friends for a legacy!'

Ellie blinked. 'I explained to you that—'

'As if I believed that garbage! How do I know that you didn't help Monique into an early grave? If you don't help us out, I shall ask the police to investigate your movements with regard to her death. They'll find a link, I'm sure of that. You could have sent her something or met her for lunch and put something in her drink. They'll have to exhume her body and test it for poison!'

'If you please,' said the grey man, 'Monique died of natural causes, and her body was cremated this morning.'

'You would say that! But you'll change your tune when the police start asking questions about your role in this affair!'

'I can see you are angry,' said the grey man. 'Take care that you don't slander anyone.'

There was a long silence. The grey man clicked his briefcase shut. 'Mrs Quicke, would you care to ring and make an appointment with me? My card.' He handed it over.

'I believe that the sooner we meet, the better.'

Ellie found herself ushered outside into the street without knowing quite how she'd got there. She held the grey man's card in her hand. She had, for the moment, no idea where she was.

She'd come in a car, hadn't she? With Rafael? He was supposed to have phoned her, or she to have phoned him? She took her phone out of her bag. She'd failed to switch it on when she left the church. Oh, dear.

Someone called her name. Rafael crossed the street to meet her. 'I had to move the car. It's over the road.' And then, 'Take my arm. You look as if you've been sandbagged.'

Yes, that's what it felt like. 'Thank you, Rafael.'

'You're shaking. Are you all right?'

'I'll be all right in a minute.'

He inserted her into his car, handed the seat belt to her, went round to the driver's side, and got in beside her. And frowned. 'What's up?'

She held the seat belt in one hand and her phone in the other. 'I've missed several calls. Or perhaps they're old ones that I haven't deleted?'

He took the phone off her and checked. 'A missed call from Thomas and one from your police friend, Lesley. Do you want me to listen to them for you?'

She nodded. She couldn't think straight. All that money . . .? Rafael played the voicemail. First was Thomas.

'Ellie, I'm not feeling too good. Stomach cramps. I rang the surgery and they haven't a slot to see a doctor today, but they said if it was bad I should go straight to A&E. I don't think I'd be safe to drive, so I'm calling a cab. I'm sure it's nothing much. I'll ring you again when I've seen someone at the hospital.'

Ellie gasped. 'Oh, Thomas is sick. He's gone to hospital!'

Rafael handed the phone back to her and started the car. 'On our way. It won't be anything much. He suffers from indigestion sometimes, doesn't he? Ten to one, it's wind.

'Don't you want to listen to what Lesley has to say?'

Ellie couldn't care less what Lesley had to say. Thomas was ill! But he was never ill. Well, yes. He did have indigestion, but . . . No, he was never ill. It couldn't be anything serious. *Dear Lord. Look after him!*

'There was another message on your phone,' Rafael reminded her. 'From Lesley. It might be important.'

He was trying to distract her. Well, all right. She'd listen to the message.

Lesley sounded tired. 'Ellie, I've had the most extraordinary phone call. I can't make head nor tail of it. Someone has accused Thomas of stealing from his parishioners. That must be rubbish but it's landed on the desk of my unbeloved superior so it'll have to be investigated. I'll pop round later to have a word.'

ELEVEN

Friday, early afternoon

Ellie dropped the phone in her lap. She told herself not to panic. Thomas was ill! Thomas was on his way to hospital. It must be serious. He wasn't the sort to complain.

The message from Lesley didn't make sense. Thomas was being investigated by the police? But . . . how? Who would have dared to . . .? Well, Diana did threaten, but . . . No, it can't have been Diana! She hadn't had time to ring the police. Or had she?

It must be some relative of the people who'd left Thomas money and who'd heard that he'd been given money from lots of different sources. No one who knew Thomas would wish him ill, would they?

Thomas is ill. Thomas is in hospital.

She could feel her heart going *Thud, Thud, Thud!*

She looked at her watch. 'Rafael, how quickly can we get to the hospital?'

'Forty-five minutes. Half an hour if the traffic's light. Do you want to ring Lesley, tell her what's happened? Otherwise she might turn up at the house, and neither you nor Thomas will be there.'

Ellie couldn't think straight. Thomas was ill. He was two days off putting the magazine to bed. What would happen to the magazine if . . .? No, he was *not* going to die. He had stomach ache. Indigestion. Wind. They'd give him something to relieve the symptoms and he'd be perfectly all right. She had to believe that. How would she cope, if he were to die?

Rafael said, 'Don't worry. His guardian angel will be looking after him.'

Ellie tried to follow his lead. 'I didn't know you believed in guardian angels.'

'I'm not sure I do. Except in moments of difficulty when I find out that I really, really do believe in them. Pray, Ellie. Pray.'

Good advice. *Dear Lord, dear Lord, dear Lord. Look after him.*

The traffic was heavy. They slowed to a crawl. Rafael was a good driver, and patient. She wanted to urge him to find an alternative route to the hospital but stopped herself just in time. Rafael knew all the shortcuts. She must sit tight. And pray.

Thomas is in danger. I can feel it in my bones. Dear Lord, look after him, please!

The traffic had come to a standstill. There was no way they could have moved off the motorway even if they had wanted to do so. They were completely boxed in.

Rafael said, 'Let talk about cabbages and kings. Who would have told the police that Thomas had been involved in something criminal?'

Ellie tried to keep calm. Rafael wanted to distract her by talking. It was probably a good idea to go along with his idea. It might keep her from going mad with frustration, locked into traffic with no way out.

'I don't know who would have it in for him to such an extent. Someone who's jealous of him? Someone who wanted more money than they themselves got from a will? Someone who's heard that Thomas has been given more than they have?'

'To what purpose? Envy isn't a strong enough reason to accuse him of theft, is it?'

'It might be. Someone might think he had far too easy a life, married to a woman who owns a big house. It might be just spite. They'd think that an anonymous phone call to the police would cause them to give Thomas a hard time. You know how mud sticks. Thomas had been thinking of taking the matter to the police, but they wouldn't know that. If the police get involved, his finances and the finances of the magazine will be scrutinized up hill and down dale. Every scrap of paper, all his bills, will be referred to auditors and if they find one bill unpaid or overpaid . . . He works so hard! He does so much good!'

He's in hospital, in pain, and I'm stuck in a traffic jam.

Rafael said, 'He's squeaky clean. No one who knows him could possibly think he'd done anything wrong.'

'It doesn't matter. Once the word gets out, even if the police can't find anything wrong, his name will be mud. You know the way it goes; they'll start by saying that Thomas could never, ever have killed anyone for a few pounds here and there. But unless they have more luck than I did, the police won't discover any good reason for so many people giving money to a man they hardly knew, if indeed they ever did know him. Public opinion will begin to change.

'They will start to say there's no smoke without a fire, that they always knew there was something dicey about a man of the cloth whose acquaintances died off in droves. They'll bring up the business of that doctor who got his patients to make a will in his favour, and then killed them with lethal doses of medicine. The rumours will mount and gain strength. People will start to remember that Thomas "boasted" about having money to visit his family in Canada, and about living in a big house. He will not be asked to take any more services. People will fail to recognize him in the street, and finally the church authorities will suggest he resign as editor of the magazine and ask him to account for every penny he's spent on it for the last umpteen years. It will break him.'

Rafael edged the car forward. 'It won't break him, Ellie. He's a good man, and a strong one.'

'No, perhaps it wouldn't break him, but it would hurt him. If his friends were to desert him, he'd feel it.'

'I wouldn't. Nor would Susan.'

Ellie thought that Rafael probably meant that, but he didn't know how hard it could be to stand against public opinion. Rafael was a businessman but he had never had the pressure of public opinion brought against him, and neither had Susan. If their families turned against Thomas, if his business contacts did too, then Rafael might well . . . bend. He meant well now, but it might be another matter some months down the line.

Ellie started to laugh. Then stopped abruptly. That way, hysteria lay. She said, 'There's worse. Monique has left me almost her entire estate, or rather, she's left it to the trust with a couple of strings attached. Diana thought it would mean I'd bale her out of her spot of financial problems, but I refused so she's going to accuse me of causing Monique's death.'

Rafael gave a short bark of laughter. 'You're joking! Just wait till I tell Susan!'

Ellie clung to common sense. 'No one would believe it of me, would they? I mean, how could I ever . . .? Of course, the same thing applies to me as to Thomas. If Diana does go ahead and accuse me of murdering Monique, there'll be someone who will believe her, and then . . . and then . . . Oh, the trust would have to get rid of me, or rather, I'd have to resign. I don't know whether to laugh or cry!'

'Why not both? Except . . . would you mind waiting to have hysterics until we start moving forward again? Sitting here in traffic, someone's bound to see you throwing a wobbly, and then they'll think it's me who's made you cry. They'll call the police, and I'll be had up for making off with you against your will and end up in a prison cell.'

Ellie sought for a hankie, because she was indeed both laughing and crying. 'Oh, you! Anyway, the grey man who's the executor said that Monique has been cremated, so they can't prove I killed her, as if I would! I liked Monique.'

There was a small movement in the traffic ahead, and they inched forward a few feet. Rafael said, 'I liked her, too. Didn't she ever hint that she wanted to leave her money to you?'

Ellie corrected him. 'To the trust. No, I'm trying to think when we last met, but . . . well, she'd had an op which hadn't gone well, and then there was that horrid affair when Diana and her friends were accused of killing off their husbands, and Monique helped us to sort that out. After that we sort of lost touch. I sent her a Christmas card with a note asking when she might like to have lunch with me, and she sent one back saying she wasn't feeling too bright but hoping some new treatment might help and that was the last I heard from her. I wish we'd managed to meet up again, but we didn't.'

He grinned. 'Is Diana going to say you sent Monique a Christmas card soaked in poison? I don't see how else you could have killed her.'

'Silly! She fell and broke her thigh, was taken to hospital, deteriorated and died. Diana told me that herself. It seems to have happened very quickly at the end. I'm glad for her. I mean, I'm glad it was quick, but I'm not glad that she died. If you see what I mean.'

'Then you're in the clear.'

'Mud sticks. If she says I was there when Monique fell . . . oh, I know it's ridiculous. I don't even know exactly when it happened.' She saw Rafael glance at his watch. She looked at hers. However long was this journey going to take?

She picked up her phone and tried Thomas's mobile number. It had been turned off. Of course, they asked you to turn off your phones in hospital, didn't they?

She made herself relax, muscle by muscle. The bubble of fear she'd been repressing rose up and hit her. She gasped, closed her eyes tightly.

'Mrs Quicke, are you all right?'

'Yes,' she said, digging her nails into her palms. 'Take no notice. I'm just rather frightened. Not for me, but for Thomas. For me, too, I suppose. I'll be all right in a minute.'

He looked around at the stationary traffic. 'If there were a pub in sight, I'd let you out of the car so that you could get yourself a stiff drink. See how gridlocked we are. I'd probably be sitting in the same place by the time you got back. I'll have to remember to keep something in the glove box for medicinal purposes in future. Why, may I ask, do they still call it a glove box? Who wears gloves nowadays?'

He was burbling away, trying to distract her. She gave him full marks for it. She took some deep breaths. He waited for her to regain her equilibrium. At length she said, 'I'm all right now. Sorry for making such an exhibition of myself.'

They moved forward a few feet. The traffic eased ahead of them, and they almost managed thirty miles an hour before they slowed down and stopped again.

He said, 'You'll be all right when you get back to Thomas. He's a rock, isn't he?'

She nodded. Yes, Thomas was a rock, but he was a rock which was about to be blown up by person or persons unknown. If he survived this attack of whatever it was, if they let him out of hospital, hopefully cured, then he'd have to face a police investigation. He'd come down again in one piece, but perhaps with some bits chipped off him. She struggled to think in a positive fashion.

Rafael said, 'Changing the subject: I wasn't going to mention it so soon, but would you like me to suggest myself for . . . no, it's too early. Isn't it?'

'What is? Oh. Ah.' Ellie almost managed a smile. 'Why, Rafael! I've thought for some time how good it would be to have you join us in the trust. That is, if you could find the time to do so, what with the baby coming and your having to find a permanent place to live. I've already sounded out the other members of the trust about it and they liked the idea. I'm thrilled that you should think of doing it. But you mustn't join us yet.'

'You need me more than ever now you've got all that extra money coming in. Susan suggested it first, by the way. You know me; if left to myself, I'd only think of making money. Heaven only knows what would have become of me if I hadn't met Susan, who introduced me to you and Thomas and taught me that there were better ways of getting through the day than that. Susan tells me I need to spend more time thinking about others, and I'm beginning to think she's right.'

Rafael always paints himself worse than he is, doesn't he?

She tried for the light touch. 'It warms the cockles of my heart that you should offer but you don't realize how difficult life would become for you if your family and friends heard you were sticking up for a man accused of murder.'

'Let me tell you something about my family, Mrs Quicke. My mother may have been born in Italy, given me her father's name and passed on his genes, but she would never oppose my father in any way. He's a throwback to the Victorian age: upright, conscientious, and rigidly Puritan in his thinking. He regarded my buccaneering days with dismay. He found it hardly believable that he could have produced someone who dillied and dallied with girls, he was horrified when I rejected a career in academia and turned to making money by developing a rundown block of flats. I am not what he thought a son of his ought to be. Don't get me wrong; he's fond of me in a way, and I of him. I respect his values, on the whole. We're always polite to one another, but I won't melt if he tries to blast me with a flame-thrower.'

'You inherited the money to buy the flats from an uncle?'

'My father's brother. Another buccaneer. Made his money in some Get Rich Quick Scheme, got out just before the police moved in on him, narrowly avoided spending some time in jail and drank himself to death. Yes, he left me what was left of his money, with a recommendation to buy the best wines and never to listen to my father's advice.'

Ellie began to smile, and then to laugh out loud. 'Does Susan know all this?'

'Of course she does. She knows she's got her work cut out to make a human being of me, to which I say that I'm a work in progress. So, Mrs Quicke, you'll present me to your trust as soon as you like. Next week, perhaps? I know you usually meet on a Thursday morning. Are you going to have to call an extra meeting, or shall we make a date for it now?'

'You're quite mad. You know that, don't you?'

'Mm-hm. I'll take that as a "yes".'

Ellie was silent. Her stomach was playing up. Fear was doing horrid things to her digestion. As it had done to Thomas's? He'd been suffering from indigestion for some time, hadn't he? They'd put it down to Hetty's cooking and it was true that her pastry did lie heavily on the stomach, but the sort of pain which would have driven the stoical Thomas to hospital was something else, wasn't it?

Something was very wrong. Ellie didn't believe in omens and superstitions. Of course not. But there was a nasty pressure, not exactly in her lungs, but thereabouts. Something thudding away, telling her that all was not well. She said, 'Is there any way we can get off this motorway, Rafael? I'm so sorry, I don't drive, and you know what you're doing, far better than me, but . . . I'm really worried about Thomas, which is quite stupid, I know that. He's in the best of hands.'

'Nearly there. Approaching the turn off to Ealing now. When Susan hears what's happened, she'll be blaming herself, thinking it was her cooking giving him a tummy ache.'

'It's probably the black coffee he drinks before he goes to bed at night. I've never understood how he can do that and sleep soundly.'

Rafael said, 'Do you want to see if you can contact Lesley, tell her what's happened to Thomas and that you don't know how long you'll be at the hospital?'

Of course. That was the sensible thing to do. She didn't do it. Her hands were shaking too much. She said, 'I'll do it in a minute.'

Finally they reached the hospital. Ellie shot inside while Rafael parked the car, and they chased one another through the different sections till they found Thomas in a bed in Accident and Emergency. He was wearing a hospital gown, with a bouquet of needles in the back of one of his hands. He looked tired but pleased to see them.

'Sorry about this. The pain got too bad to ignore. It's never been as bad as this before. They suspect a stomach ulcer. They've done some tests and are awaiting the results.'

Ellie had hold of his hand as if she were afraid he'd slip away if she didn't hold on to him. 'It's Friday afternoon. Will they do anything over the weekend?'

'Probably not,' said Thomas. He closed his eyes for a moment and it looked as if he'd drifted off to sleep. Then he struggled awake. 'How stupid of me. If they keep me in, there's a couple of things that need seeing to. Ellie, don't wait around. Hospitals are such depressing places. I'll ring you when there's any news. Can you get hold of my secretary, tell her what's happened? I was going to go through everything one more time before I sent it off to the printers on Monday. So, just in case I don't get back in time, tell her to have a quick shufti if she will, and send it all off.'

Something was wrong with Ellie's throat. She tried to speak. Failed. Coughed. Managed it. 'Don't you dare die on me!'

'Wouldn't dream of it.' His eyes went beyond Ellie to Rafael. 'Look after her for me.'

Rafael said, 'I'll ask what's happening at the desk.'

Ellie kept hold of Thomas's hand. His eyes closed again, but he said, 'How was the funeral?'

'Fine. Evan made a bit of a scene. Par for the course, I suppose.' She didn't tell him about being left Monique's money. Time for that later, when he was feeling better. A stomach ulcer was painful but not life-threatening, right? They'd give him some jalop and send him home. Hopefully.

He looked ill. He hadn't eaten anything which would have brought this attack about, had he? It must have been brought on by anxiety about the money . . . and he didn't know someone had been to the police about it.

She wasn't going to tell him.

Rafael returned with a porter. Thomas was being whisked off for more tests. No, Ellie couldn't go with him. She was told to ring later, much later. They'd probably be keeping Thomas in overnight. Yes, yes. Ring later. Now, off we go . . .

Rafael put his arm round Ellie as Thomas was borne away. Rafael's arm was strong.

Ellie said, 'I am not going to break down and weep. No. That would be totally counter-productive. Stomach ulcers are quite common. Doctors know how to treat them. They do it all the time.'

Rafael said, 'Good girl. That's the ticket. Let's get out of here and ring Susan. Look at the time! She'll want to know what you've been doing with me.'

'Lesley! I'd forgotten that Lesley wanted to come round. What on earth am I going to say to her? Will she think Thomas is malingering, that he's managed to get himself admitted to hospital to avoid being questioned by the police?'

'No, of course not.'

'No, of course not,' echoed Ellie. 'Pull yourself together, girl!' And then tried to laugh at herself. 'Hark at me. Going senile.'

'Not you, Ellie. Let me reassure Susan that I've not met with a fatal accident on the way back from the funeral, and then I'll take you home. By that time, they may well have some news for you from the hospital.'

'They'll let me come back this evening for visiting time, won't they?'

'I have no idea. I'll hang around for a bit, anyway, in case you need ferrying to and fro again.'

'You talk as if I'm two years old,' said Ellie, hanging on to her dignity. 'I'm perfectly able to cope. I can't afford to give way to the vapours, or whatever it was that Victorian ladies were always doing in moments of stress—'

'It was the corsets that did for them, wasn't it? If they tried to take a deep breath, they passed out.'

'Well, I'm not going to do that!' She crossed her fingers.

Rafael made his phone call and drove them both back to Ellie's place.

She let them into the hall. All was quiet and peaceful. The grandfather clock ticked. Midge the cat was curled up on the hall chair, asleep.

Her police friend, Lesley, appeared in the doorway to the sitting room, saying, 'Hello, there. Your housekeeper let me in!'

And it was at that point Ellie gave way to a flood of tears.

TWELVE

Late Friday afternoon

Lesley hastened to Ellie's side. 'My dear, whatever is the matter?'

Ellie tried to speak and failed. Found a hankie and used it. 'Sorry, sorry. Such a cry-baby. Lesley, Thomas is in hospital, and they don't know why and they're doing tests and they've sent us home. It's probably just a stomach ulcer, but he looks dreadful and I'm so afraid!'

'There, there. Thomas is strong. I'm sure he'll be all right.'

Ellie sobbed. 'Nothing's right! Diana's going to accuse me of murder!'

Lesley was shocked. 'Diana's going to do *what*?'

Ellie was too wound up to stop now that she had started. 'She says I murdered Monique, which I didn't, I swear I didn't. How could I have done so, anyway? I haven't seen her for months. Diana makes herself believe whatever she wants to believe and oh, I can't bear it!'

'Wait a minute! I don't understand. I've been told to speak to you because someone rang the police station to say Thomas had been embezzling funds, which I didn't believe for a minute, but murder? That's so ridiculous it's . . . Words fail me! Let's sit down and you can tell me all about it.'

Rafael said, 'I'll make a pot of tea, shall I?' He departed for the kitchen quarters.

Ellie couldn't stop talking. 'I'm sorry, I'm so stupid, but it's been a terrible few days, and when Diana said that . . . She wants money as always, and when she found out that Monique has left me some . . . Do you remember Monique? Perhaps you don't. She was Evan's first wife, long divorced and she's left all this money not to me but the trust, and Diana's furious and she said she was going to tell the police that—'

'From the beginning,' said Lesley, steering Ellie into the sitting room and depositing her in her high-backed chair.

Ellie struggled to speak clearly. 'Diana's going to say that I killed Monique, because I wouldn't help her. Wouldn't help Diana, I mean. Financially. As if I could, because it has to go through the trust, anyway, and they wouldn't agree to help Diana. Why should they? And I didn't kill Monique. I don't even know exactly when she died!'

Lesley pulled up a chair and held her hand. 'Take a deep breath, girl! Get a grip.'

Ellie gulped and tried to calm herself down. 'Sorry, sorry. I know it's ridiculous, and Diana does too, really. At least, she would if she were thinking straight, but I do see that she's in a bit of a hole. What's happened is that they bought an option on a piece of land by the river, thinking they could get permission to develop it. Now they need to complete the deal but can't, so they'll lose what they've already invested. It sounds as if their finances are in a dreadful mess and they ought never to have committed themselves to such a deal, but what do I know about such things, anyway?'

Rafael clanked in with the hostess trolley. Teapot, mugs instead of cups and saucers, milk, sugar and the biscuit tin.

'Carbohydrates for shock. I'll be mother, shall I?' He poured out mugs of hot, very strong tea, added sugar and handed them around. 'No talking, by order. Not till we've drunk the tea and had several biscuits each.'

Ellie felt in her pockets for her phone. Had she put it back in her handbag, and if so, where had she dropped that? 'I have to ring the hospital.'

Rafael said, 'You drink your tea, and I'll do it.' He got out his smartphone, rang the hospital and was switched here and there. And listened. He clicked his phone off. 'They've admitted him to a ward. You can visit this evening.'

Ellie drank her tea and tried to relax. 'Understood. I'll be all right in a minute.'

Lesley took a second biscuit and said, 'Rafael, would you like to fill me in while Ellie recovers her wits?'

Rafael replied for Ellie. 'Monique – you remember her, don't you? Impressive woman, owned a successful estate agency in Kensington, walked with a stick. Married to Evan for a short time, twenty-odd years ago. Monique had a fall some weeks ago, was hospitalized, went downhill and died. She was cremated early this morning. Ellie and I went to the service in church at noon. The will was read this afternoon. Mrs Quicke's trust gets practically everything with strings attached. Said strings are that the trust must look after the son Monique produced with Evan, if he is ever well enough to live in the community again. Evan and Diana were furious and uttered threats which were probably libellous, knowing them. Incredibly, they accused Ellie of murdering Monique. Ellie is distressed because she liked Monique. End of.'

Lesley drank tea and ate her second biscuit. 'Let's get this straight. Diana is going to lodge an official complaint against her mother? Not against Thomas?'

Rafael shrugged. 'So Ellie said.'

Ellie set aside her sodden hankie and reached for the box of tissues on a nearby table. She mopped herself up and blew her nose. 'There's no reasoning with Diana. She lashes out without thinking. Evan's getting old and losing his touch and she has two small children under five. She's under a lot of stress. But to accuse me of murder!'

'How many other people have you and Thomas upset recently?'

Ellie took a deep breath. 'Thomas didn't upset anyone. Six people have died recently and left him varying sums of money. Plus their relatives and friends.'

Lesley blinked. 'How odd, Ellie, really?'

'Have you got half an hour to tell you what's been happening? We've been trying to sort it out ourselves this week and got nowhere. Thomas was going to take the whole business to you tomorrow, but now he's in hospital and I don't know how . . .' She restrained tears with difficulty. 'Let me fetch the paperwork we've been collecting and you can see what's been going on for yourself.'

She got to her feet, trying to think where she'd left the papers. 'Now, I know some of the letters are in Thomas's study and some in mine . . . Which reminds me that I must speak to his secretary urgently. Give me a minute, will you, Lesley?'

She left the room as Rafael said, 'Shall I pour you another cuppa, Lesley?'

Ellie dashed down to Thomas's study at the end of the corridor and was not surprised to find his secretary's desk unoccupied. It was getting latish on a Friday afternoon, and the woman didn't usually work long hours. Of course, she didn't know Thomas was in hospital, did she?

Ellie rubbed her forehead, trying to think. Ought she to get in touch with his secretary and ask her as a favour to work on the magazine over the weekend? Ah, but the woman wasn't usually around at weekends, was she? Didn't she go up north to visit her mother, who was ailing? In which case, she was not going to be dragged back to London till Monday when they were due to send the stuff to the printers.

Ellie decided that if the magazine went out two days late, it wouldn't matter.

She collected some of the relevant papers, took them to her study and with trembling fingers booted up the photocopier.

Rafael tapped on the door and she started. He said, 'Lesley suspects you're going to take photocopies, but she's letting you do it. If she'd disapproved, she'd have accompanied you to your lair and stood over you till you handed the stuff over. Do the earliest ones first. I'll take them back to her, saying you've put them in different files and you're taking a while to find where you've put everything.'

Ellie nodded, putting an original into the copier, and pressing buttons. When two had been done, she handed the originals to Rafael, who took them back down the corridor to the sitting room.

Ellie proceeded with the next lot, and the next . . .

Rafael returned, ironing out a grin. 'She knows exactly what you're doing, but she's not going to say anything.'

Ellie turned off the copier. 'I don't know why I'm bothering. What good is it going to do to have copies?'

'You'll think of something. By the way, I think your house-keeper's just come back. I heard someone come in the front door as I delivered the first papers to Lesley. Whoever it was didn't go upstairs but went straight along to the kitchen.'

Ellie groaned. 'Another problem. I've got to find somewhere else for her to live. You wouldn't have a spare room to let, would you?'

'I'm not that stupid. Let her throw herself on the mercies of the borough council. They have facilities for waifs and strays.'

He was right. Hard-hearted, but right.

They took the rest of the papers back to the sitting room and delivered them to Lesley, who looked through them and said, 'Talk me through this, will you?'

So Ellie did so. She began at the beginning, when the first cheque arrived from the estate of a parishioner. Ellie said, 'It was unexpected, but he'd known and liked her. He was grateful, if slightly surprised, that she'd remembered him. The same with the second one. Well, that wasn't a parishioner but someone who lived locally and got in touch with Thomas through the charity Age UK. She was pretty well housebound. Thomas used to visit her, not every week but every now and then.'

Lesley spread the paperwork out on the gateleg table in the window and put the documents in order as Ellie talked her through the arrival of numbers three to five and Thomas's growing bewilderment as to why he'd been selected as a recipient of this bounty.

Ellie said, 'He was beginning to think something was not quite right when he got a cheque from the estate of an old friend for a much greater amount, in fact for twenty thousand pounds. He'd known the man well for many years. He believed that that last cheque was all right but, knowing that number six was all right made the others more and not less suspect.'

Lesley eyed the paperwork. 'Yes, I see what you mean. None of the early ones are for large amounts, but number six is for twenty thousand pounds and that is a different matter. You say that's genuine. Have you checked?'

'We haven't had time. It was Thursday afternoon – only yesterday! – that Thomas received that big cheque. His reaction was that he was going to ask you to look into the matter, and that he didn't feel he could possibly accept it, or any of the other cheques he'd been sent. I didn't agree with him entirely. I thought that he should accept the money from his friend, but . . . Yes, I had to admit that there was something very strange about the earlier ones. I suggested trying to find out some link between the testators which would account for them leaving Thomas money, and he agreed. We discussed the matter with Rafael and Susan, and they came up with some information which may or may not be helpful.'

Rafael said, 'Number four. I knew him slightly. If I say he was a corrupt councillor, you'll probably know who I mean.'

Lesley looked startled. Then thoughtful. Finally she leaned down and picked one particular set of papers up off the floor. 'Councillor Thornwell?'

'Rumour indicates he was far from squeaky clean, but you didn't hear that from me.'

Ellie glanced at Rafael, wondering if he were going to mention the possibly corrupt deal Diana and Evan had been involved in with Councillor Thornwell, but Rafael's expression remained guileless.

Lesley narrowed her eyes at Rafael. 'You have no proof of anything untoward?'

Rafael widened his eyes. 'About what?'

Lesley said, 'Humpf. All right. So where's the connection between Thornwell and Thomas?'

'That's just it,' said Ellie. 'I don't know. Thomas didn't know. I haven't a clue where to start on that one.'

Thomas is in hospital and I don't know how I can remain sitting here, talking calmly about these cheques as if they were important.

Lesley said, 'At ten this morning someone rang the station to claim that Thomas had been stealing from his parishioners. It was a woman who refused to give her name. The call was recorded. It landed on my desk with a thud. My boss was thrilled to hear that Thomas was being accused of something criminal and asked me to investigate. I don't think it was Diana, because she speaks in a clipped manner. I'll see if I can get permission for you to listen to the tape. You might recognize the voice. Do you think it could be one of the people you've interviewed about Thomas's cheques?'

Ellie shook her head. 'I only saw two of them, and I can't think it would be either. I met Bob and Dawn Pullin, the stepson and stepdaughter of Mrs Pullin – she's number five – the woman who left him a thousand pounds. Neither of them knew Thomas. Neither of them thought there was anything odd about their stepmother's list of bequests. They spoke openly to me about their problems in life, but there was no hint of resentment. Well, except that Bob Pullin – who is not the nicest of men – did say that if the lawyers hadn't had to pay out a number of bequests, they'd have had enough in the bank to get the house ready to put on the market. I offered to help with a loan, an offer which they accepted with pleasure. Neither of them would have complained about me or Thomas.'

Lesley said, 'I'll have to see them, though.'

'Granted. I also went to see a long-time old friend of mine, Gwen Harris, Harold's widow. I don't think either Gwen or Harold ever met Thomas. They knew me, but not him. When I raised the matter of Harold's bequest to Thomas, Gwen wasn't at all perturbed about it. Poor dear, she's in a bad way. On anti-depressants. Those are the only two families I visited. Maybe the police can get further, but I'm stuck.'

Lesley shuffled the papers together. 'You have a knack of getting people to talk and I suspect I'll get less out of them than you. Have you got their phone numbers?'

'I can give you those for the Pullins, brother and sister, and for Gwen. I haven't had time to do any more.'

Lesley was soothing. 'Don't worry. I can get their details easily enough.'

Ellie looked at the clock. Was it running slow? She looked at her watch. When had Rafael said that visiting hours started?

Lesley pushed the paperwork together. 'You'll want to get to the hospital. I'm sure it's nothing serious with Thomas. In the meantime, you do understand that you mustn't try to contact any of these people about the bequests? Leave all that to me.'

Ellie said, 'Oh, but I have to lend the Pullin family some money and arrange for their stepmother's house to be cleared. I promised!' She ran her fingers back through her hair.

How long will it take me to get to the hospital? It's a bus to the Broadway, and then another to the hospital. Perhaps I'd better take a cab.

Lesley tapped the papers into a neat pile. 'I know nothing about that.'

Did Lesley mean that she didn't want to hear about it, or that she didn't want to know about it? Confusion . . .!

Rafael said, 'Suppose Ellie arranges the loan and the clearing up through a solicitor. That would be all right, wouldn't it?'

'I haven't a clue what you're talking about,' said Lesley, slipping the papers into a folder, and getting ready to leave.

Ellie wasn't sure what this meant, either. 'Do you mean, "out of sight, out of mind"?'

Lesley said, 'Give Thomas my love,' and took herself off.

Rafael put the last of the tea things back on the trolley. 'I'll take you to the hospital. Saves time.'

'You're a busy man. You can't just—'

'Yes, I can. If I didn't, can you imagine what Susan would say? I'd be sleeping on the settee tonight. I'll ring her, tell her what's happening.' He got out his phone.

Ellie pushed the trolley across the hall and down to the kitchen from which came a smell of burning and the sound of the radio going at full blast.

Oh dear! Yes, there was Hetty, hair all over the place, a smudge of flour on her cheek, giving vent to little screams of horror, attempting to lift a baking tray full of burnt scones out of the top oven. The table was littered with pans and jars and a bag of flour, spilling its contents everywhere.

Also, there was a whirring sound. What could that be? The liquidizer, overdoing it? Scraps of uncooked pastry clung to the board on which Ellie usually made sandwiches, and there were coils of apple peel everywhere.

On the floor by the oven was a puddle with a broken eggshell in it. If someone slipped on that, they could do themselves a serious injury. As if that were not enough, something boiled over on the stove.

'Oh, oh, oh!' cried Hetty, dropping the tray on to the table, which overturned half a bottle of milk. The liquid ran thither and hither over the surface, found its way to the edge and dripped down to the floor.

'Oh, oh, oh! Everything's gone wrong!' Hetty flung herself into the big chair at the head of the table and rocked to and fro in a nicely judged case of hysteria.

Ellie told herself to keep calm. Very calm. She abandoned the trolley to switch off the radio first, and then the gas under the pot on the stove. And lastly, the liquidizer.

A beautiful silence flooded into the room.

Ellie righted the milk bottle, seized some kitchen towel and wiped up first the egg on the floor and then the milk.

Hetty wept, jetting out words that sometimes made sense and sometimes didn't. 'But I didn't know you were coming back so . . . I thought to surprise . . . I know it's all a mess, it's all gone wrong. But I thought you'd be so pleased if I made you a lovely pie and some scones for tea, and it would make up for . . . Because I know how hard you work, and I thought that if I made you a really nice supper, you'd give me another chance.'

Ellie tipped the burnt scones into the bin and put the baking tray in soak. A pan full of apples cooking in a sugary liquid had boiled over on the stove. The sugar in the pan was going to make clearing up that mess difficult.

Ellie got out the mop and cleaned the floor where the egg and the milk had been. The egg box was now empty, which meant there wouldn't be any eggs left for breakfast.

Hetty wept louder than ever.

Rafael came in. He exclaimed something which Ellie decided not to hear, seized the mop from Ellie and proceeded to give the floor a better clean. Ellie tackled the mess on the table.

Then she remembered that Hetty said she'd put a pie in the oven? Ellie opened the bottom oven door and black smoke flooded into the kitchen.

Rafael said something else sharp.

Ellie looked at the clock. Oughtn't she to be on her way to the hospital by now?

Rafael intercepted her look. 'I'll take you. Let's clear this lot up, first.'

Hetty was gulping, red-faced. But no longer in tears. 'I was only trying to help!'

'Yes,' said Ellie. 'I know. I did ask you not to. We let you have the flat upstairs until you could get yourself sorted, and we never expected you to use our kitchen. We haven't asked for rent which makes you a guest and not a tenant. Your stay here hasn't worked out. We wish you nothing but good, but you are no longer welcome. I have been trying to find somewhere else for you to go locally and had no luck. I must ask you to make an effort to find something for yourself. Now!'

Hetty was back to sobbing again. 'You can't just turn me out like that.'

'If you go down to the council they will find you somewhere to live. It may only be temporary, but that's the best advice I can give you. I really can't have you in my kitchen again.'

'You only say that because . . . It's because Thomas has turned against me, I know! If it weren't for him—'

'Nonsense,' said Ellie, beginning to feel heated. 'It wasn't Thomas, and in any case he's in hospital at the moment with terrible stomach pains. They're keeping him in, and I don't know how long or what . . .' She mastered herself with an effort. There was no point in her breaking down, too.

'Is he?' Hetty's tears dried up. 'Really! Well, I'm not surprised. His stomach's always been weak, and *you* don't know how to feed a man who likes his food, do you?'

Ellie lost it. 'That's enough, and more than enough. Hetty, I must ask you to leave my kitchen now, this very minute! I am going to the hospital as soon as I've cleared up here. While I'm out, I want you to pack your things up. You can stay here tonight, but tomorrow you must find yourself somewhere else to go.'

Hetty shrieked, 'You don't mean it!'

'Yes, I do,' said Ellie, sweeping pans and bowls into the sink. 'Out! Out! Out!'

Hetty fled, with a scream.

Rafael put his hands on Ellie's shoulders and turned her around. 'Let me finish up here. Go and powder your nose or whatever. We're leaving for the hospital in ten minutes flat.'

Ellie thought that she could do with a stiff drink, only she didn't indulge except for the odd half glass of something at a party, or for an evening meal when they had friends round and they didn't have anything but beer in the house. And she'd never liked beer.

Would a drink help now? No, probably not. She put out a hand to the back of a chair to steady herself. She said, 'I think I'm rather upset.'

Rafael guided her into a chair and pushed her head down.

She wanted to say, 'I'm perfectly all right,' but found she couldn't say anything at all.

THIRTEEN

Friday, early evening

Back to the hospital. Thomas was no longer in A&E. He'd been admitted to a ward . . . but which one?

He was in Intensive Care.

Ellie clutched Rafael's hand as they approached Thomas's bed. He was hooked up to this and that piece of equipment. Heart monitor? Some fluid was dripping into a vein?

His eyes were closed. His skin looked pallid.

Rafael pulled up a chair and made Ellie sit down. At least there were no curtains drawn around Thomas's bed, so he couldn't be in dire straits. Or could he?

Thomas lifted heavy eyelids and smiled at Ellie. 'It's nothing serious. Be home tomorrow.'

Rafael vanished. Ellie held Thomas's hand. He closed his eyes and slept.

Eventually Rafael returned with a nurse, who took Ellie a little distance away from the patient to deliver the bad news.

It appeared that Thomas had been nursing an ulcer for some time, but this was not in itself a major cause for alarm as he was a strong, healthy man in all other respects and could be expected to respond well to treatment. However, the nurse said he'd recently ingested something which had attacked the lining of his stomach and caused his condition to become more serious. Could Mrs Quicke think of anything he might have eaten recently which would have had such an effect?

Ellie shook her head.

Rafael shook his head, too.

'What medication is he on?'

'Indigestion tablets now and then,' said Ellie. 'Nothing else.'

'No arthritis, joint pains?'

She shook her head.

Rafael asked, 'Why do you ask about arthritis?'

'Occasionally people have a bad reaction to something they can buy over the counter if they have joint pains. It has been known to upset the stomach.'

They looked back at the bed where Thomas lay, asleep or nearly so.

Ellie said, 'He hasn't complained of any joint pains. I haven't seen him take anything except indigestion tablets. He does have a stressful job. It makes sense that he has an ulcer. What . . .?' She faltered, unable to ask what the prognosis was.

The nurse was brisk. 'We should have it under control pretty soon. By tomorrow he should be feeling a lot better.'

'You're keeping him in?'

'We're monitoring him closely. When you go home it might be an idea to check his pockets to see if you can find any tablets other than the ones for indigestion. If you find anything, bring it in to us or, better still, telephone through to say what it is.'

Off went the nurse, professionally detached in manner.

Ellie propped herself up against the wall. 'The nurse thinks he's taken something he shouldn't. I don't get it. If Thomas had a pain, he'd say so, wouldn't he?'

*   *   *

Rafael drove Ellie home at the end of the visiting hour.

He said she wasn't safe to be let out on the streets on her own. She was glad of his support. Thomas was her rock but, as she'd sat by his bed holding his hand, she'd had the impression that he was drifting away from her . . . if a rock could drift. Which it couldn't. No.

She was overtired.

Rafael took her key from her hand and opened the front door. 'I don't think you should be alone. I've rung Susan and asked if she can pop over with some food for us. That is, if you don't mind.'

Mind? No, she didn't mind. She thought it was an excellent idea. Food? When had she eaten last? At breakfast, probably. She hadn't had anything after the church service, had she? Yes. One small sandwich. Not enough.

Somewhere a fire alarm was ringing. Not here, obviously. Perhaps next door.

Oh. A blue haze seeped out of the corridor to the kitchen.

Ellie blinked. She was seeing things. How could a blue haze be in her hall?

The alarm in the hall was ringing. Not next door. Here, in her own house!

The sound sliced through her head, cutting off all possibility of thought.

Rafael dashed down the corridor through the haze, which she hadn't imagined but which was real. As far as hazes can be real.

The clamour of the fire alarm!

She followed Rafael. Yes, something was burning in the kitchen. Ellie couldn't understand that. Hadn't she and Rafael cleaned up before they'd left for the hospital to see Thomas?

The fire alarm was insistent. Its beat went right through her. Whatever . . .?

She could see Rafael's mouth moving. He found the oven gloves and put them on. He was mouthing curses, fumbling with something at the stove. Something had boiled over on the stove, something that was alight? No, that couldn't possibly have happened, because they'd turned everything off before they left, hadn't they?

Rafael took a pan from the hob, put it in the sink and turned the tap on its contents. Steam rose, hissing. He unlocked and opened the back door.

Ellie attacked the windows in the kitchen, thrusting them open as far as they would go. The haze dissipated. The noise of the alarm finally came to an end. The silence was intense.

She could hear herself breathe.

She could hear something else. Someone was snoring. What!

On the big chair at the head of the table lay Hetty, hair all over the place, legs akimbo. Asleep and snoring. On the table in front of Hetty lay an empty packet of pills and a note.

Ellie picked it up and read it. It said, *I did my best!*

So, Hetty hadn't taken the pills by accident. She'd tried to commit suicide.

Rafael said something in a vicious undertone.

Ellie sat down on the nearest chair with a bump.

Dear Lord, I can't cope with this. It's too much! Poor Hetty! I didn't mean to drive her to this. I'm too tired to move. I haven't the strength to deal with a suicide attempt. And, you won't forget to look after Thomas, will you?

She'd dropped her handbag on the floor. She picked it up to get out her phone, only to find that Rafael was already on his, calling for an ambulance.

Thank the Lord, Rafael had known what to do whereas she had sat there like a dumb thing. She was useless, always had been.

Rafael spoke into the phone. 'Yes, she's breathing. No, she's not conscious. She's taken something. Lord alone knows. There's a packet of . . . Dunno. Sleeping tablets, I think?' He picked the pack up and turned it over. 'Yes, sleeping tablets. The pack is empty. It's not an over-the-counter remedy, not one I recognize, anyway . . . How long ago? I've no idea. We've been out for a couple of hours, I suppose . . . You want me to walk her around, keep her conscious? You must be joking. I'm not touching her. She's caused so much trouble, you've no idea.'

Ellie put her handbag on the table and brushed one hand off against the other. The paramedics wanted them to keep Hetty moving so Ellie must try to do that. She might not like Hetty, and yes, Hetty had caused a lot of unnecessary trouble, but she was a human being.

With an effort, Ellie pushed herself off her chair and got her arm under Hetty's shoulders. Come on! Heave ho!

She failed in her attempt to lift the woman, who slumped back into the big chair.

Rafael let rip another couple of swear words, tucked his phone between his shoulder and his neck, and came to help her. 'This is against my better judgement. We should let the woman die if that's what she wants to do. What with Thomas in hospital and all . . .'

Nevertheless, without letting go of his phone, he helped Ellie get Hetty upright. The woman lolled between them, her feet all over the place. Totally out of it.

Rafael continued to speak on his phone. 'Yes, we've got her upright, but no, she's nowhere near conscious. You'd better hurry!'

Hetty's body had a slightly unpleasant odour. Not curry, but perhaps some herb or other? Perhaps the scent came from her hair? An unusual shampoo?

Rafael said to Ellie, 'You can let go. I've got her.' He gave Hetty a little shake. 'Come on! Wakey wakey!'

Hetty mumbled something. So she was still alive?

Ellie shivered. The evening had turned cooler and, now the blue haze had dissipated, there was no need to leave all the doors and windows open. She went round, closing them. Her steps dragged. She wanted to lie down and die.

Rafael hauled Hetty three steps along the floor.

Hetty moaned and sobbed, 'No, leave me be!'

Ellie thought that they'd caught her just in time. The hospital would pump out her stomach and she'd be as good as new. Ellie let herself down into a chair and closed her eyes.

It occurred to her that Hetty had known Ellie would be back soon. Had she timed a suicide attempt knowing that Ellie would be in time to rescue her?

Er, yes, probably.

Hetty could have taken pills and laid down on her bed in the top flat and no one would have missed her until the following morning and possibly not even then. That way, she'd have made sure to die.

But no, she'd taken the pills and laid down in the kitchen where Ellie would be bound to find her as soon as she returned home. What's more, Hetty had left something on the stove which would produce smoke and set off the fire alarms, alerting anyone in earshot to an emergency.

So it wasn't a suicide attempt as such. It was what they call 'a cry for help'.

Ah, but that note had been written with malice aforethought. It was designed to make Ellie and Thomas feel guilty about the way they'd treated Hetty.

Ellie didn't feel guilty. Like Rafael, she felt considerable annoyance with the woman. Or, well, perhaps she did feel a bit guilty. She could have taken a little more time and trouble to soften Hetty's dismissal, but the upshot would have been the same.

Someone knocked on the door.

Rafael was still dragging Hetty around like a lifesize doll.

Ellie tottered along the corridor to let the ambulance men in. The taller of the two paramedics had a shaved head and looked as if he worked out. He said, 'Where's the patient?'

Ellie pointed the ambulance men in the direction of the kitchen. 'Down there. My friend is walking her around. I think she's faking it. Yes, she's probably taken some pills, but not very long ago. Perhaps within the last fifteen minutes.'

A taxi drew up and a very pregnant girl got out of it. Susan, carrying an insulated bag. 'What's the ambulance for? Is it Rafael? Is he hurt?'

Ellie pulled Susan indoors. 'He's fine, Susan. Have you brought us something to eat? Bless you for that, but I don't think we can eat in the kitchen. It's Hetty. Faking it. At least, I think she is. Only, I might be wrong. I don't know whether I'm on my head or my heels.'

Susan dumped her bag on the hall table and put her arms around Ellie. 'The paramedics will sort it out. Rafael said you've had a perfectly horrid day. You'll feel better after you've eaten. Now, what is the latest on Thomas?'

Ellie tried to smile. 'That's one thing about you, Susan; you always get your priorities right.'

Rafael appeared, to kiss Susan and report. 'Hetty's talking, sort of. Insists she wants to die. Says she took four sleeping tablets.'

Ellie said, 'I think she timed it so we'd find her as soon as we got back from the hospital. I'm wondering if she only took them when she heard our return.'

'If that's the case, then she's a good actress,' said Rafael. 'She fooled me.'

Ellie said, 'I'm beginning to think she's an excellent actress. What worries me is that she might have given Thomas something to make him so poorly.'

Susan said, 'Why would she do that?'

'Well, the hospital asked me to look for something which Thomas might have taken, to put him in such pain. Hetty had some sleeping pills which you can only get on prescription, so now I'm wondering what else she's got upstairs. As to why she'd give anything harmful to Thomas, I'm probably imagining things but she might think she has a reason. It was Thomas who asked me to let her have the top flat for a while. Within a week I could see it wasn't going to work, but it took him a lot longer to come to the same conclusion. Now he's as anxious for her to go as I am. I have asked her to find somewhere else. She appealed to Thomas to reverse my decision and failed. No, I know I have no evidence, but I'm thinking she might now have turned on Thomas. If I'm right . . . Well, first, I need to look at what other medication she may be hiding upstairs.'

The paramedic with the shaven head emerged from the kitchen. 'We're taking her in. She's pretty confused about how many tablets she's taken, and we have to be on the safe side in such cases. She says the tablets belong to someone called Ellie, who gave them to her when she couldn't sleep. Is that right?'

'I'm Ellie, but they're not my tablets. Neither my husband nor I have any need for sleeping tablets. I've never seen them before.'

That paramedic twitched his eyebrows. Maybe he believed Ellie and maybe he didn't, but it wasn't his job to apportion blame. He said, 'Who's coming in the ambulance with her?'

'Not I,' said Ellie.

'Nor I,' said Rafael.

Perhaps the paramedic thought them callous in their refusal to care for a woman who'd just tried to commit suicide, but he was too well-trained to show it. He said, 'You'll contact her next of kin, then?'

'She hasn't got any,' said Ellie. 'She needs referring to a counsellor and to find somewhere else to go when she's discharged. A hostel or something. I'll pack up her belongings and they can be forwarded to wherever she goes when she leaves hospital. Yes, that does sound hard-hearted, but you've no idea how much trouble she's caused. And don't say I can't turn her out into the cold because I've given her plenty of notice to find somewhere else.'

'Not my problem.' The paramedic collected a wheelchair from the ambulance, took it down to the kitchen and collected Hetty and his mate.

As they passed through the hall, Hetty cried out, 'Oh, Ellie! Forgive me! Give me another chance!'

Ellie didn't respond. Perhaps she'd feel guilty about it later, but no, the woman must go.

Hetty was packed into the ambulance and driven away.

Rafael shut the front door. Peace and quiet descended.

It was getting dark. Susan switched on the lights and said, 'Let's eat.'

Rafael said, 'The kitchen's still in a mess. When do your cleaners come, Ellie?'

'Tuesday. I'll clear up tomorrow. I want to get back to the hospital this evening, but first—'

'First we eat,' said Rafael. 'In the living room. The table and chairs are still there from last night, aren't they?'

They were. Ellie was persuaded to sit and eat. They gave her only a small portion of the chicken casserole at first. She ate that with one eye on the clock. Then had another spoonful. It was delicious. Then, when she said she must go up to search Hetty's rooms, Susan persuaded Ellie to taste the creamy dessert she'd brought with her. Finally, Rafael brought them all mugs of tea from the kitchen.

It was only then that Ellie realized how tired she was feeling. She smiled at their two anxious faces. 'I'll live. I'm sure Thomas will, too.'

Rafael looked at his watch. 'Three quarters of an hour till we need to leave the house for the hospital. You sit still, Ellie. I'm going to go upstairs and search that little madam's quarters for suspicious items. Do you know what medication she's on, if any?'

Ellie was happy to sit still for the time being. Worrying about Thomas was tiring her out, even though she kept telling herself he was in the best possible place and would be perfectly all right in a trice.

What had Rafael asked her? Ah, what medication Hetty could be on. 'She takes something for hay fever occasionally. She boasts she's as strong as an ox, sleeps like a baby, works harder than most people half her age. I've never heard her mention any other health problem.'

'So where did she get those sleeping tablets from?'

'No idea. They aren't mine, nor Thomas's.'

'I won't be long.' He caught Susan's eye, and some message seemed to pass between them for Susan said, 'Take care,' and blew him a kiss.

He left and Ellie transferred to her own comfortable, high-backed chair while Susan swept the supper things on to the hostess trolley.

Ellie said, 'So what was that nod and a wink about, Susan? Rafael wants you to do something for him?'

Susan clattered knives and forks. She was frowning. 'Maybe now is not the right time to talk about it.'

'We have three-quarters of an hour and anything that takes my mind off Thomas would be a good thing.'

Susan let herself down on to a chair and stroked her bump. 'All right, I'll tell you. You may think it's a terrible idea. If so, we won't mention it again. Way back in the beginning, when we first met and he came to the house, Rafael's business mind told him that right here in this house there was an opportunity to make a lot of money.'

Ellie started. 'Oh! He wants to pull down this house and develop the site? No, my dear. No.'

'No, not that. Yes, he did see the potential but I soon put him right on the subject. It's your house, you and Thomas love it and fit into it like two peas in a pod. Right?'

'Yes, we do,' said Ellie.

Susan cleared her throat. She was nervous about this. 'He's noticed, and I have, too, that you're not keeping up with the maintenance, and that a lot of the rooms aren't used at all. We wondered if perhaps the house were becoming a burden rather than a blessing.'

'Well, yes,' said Ellie. 'We did plan to do this and that by way of maintenance, but then things happened. It's true I do feel guilty about the two of us rattling around in such a big place, but we love it and I can't imagine us moving into a small shoebox somewhere or having no garden.'

'We absolutely understand that,' said Susan, 'but I thought it might be a good idea to let you know what Rafael was thinking about for the future. Do you want me to go on?'

Ellie's heart beat went into overdrive. She wasn't at all sure that she wanted to hear what their idea might be. She sensed it was going to mean a big change in their circumstances. What would Thomas feel about this?

Oh, Thomas! Don't die on me!

Ellie said, 'I know this house is too big for us, I know it needs money spending on it, but—'

'But it's your home,' said Susan. 'We both understand that. His idea was that, perhaps in a few years' time, you might think, eventually, not straight away . . .'

Ellie said, 'I'm listening.'

'Dividing the house in two, each having its own front door and stairs.'

Ellie began to be angry. She had taken Susan in because the girl had needed somewhere to live while she was going through college. Susan had suffered from being bullied and laughed at because she had an outstandingly beautiful bosom. Ellie had got the girl to realize what an asset her boobs were, Susan had gradually gained in confidence, had become a sort of daughter to Ellie and Thomas and landed Rafael as a husband. Now Susan wanted to turn Ellie out of her own house? Ellie wondered if she might faint. As in a dream, she heard her own voice saying, 'How could we do that?'

'Downstairs you keep this side, with the exception of the library and the Quiet Room. You only use the dining room one morning a week, so that becomes Thomas's study and Quiet Room. You can have your weekly meetings in the sitting room or hold them at the offices of the trust. The kitchen quarters could do with some upgrading, but the rest of this side stays as it is: that is, the hall, conservatory, sitting room, and your study on the ground floor.

'Upstairs you keep your own en suite and the guest en suite next to it. You already have a second spare bedroom en suite over the kitchen quarters, which you can refurnish for use by visiting grandchildren. And you keep half the garden.'

Ellie followed that with painful interest. And incredulity. 'We'd end up with a three-bedroom house, all bedrooms en suite, while Thomas spreads himself out in the current dining room? But . . .' She didn't know what to say.

Susan looked anxious. 'I thought we might just talk about it, toss the idea around, consider the best and the worst sides of it.'

Ellie put her hand to her throat. 'I can't think straight!'

'We'll say no more. I'll just dump everything in the kitchen for now, shall I?' Off she went, leaving Ellie wondering if she were on her head or her heels.

What a stupid idea! How dare Susan suggest . . .! It was ridiculous.

I wouldn't have to worry about all the rooms I never go into.

No, you couldn't possibly divide up a big old house like that. For one thing, Thomas loves his Quiet Room. It's the place he retires to several times a day to talk to God and to think about things.

Come on! I've heard him say that any place in which prayers are said soon becomes a Quiet Room.

Rafael appeared in the doorway, looking bothered. 'I found a pack of Ibuprofen tablets under the chair in the kitchen where Hetty was lying. I suppose they may have fallen out of her pocket or her handbag and she hadn't noticed. They're strong stuff. Neither you nor Thomas suffer from rheumatism or arthritis, do you?'

Ellie shook her head. 'Ibuprofen upsets my stomach. I tried it once, but never again. Thomas is the same.'

'I use it occasionally with no ill effects and so does Susan, but I know it can be murder to a few unlucky people. Did Hetty take it?'

'I've never heard her complain of aches and pains, so why would she? You think that's what's upset Thomas's stomach? He wouldn't have taken them of his own accord, which means . . .' She took a deep breath. 'There's only one thing which Thomas eats or drinks and I don't, and that's a brand of instant coffee which he buys from a specialist shop. It's far too strong for me. I have one of the milder ones from the supermarket. If Hetty had ground up some Ibuprofen tablets and put them in his jar of coffee he wouldn't have known he was taking them, would he?'

'He wouldn't.'

'You think we should take the coffee jar into the hospital with us?'

'The packet, certainly. Now, I went upstairs intending to look around Hetty's flat for any other medication, but I couldn't get in. You didn't tell me you'd put a lock on the door at the bottom of the stairs that leads up to her place. If you'll let me have the key, I'll—'

'What! There's never been a lock on that door.'

'Well, there is now. A new one. So what do you want me to do about it?'

FOURTEEN

Friday evening

Ellie was bewildered. 'I don't understand. Hetty didn't ask me if she could put a lock on that door.'

Susan appeared in the doorway. 'I suppose she got it done while you were out one day?'

Rafael said, 'If she'd paid rent she'd have a right to privacy and a lock on the door to her quarters, but she would have had to ask your permission and given you a spare key for emergency access. If she didn't pay rent then she's a guest in your house and has no right to put in a lock.'

Ellie threw up her hands. 'She never asked. Horrors! Suppose we'd needed to attend to a leak up there! That's where the big tank for our water is, and the feeder tank for the central heating. We need access.'

Rafael rubbed his chin. 'New locks are usually supplied with several keys, so she must have at least one spare. The thing is we can't get in tonight unless we break down the door. Presumably she's got her own keys with her?'

Ellie thought back to the moment when the paramedics had wheeled Hetty out through the hall and into the ambulance. Hetty had been clutching her handbag on her lap.

Susan got there ahead of Ellie. 'She had her handbag with her, so yes.'

Ellie wondered what other medication Hetty might have been hoarding. Was it possible that there was a link between Hetty and the deaths which had been following Thomas around? No, surely not. The idea was absurd. But, once lodged in her mind, it refused to disappear.

Rafael said, 'It's a nuisance. I'd like us to have packed up her things and put them out for her to collect tomorrow. I suppose they'll keep her overnight at the hospital, so there's no immediate hurry to get into her rooms. Tomorrow I'll get a locksmith to open up for you.'

Susan said, 'This isn't a tragedy. It's a hiccup. Of course, Hetty shouldn't have put a lock on her door without asking permission and giving you a spare key, but some people have a thing about privacy.'

Ellie said, '*You* never thought of asking for one when you lived here.'

'It never occurred to me, but she's older and values the security of having her own front door.'

'Yes,' said Rafael, 'I suppose that's it. There's nothing sinister about it, is there?' But he still looked troubled.

It occurred to Ellie that Hetty could move in and out of the house as she pleased, but that she, Ellie, couldn't prevent her doing so. It was not a comforting thought. She twitched her lips into what might pass for a smile if you were losing your sight or wearing dark glasses.

'No need for a locksmith. I'm sure it's just a misunderstanding.

I'll have to have words with Hetty about it tomorrow when she gets back from the hospital. Now, you two have done more than enough for me today so off you go home. I'm taking a cab to the hospital.'

'No,' said Rafael, checking with Susan that she agreed with him. 'We're not leaving you alone. Susan and I will give you a lift to the hospital. Then, while you're seeing Thomas, we'll collect some overnight things from our flat and get back to the hospital in time to fetch you when visiting hours are over. We're going to cadge a loan of your sofa and Thomas's La-Z-boy, so that we can sleep here tonight.'

Ellie felt tears were on the way. 'Oh, I'm sure there's no need for that, though I must admit I could do with the company, which is totally stupid of me, but there it is. I mean, suppose Hetty were to . . . No, I'm sure they'll keep her in tonight, and there's no reason to worry about her, or anything else.'

Ellie shivered, thinking of that locked door and the possibility of prescription medicines popping up here and there.

Susan put her hand on her tall husband's arm and smiled up at him. 'Bags I the settee. The baby makes me toss and turn so much at night that you'd be better off on the chair.'

Ellie said, 'Now, now. There's no need for either of you to doss down in the sitting room. The guest room bed is already made up and Susan knows where the clean towels are kept. Just in case, though I'm sure there's absolutely no need and it's totally overreacting, we'll bolt the front door and the kitchen door before we go up for the night.'

'Let's go,' said Rafael. 'Hospital first . . .'

Friday evening

Thomas had been moved to a four-bed ward high up in the hospital. He was looking pale and there was a drip still going into his arm, but his eyes were brighter and he struggled to sit more upright when Ellie arrived.

She sat beside him and took his hand. 'You're feeling better?'

'Much. They say it was an ulcer. It's responding to treatment and they'll probably let me go home tomorrow.'

'Good. I've missed you. Nothing's the same without you.'

'Believe me, the moment they let me get back on my feet, I'm out of here. I said I'd take any pills they'd like to give me if they'd let me out this evening, but they refused. They're really busy, too. They could do with the bed.'

Ellie didn't think he was well enough to leave yet and she was glad that they were keeping him in, while being more anxious than ever about his health. Thomas didn't know there was a query about the source of his problem, either. Would it make him more or less anxious to know about the Ibuprofen?

She produced the pack of Ibuprofen. 'We found these in the kitchen. They're not yours, are they?'

'No. I tried them once. Gave me the most horrendous tummy ache.'

Ellie said, 'I thought not,' and put them away in her bag. So they must be Hetty's. But Hetty hadn't suffered from back or muscle pain, had she? It looked as if the ulcer had been caused by Thomas's heavy workload and Hetty's pastry, which he had treated with indigestion tablets. So far, so good. But his recent collapse was due to something more than an ulcer, wasn't it? She patted his hand. 'I'm just going to see the nurse. Back in a minute.'

She found the ward sister at her station in the corridor and managed to attract her attention. After identifying herself, she handed over the almost empty packet of Ibuprofen, explaining that the nurse had asked earlier if Thomas might have taken something to upset his stomach.

The ward sister gave her a needle of a look. 'You fed him these?'

'No. I never take them and neither does Thomas. They don't agree with us. However, it is possible that our lodger . . . Long story short, but he's not in her best books at the moment. We found the packet where she'd been sitting.'

'Has she admitted—?'

'No. She's taken some sleeping pills and they brought her into this very hospital a short time ago. We didn't find the Ibuprofen till after she'd gone.'

The nurse's eyes narrowed. 'She made a suicide attempt?'

'Not a very serious one, in my opinion. It was more like a cry for help. We found her very soon after she'd taken the pills and called the paramedics.'

'What's her name?'

Ellie gave it. She glanced around. 'I suppose she might have ended up on this floor.'

The nurse consulted a whiteboard. 'No, she's not been admitted up here. I'll show the packet to the doctor when he comes on his rounds in the morning.'

'Can my husband be discharged tomorrow?'

'Perhaps. We'll see. Now we know what he's taken . . . This stuff can strip the lining of your stomach. We'll have to see how he gets on.'

Ellie looked into the other bays as she returned to Thomas's side. All the beds were filled, and visitors were pouring in to sit with the patients. Ellie didn't see any sign of Hetty. Well, that was a relief.

Even more of a relief to see that Thomas was sitting more upright when she returned.

'What's the news?' he asked. 'I've only been here a few hours and I'm beginning to feel I'm in an alternative world.'

'You're feeling better.'

'Don't avoid the subject. What's happening? Has Lesley been round? What is she going to do about the money? How did Monique's funeral go? Did Evan make a scene? Tell me all.'

So much had been happening that he didn't know about. She hesitated. Should she tell him about Hetty's suicide attempt now, when he still looked like death warmed up? She thought not. Sufficient to the day is the evil thereof, et cetera. He needed reassurance, not more worry.

'The funeral went off like clockwork. Monique had a good send-off. She was respected and held in affection. Evan did try to make a scene in the church but was duly squashed. His daughter, Freya . . . Do you remember her? The best of the bunch. Anyway, Monique has left Freya enough to buy a place for herself when she's a bit older. I'm so pleased for her. Monique has also left some money to the trust fund, with strings attached. We'll be able to do some good with that.'

He smiled and pressed her hand. 'Good, good.' He was tiring, his eyelids at half-mast. He would soon be asleep. She wouldn't bother him with any of the bad news.

He said, 'Usually I can pray anywhere. I found it difficult to concentrate in here at first. My mind kept going round and round, worrying about all those deaths. Then I settled and I could pray again. It's not the same as being in my Quiet Room, but—'

She must have jumped, for he said, 'What is it?'

She shifted in her chair. She didn't know what to tell him. Nothing, probably. He didn't need to be worried about the house, or anything. She said, 'Oh, nothing really. Just a stupid idea that Rafael and Susan had about the house.'

He stroked the back of her hand with his thumb. 'They are an unusually intelligent young couple. I'd listen with interest to any ideas they might have.'

'Well, not if it affects your Quiet Room.'

'*My* Quiet Room? It's not mine. You use it, too, and Little Evan likes to take a nap in it. What do they want to do with it?'

'They are thinking it might be possible to divide the house in two, with you having the dining room as your study and Quiet Room. I told them it was a ridiculous idea.'

'What?' He frowned, still stroking her hand. 'Say that again. I don't quite see how . . .?'

She told him what they'd suggested.

For a long time he said nothing. Then he nodded. 'Well, well. It's an idea which has some merit. What do you think of it?'

'I've had three homes in my life. The one I was brought up in, the one I lived in during my first marriage, and now this one. I've loved all of them but this one is the best. I love the big rooms and high ceilings and the garden, and the . . . I don't know how to put it, but I love the solid feel of it. Of course I could move again if I had to, and I'm sure I could get to love that house, too. My home is where we live together, you and me.'

'I feel like that, too.' He thought for a moment, and then he smiled. It was a feeble echo of his usual grin, but it did indicate that he found something amusing about the situation. 'Did you ask them what they planned for the other half of the house?'

'Well, no. Of course not.'

He laughed. Really laughed. 'Ellie, my love, when you took young Susan in, little did you think you were harbouring an angel unawares.'

'I don't get it. You can't like the idea?'

A bell rang. The end of visiting hours.

He flopped back on his pillows. 'Ask her. Tell them from me that anywhere I pray becomes a Quiet Room, even in this noisy hospital. You must go now. I have my phone with me. I'll ring you tomorrow morning to let you know if I'm going to be released and when.'

Friday evening

Rafael and Susan collected Ellie from the main entrance of the hospital and took her back home. As soon as she stepped inside the hall, Ellie felt tiredness descend upon her. The light was blinking on the phone in the hall, indicating telephone messages. She couldn't deal with them. She wanted to sit down and weep, while aware that that would do no good whatsoever.

Susan eased Ellie towards the stairs. 'I'm telling you what to do for once. You're going to have a nice hot bath and get into bed. I'm going to bring you up a hot drink, possibly with a tot of something in it to help you sleep. I'll help Rafael clear up in the kitchen, and then we'll see that the house is shut down for the night, all right and tight. If you want anything, just call out and we'll hear you.'

'I am not in my dotage. I can manage perfectly well by myself.'

Rafael put his arm around her to help her up the stairs. 'Yes, Granny. Of course you can. You're perfectly fit and ready to run a marathon. But not tonight. Tonight Susan is coming to tuck you up in bed, hear your prayers and read you a fairy story.'

Ellie said, 'Oh, you!' And wiped tears from her cheeks.

The phone rang. They let it. Diana's voice rang out through the hall.

Ellie stopped, and so did Rafael. They all three listened to the message Diana was recording.

'Mother, where are you? We're just back from the solicitor. We've been advised to hold off going to the police about Thomas stealing all that money until we've given you a chance to sort things out. I suggest you get me appointed as a member of your board of trustees straight away. That should solve all our difficulties and mean that Thomas's thefts need not be trumpeted from the rooftops. I expect you to arrange for me to be at the next trust meeting, with a firm proposal to tide us over financially. Oh yes, and you must arrange to give us the title deeds of our house. That's it. I'll ring you again tomorrow.'

Ellie missed a step and hung on to Rafael's arm. 'It never rains but it pours. She goes on the board over my dead body, though, come to think of it, she'd quite like to do it that way. It's ridiculous! Why am I crying? The other trustees would never accept her.'

'I said, put me up instead.'

'Are you sure, Rafael?'

'I could neutralize the wicked witch of the west for you.'

Meaning Diana?

Susan giggled. 'That I'd like to see.' She held on to the banister, puffing a bit. 'Baby's anxious to get going.'

The police are not going to let the accusation against Thomas go. Whether Diana carries out her threat to accuse him of theft or not, there is still that complaint from a female caller and the other cases which the police will have to consider. There's Gwen and Harold. Why on earth did Harold leave money to Thomas? What about Mrs Pullin with her cats and her awful family, whom I've promised to help? Oh dear, I ought to have done something about that today, but I haven't. What else have I forgotten?

She said, 'The inside of my head is like a merry-go-round. My thoughts go round and round and up and down.'

Rafael pushed her gently on to her bed and knelt to take off her shoes. 'I like merry-go-rounds. Are you riding on a fiery steed, or a cockerel with a tail of feathers?'

Ellie thought about that. 'A horse. A beautiful dappled grey with a black mane and tail. There's music blaring out from the centre, and my horse has flaring red nostrils, and he's loving the speed we're doing. There's mirrors in the centre around the organ pipes, catching the light, and a disdainful young man collecting the money. He balances on the edge of the platform, enjoying the danger. There's a bell that clangs, and children wide-eyed with terror, clinging on with all of their might to the barley-stick poles which must be gilded. It's no good if there's not enough gilding.'

'I like it,' said Rafael. 'Bags I the cockerel, though.'

Susan crowed, 'Cock-a-doodle-doo!'

Ellie said, 'You know what? You're both mad.' She reached out to take their hands. 'Tell me; what do you want to do with the other half of the house?'

Susan said, 'Didn't you guess? We'll live in it, of course.'

Light dawned. 'Of course,' said Ellie. She laughed out loud. 'Why didn't I think of that? Thomas guessed straight away. He's all for it, though I can't say I've thoroughly grasped what it is you plan to do.'

'There's plenty of time for that,' said Rafael. 'Now you must get a good night's sleep.'

Susan said, 'Thomas will be all right, you know. He's strong.'

'That's what I keep telling myself,' said Ellie. 'But if he's been poisoned . . .?'

Rafael said, 'The doctors will know what to do.'

Ellie looked at them, and they looked back. She could see in their eyes the watchfulness that was also in hers. She said, 'We're thinking along the same lines?'

Rafael nodded. 'We'll talk about it tomorrow.'

Ellie slept well enough. Waking at two, she remembered her friends were sleeping next door. She ordered herself not to start thinking about the problems that beset her, knowing that if she did, she'd not sleep again. And turned over . . . only to realize that she'd been woken by someone pounding on the front door downstairs. She sat up, alarmed. And the phone downstairs shrilled.

She couldn't think what was happening. Who would knock on the door at this time of night? Oh, where was Thomas? She put out a hand for him and remembered that he was in hospital.

Was it the police at the door? But why? In the middle of the night?

There were voices in the corridor outside. 'What?'

'I'll go.'

'No, you go back to bed.'

Ah, Rafael and Susan had been sleeping next door to her,

hadn't they? Ellie pulled on a dressing gown – it happened to be Thomas's – but what did that matter?

Oh, Thomas, don't die on me!

She stepped out on to the landing. Someone switched the lights on down in the hall.

The phone stopped ringing and went to voicemail. And was silent. No one was leaving a message, were they?

Rafael and Susan stood at the top of the stairs, wearing one suit of pyjamas between them. One wore a top, the other wore the trousers. Ellie blinked. Which was which? Oh, what did that matter!

Ellie said, 'You two go back to bed. I'll deal with it.'

'But . . .!' said Susan, and was quieted by a gesture from Rafael.

He said, 'I hate to sound sexist, but this is a man's job.' He left Susan on the landing to make his way down the stairs on slippered feet, followed by Ellie at a slower pace.

The phone started to ring again. Ellie got there just before it went to voicemail. She said, 'Who is it?' Although she knew who it was really, didn't she?

'It's me.' A faint, die-away voice. 'I'm perfectly all right now. They pumped me out and they needed my bed, so I discharged myself, I got a cab to come home because the hospital transport doesn't work at this time of night. I knew you'd be all alone and frightened, and I had to make the effort to get back to look after you, didn't I?'

'I'm not alone,' said Ellie, thankful for her friends' presence.

Hetty wasn't listening. 'Only now my key won't work and I'm freezing out here, and I haven't enough money to pay the cab, so please let me in so that I can take care of you and then everything will be all right again.'

'I don't want to open the door at this time of night. Can't you go to a B and B somewhere?'

'I haven't any money. You know I haven't any money! Ellie, for pity's sake!'

For pity's sake? Ellie didn't feel like pitying Hetty. Or rather, she did, in one way. But in the other way, she felt she'd rather let a live rattlesnake into the house. She said, 'All right, I'll let you in. We'll talk in the morning.'

She put the phone down and nodded to Rafael. 'Let her in. She's nowhere else to go.'

Rafael drew back the bolts and pulled the door open.

A bundle of misery and distress stood in the porch, shivering. Clutching her handbag. No one could fail to feel sorry for her, could they?

When Hetty saw Rafael, she took half a step back. 'Oh, but . . . What are you doing here? You don't belong here.' She pushed back her hair from her face with a hand that shook.

'Come in if you're coming,' said Rafael.

Hetty hesitated. 'Could you pay the taxi for me? Please?'

Ellie found her handbag, handed the purse to Rafael, and asked him to do the honours. Which he did. Then he shut the door and bolted it again.

Hetty skirted around Rafael as if he might attack her. Once she'd gained Ellie's side, she said in a conspiratorial tone, 'You don't need them now I'm home, do you? Tell them to go. Just you and me, we'll be fine. We don't need anyone else, do we?'

Ellie said, 'They stay. I asked them to. Now, Hetty, I'm letting you remain for the rest of the night, but you must go in the morning.'

'Are you cross because I came back in the middle of the night? I didn't want to wake you up at this time but what else could I do? I couldn't leave you all by yourself in this big house.'

Ellie said, 'We can't talk now. I want you to go straight up to bed.'

'Oh, but can't I make you a nice hot drink? It's the least I can do now I've woken you up. And Mr Rafael, too. And his pretty wife. They're not in my rooms, are they?'

'They are my guests. As you are, Hetty. Oh, I've just thought. Rafael, will you go up with Hetty and once she's unlocked the door leading up to her flat, will you take the key off her? I don't like part of my house being barred to me.'

'Oh, if that's all! I have a spare key, and of course I'll let you have it. You only had to ask!'

'I'm asking for it now, Hetty. This minute.'

'Oh, but I'm not quite sure where I've put it. The spare, I mean. I can't let you have my own personal key, can I? Or I wouldn't be able to sleep soundly in my own sweet bed.' She gave a tinselly laugh, which grated.

Ellie looked at Hetty and saw not the pathetic little woman who was always so anxious to please but a sinewy snake whose fangs could poison her victims.

Ellie closed her eyes for a moment. Was she so tired that she was hallucinating? Had she really, even for a moment, believed that Hetty could be behind the deaths which had so conveniently showered money on Thomas? No, surely not.

The suspicion would not go away.

If Hetty had indeed been behind the deaths, then how . . .? And why?

Answer: because in the beginning Thomas had taken her part, had introduced her to Ellie and arranged for her to occupy the flat at the top of the house. Hetty had been grateful. Had she been grateful enough to arrange for his name to be included in the wills of various people, some of whom Thomas had known, and some of whom were complete strangers to him?

How could she have managed that? And how on earth could she have been responsible for all those deaths?

Answer: she couldn't. The very thought was ridiculous.

But always supposing she had been involved in some way with the deaths, then why would she have turned on the man who had done so much for her and tried to poison him?

Answer: because he'd changed his mind about letting her live with them.

Ellie shivered. She told herself she was overtired and imagining things. Hetty was no killer. But still. 'I'd like the key tonight, please. Rafael, will you see to it?'

Hetty wept, 'You can't mean it. Don't you trust me?'

'Oh, go up to bed,' said Ellie. 'We'll all feel better in the morning.'

'Yes, and I'll bring the spare key down with me to breakfast, shall I? Then we can have a nice cosy chat and make a plan for the day together.' So saying, Hetty went on up the stairs at a fair old pace.

Rafael arched his eyebrows at Ellie. Should he follow Hetty, or not?

Ellie nodded. 'Yes, get the key.'

Hetty was too quick for him. Even as Rafael reached the landing, they heard the door to Hetty's stairs open and shut with a click.

Rafael hung over the landing. He was annoyed with himself. 'Foiled again!'

'Never mind,' said Ellie. 'We'll get it sorted in the morning.'

FIFTEEN

Saturday morning

Ellie woke to a feeling of depression. At first she couldn't think why she was feeling so down, and then she did.

Thomas was ill in hospital.

Hetty had tried to commit suicide – or had she?

Diana was out of control.

The police were going to investigate everything that Thomas had said or done for the last goodness knows how many years.

Plus, it was a grey morning outside.

She drew back the curtains and looked down on her much-loved garden. Midge, her marauding ginger tomcat, was on the lawn stalking an unwary sparrow . . . Which suddenly realized it was in danger and flew up in the air with a squawk. Frustrated, Midge spat a couple of swear words at the bird and slunk off to find easier prey.

Ellie found herself smiling until she reminded herself that she really must cut the grass that day. Her gardener was a testy old soul who came when he felt like it and did as little as he could. Recently he'd been complaining the petrol mower was getting too much for him. Oh, but she'd be spending most of today at the hospital.

Oh, Thomas! Dear Lord, look after him.

What am I to do about Hetty? Do I tell Lesley my suspicions about her? I have no proof. Lesley would never believe me. Why should she? I don't believe it, myself.

There was a stir on the other side of the bedroom wall and

then, as Ellie made her slow way into her en suite, she heard the shower start up next door. It was a great comfort to know that Rafael and Susan were in the house.

What about that crazy scheme of theirs to cut the house in half?

'I can't cope with that at the moment,' said Ellie, as she got ready to face the day.

In the kitchen, she turned on the radio for company only to find it pumping out the raucous music which Hetty preferred. Gritting her teeth, Ellie changed it back to Radio 3 and a Bach concerto. Soothing. A good tune. Orderly. She needed 'orderly'.

Rafael and Susan appeared, looking flustered.

Susan said, 'Rafael's remembered he's got an important meeting this morning. He'll drop me off at the flat first. I'm on maternity leave now, so don't have to go in for work. I don't know how long we'll be, but we'll be back as soon as we can. Can you manage, do you think?'

'I'm fine,' said Ellie, feeling as if she'd been abandoned by her only friends, while at the same time telling herself that Rafael and Susan had their own lives to lead. 'It was good of you to stay overnight and if you want to come back later, I'd be grateful. Just till Thomas returns, you know. What would you like for breakfast?'

'We'll grab something on our way in,' said Rafael, who did look worried for once. 'I'll be in touch.' He consulted his watch. 'We really must go.'

What sort of food would Thomas be having in the hospital?

They were gone and the house was quiet around her. Midge the cat plopped in through the flap and Ellie fed him. What did she want for breakfast herself? Her usual cereal and toast?

'Good morning, good morning!' Hetty carolled her way in, full of beans. 'I hear your guests left early. I suppose Thomas is still in hospital. They'll probably keep him in for a while, won't they? So it will be just the two of us for some time. Isn't that nice!' She switched the radio back to the channel she preferred.

Ellie thought of objecting to Hetty's high-handed behaviour, but instead she turned the radio off and gestured to Hetty to sit at the table. Where to start? 'Yes, Thomas is still in hospital though I hope he will come out today. No need for you to worry about Rafael and Susan. Have you got yourself packed up yet, and have you got that key for me?'

'Silly me! I must have mislaid it, but never mind, I'll get another one cut for you today so that you can feel you're King of the Castle again. You should have asked me for one before. I would never do anything to upset you, you know that!'

'Hetty, I . . .' Ellie couldn't think how to tackle the situation. If she accused Ellie of trying to poison Thomas, what would the woman say? She would deny it, and there was no proof that she had done so.

Hetty jumped up and turned the radio on again. 'Have you heard the news yet? Awful weather they're having, aren't they?' She clattered plates on to the table for breakfast, while humming along to the song on the radio.

Ellie drew in her breath. Hetty was awfully bright and cheerful, wasn't she? If she, Ellie, had had to have her stomach pumped out, she was sure she'd be feeling like death this morning. So what was going on here?

She said, 'We visited Thomas last night in hospital. He looked pretty awful. They say he's got an ulcer, but that may be the least of his problems.'

'Dearie me.' Hetty's lips curved in an unmistakeable grin of pleasure. 'That sort of thing can take ages to sort out. Men are such weaklings, aren't they? Always complaining about a toe ache or a paper cut on a finger.'

'Thomas isn't like that. Hetty, how many sleeping pills did you take yesterday? It can't have been more than one, perhaps two?'

'Oh, that was all a misunderstanding. I didn't take any sleeping pills. I don't believe in them. Let me make you a cup of coffee, shall I? It's true I was very tired yesterday and I did take a couple of those calming tablets you can get at the chemists. I must have fallen asleep in the chair down here, instead of going up to bed which would have been the sensible thing to do, wouldn't it?'

So her 'suicide attempt' had been nothing of the kind. She'd staged it all by laying herself out in the chair with an empty

packet of sleeping pills at her side. She'd left a note which
could have been read in different ways, and something burning
on the stove to set the smoke alarms off.

'How very neat,' said Ellie.

'What?' said Hetty, with a sharp glance which morphed into
one of her loud laughs. 'I didn't realize until later what a fright
you must have had when you came in and found me asleep.'
She placed a cup of coffee in front of Ellie. 'I've added two
sugar lumps. That's right, isn't it?'

Ellie only took one in coffee and she usually drank tea in the
mornings but this was no time to quibble. She said, 'I agree that
it was a touching scene last night with you laid out on the chair
and a note saying you were sorry.'

Hetty nodded. 'I was sorry for our disagreement earlier.'

'I'm sure you were,' said Ellie. 'It's a pity we had to get the
paramedics out to attend to you when they're so busy at weekends. Did they have to wash out your stomach?'

'Well, they were going to, but I managed to regain possession
of my senses and explain what had happened. They wanted to
do it anyway, but I persuaded them that the joke was on me. I
had to discharge myself, of course. They were so kind, wanting
to keep me in overnight, but I said I couldn't let you go on
thinking I'd tried to kill myself, and that you needed me to look
after you. Finally they let me go, and I'm none the worse for
wear, as you can see.'

Yes, Ellie did see. She'd been neatly tricked. Manipulated
by a master. Game, set and match to Hetty. Well, Hetty might
have won the battle, but she hadn't won the war.

Ellie finished the coffee which was a little too strong and
sweet for her taste. She said, 'Well, now that's out of the way,
I'm still asking you to pack up and leave. Today. Can you
arrange to stay with a friend somewhere? Or do you have enough
money to go to a bed and breakfast place?'

Hetty's face crumpled in distress. 'Oh, you can't mean you
want to turn me out, after everything that's happened! Not after
all I've done for you and Thomas! You wouldn't be so ungrateful!
No, it's not in you to be cruel. I promise to get you a duplicate
key today. I can get one when I go out shopping in the Avenue.
You know the man who repairs shoes? He has a key-cutting

machine. I can take my key in and he'll turn me out a duplicate in a trice.'

Hetty seized the pad and pencil they kept on the fridge. 'Let's make out a list of things that I can get this morning for you. Some of those delicious croissants from the bakery for a start, and half a dozen of those lovely white eggs we get from the butcher. And some greens, don't you think? I'll bake you one of my famous steak and kidney pies for tonight's supper, shall I? Just for the two of us.'

Ellie took the pad and pencil off Hetty. 'Hetty, we need to have a serious talk. I'm glad you haven't suffered any ill effects from whatever you did or didn't take yesterday, and I'm pleased you feel on top of the world today, but I am not feeling so happy. You keep avoiding the problem of your staying on here, but we do have to face it.'

'No need, no need. I can take a hint. You want me to be your housekeeper so that I don't have to pay you any rent for my little flat upstairs.'

'That is not what I want. In fact, Thomas and I are thinking of downsizing, so we won't need any help in the house in future.'

Hetty's jaw sagged. 'You mean, you're selling up? You're letting that awful daughter of yours push you into a one-bedroom flat somewhere? No, no! I won't let you do that. We wouldn't be at all happy there.'

For a moment Ellie entertained the possibility of Hetty turning on Diana by giving her sleeping pills and Ibuprofen. Would it work? Who would come out on top?

There was no question about the result in Ellie's mind. Diana would come out on top. Setting Hetty on to Diana would be like setting a hamster on to a fox. No, no.

Ellie told herself that she must not let her imagination run riot. She said, 'Seriously, Hetty, this is not working. I want you out of here.'

Hetty's head nodded up and down, up and down. 'Of course, of course. You want me out of your kitchen. You want me to keep to my quarters and do all my cooking up there. I understand. I will prepare your meals in my tiny kitchen up at the top and bring them down for you when you are ready to eat. There, now! That's settled.'

Frustration!

'Hetty, I am trying to be nice about this, but you have to be out of here before Thomas gets back from hospital. Today. This morning if possible. If you need a few hours to contact someplace you have to move to, then I'll allow you that but—'

'You're giving me notice! Oh, oh, oh! You're turning me out on to the street, in the cold and the rain! Oh, who will take pity on me?'

'I would have done,' said Ellie between her teeth, 'if you hadn't made Thomas ill by giving him Ibuprofen.'

A long, long silence. Hetty's eyes narrowed. 'What do you mean? How could you even think such a thing? You shouldn't say things like that, you know. It will get you into trouble. Lots of trouble. That's actionable, that is.'

'Fine,' said Ellie, crossing her fingers. 'Take me to court. I have the Ibuprofen packet with your fingerprints on it, and that's what the hospital say has poisoned Thomas's stomach.'

'There's no proof that I put anything in Thomas's coffee—'

'Who said anything about his coffee?'

Hetty's eyes went wide with shock. She'd walked into that one, hadn't she? But she recovered. 'I'm sure I'm not going to stay where I'm not wanted. It will take me some time to find somewhere else to go. Shall we say a week from today? That's a bit quick, but I dare say I can do that.'

'This morning,' said Ellie, holding out her hand, 'and I'll have that key off you now, if you please.'

Hetty threw her hands up in the air and waved them around. She acted the part of a poor, put-upon, distracted female to perfection. 'I have nowhere to go! I can't afford to rent a place! You know that!'

Actually Ellie was beginning to realize she'd been mistaken there. Hetty always boasted that she worked at lots of different jobs and even if they were for a minimum wage, since she hadn't been paying any rent while she'd lived at Ellie's then she must have some money in the bank.

Another thought occurred to Ellie. If Hetty had had contact at any time with the people who'd left money to Thomas, then they might have left money to her, too.

Ellie had a mental picture of herself going down the corridor to fetch the mail as it dropped through the letter box every day, and always finding Hetty there before her. Ellie had never seen letters addressed to Hetty because Hetty had always collected them first.

Then, somehow or other Hetty had acquired sleeping tablets of a type not available over the counter. Had she by any chance stashed more of them away upstairs? Might she have used these tablets before to shorten someone's life? What an appalling thought! And yet, there must have been some good reason for Hetty to have put a lock on the door to her quarters.

The question was if Ellie were able to search Hetty's quarters, what would she find?

At the moment there was absolutely nothing to tie Hetty in to that string of deaths and if Hetty realized she was under suspicion, she would take care to remove any evidence when she left.

Or, would she leave it behind to incriminate Thomas and Ellie?

One minute Ellie was sure that Hetty had caused the deaths and in the next minute, she told herself not to be so absurd.

What to do? She wasn't normally so indecisive, was she? She told herself that she had a right to go into every room of the house, but to search Hetty's flat she needed to get the woman out of the way. How to do that?

Offer her money, of course.

'Very well, Hetty. I do realize it might be difficult for you to find accommodation without paying rent in advance. Suppose I lend you a hundred pounds to see you over the next few days? You can repay it when your circumstances improve.'

I'll never see the money again, but it's worth it to get rid of her.

Hetty's eyes sharpened with greed. 'Oh, would you? Could you, do you think you could manage five hundred?'

She thinks I'm feeling so guilty I'll be glad to pay her off.

'Two hundred. That's all I can manage. You have a bank account?'

'Building society. Make a cheque payable to me.'

Ellie found her handbag and wrote the cheque out. 'There you are. Now I do understand you'll need the morning to find somewhere to go, and I have to go out, too. Perhaps by this afternoon you'll be ready to leave. Would you like me to help you pack?'

'Oh, no. Not in the least. I travel light, you know. I always have.' Hetty was on her feet, the cheque clutched fast in her hand. 'I suppose, if I go now, I should be able to get to the building society when they open.' She was on the move. 'I'll just fetch my coat, and I'll be off.'

Ellie shouted after her. 'Leave me your key when you go.'

'Yes, of course.' The answer came floating back.

Ellie cleared the table and set the dishwasher working. The house seemed very quiet. Midge the cat, who had disappeared when Hetty arrived, purred round Ellie's ankles asking for more food. She told him he couldn't have any more and he settled down to attend to his toilet.

Hello? Was that the front door closing, quietly?

Ellie hastened along the corridor and opened the front door only to see Hetty turn into the road, travelling at a fair pace. She hadn't left her key. Of course.

This hardened Ellie's suspicions. Why hadn't Hetty left her key? Answer: because she didn't want Ellie looking into her quarters. This made Ellie all the more determined to do so. If she couldn't break into her own rooms, then who could?

Ellie sighed. She really was not good with tools. Screwdrivers slipped and cut her wrists when she tried to use them. Hammers aimed themselves at her thumbnail. The best use for chisels, in her opinion, was to cut pieces of cake evenly. But needs must.

She couldn't wait for Rafael to get a locksmith. No. Hetty was at long last resigned to leaving and on her return would be packing to leave, taking any evidence of wrongdoing with her. It was now or never.

Ellie rummaged around in the cupboard under the stairs and came up with a large chisel and a hammer which was so heavy it took an effort to pick it up. Thus armed, she mounted the stairs to the first floor, and made her way round the landing to the door which shut off the second lot of stairs to the attic flat.

The door was firmly locked. Hetty really did not want Ellie in her rooms, did she?

Well, tough. Here comes the housebreaker to break off your lock. Except, Ellie wasn't sure how you went about it. Did you try to force open the hinges? Only, she couldn't see where the hinges were. Ah yes. They were hidden behind a piece of wood that ran from top to bottom at the side of the door. There was a similar piece of wood to the right of the doorframe, where the lock was.

In books, the hero kicks the door open.

Ellie looked down at her open-toed sandals and decided that that method was not for her.

She tried to think how Thomas might have tackled the problem. *Oh, dear Lord, look after Thomas, won't you? When would it be all right for me to ring the hospital? After the doctor's rounds, they said. In your mercy, Lord.*

Back to business. She seemed to remember that in the dim and distant past, she'd watched her father open a locked door with a hammer and chisel. Her mother had locked the door of the junk room which contained the family's luggage and they'd needed it for their holidays. Unfortunately the key had been mislaid, and drastic measures had become necessary.

Once her father had eased that strip of wood away from the frame, the workings of the lock had been exposed and he had been able to pull the door open. This method meant that the strip of wood could be replaced and that there had been no damage to the door or the doorframe.

In the here and now, Ellie noted that the door opened away from her, so if she managed to pull the strip of wood away, in theory she could get at the lock and prise the door open.

With both hands, and putting all her weight behind it, she managed to insert the fine edge of the chisel between the door and the strip of wood, and hammered it in. A small space opened up in the paintwork.

Fine. Now she had to pull the chisel out and stick it in a bit lower down. Ugh. It required a considerable effort. But she did it.

Bravo! A gap of maybe four centimetres had opened up. It was going to take ages to free the strip of wood from the frame.

She tried again. Something crackled, and another couple of centimetres was freed from paint. At this rate she'd be here for hours. Hetty would return and confront her, and then there'd be a horrid row and Hetty would leave the house and with her any chance of solving the mystery around the gifts to Thomas.

Oh, Thomas! Don't die on me! Please Lord, look after him.

Ellie looked at her watch. She'd wasted too much time already.

She picked up the heavy hammer, stood well back and swung with both hands at the lock on the door. That effort dented the wood below the lock. Her aim was poor.

Another go. This time she caught the edge of the lock.

Panting, she tried again.

Four goes later, she dropped the hammer. She was exhausted. The door looked as if it had been attacked by termites but was still firmly shut.

One more go. This time she managed to make it a bullseye. Finally, she'd shattered the wood around the lock.

She put her shoulder to the door. Protesting like mad, the wood around the lock splintered and gave way. What a mess! But she was in.

She shoved the broken door back on itself and hauled herself up the stairs. How long would Hetty be gone? How much time did she have?

On the landing at the top, she stood under the skylight. It had begun to rain, softly. The sky was grey. There were lots of shadows around.

Something touched her ankle, and she jumped a mile.

It was only Midge, the cat, who liked to be able to patrol every single room in the house, and who had been annoyed at being refused entry up here, until now.

Where to start? Ellie blinked. And lost her balance. She put out a hand to steady herself and went into the sitting room, which was in good order. Everything was clean and tidy.

The three-piece suite in its sunny apricot and white slip covers looked pristine though it had been moved to a different position in the room. Otherwise all was as it had been.

Midge tried out one of the chairs, turned round and round and settled in for a nap.

Ellie ran a finger across the occasional table to check for dust. There was none. And none on the television.

Ellie looked carefully around. Hetty had brought in only a few personal touches: a silver photograph frame showing a snap of three teenagers of whom the middle one must be Hetty; a christening mug with Hetty's initials on it; a toy horse which looked Central European . . . Brought back from a holiday, perhaps?

Ellie opened cupboards, checked the bookshelf, looked under the cushions on the settee and behind chairs. The *Radio Times* had been turned to today's programmes. There were a couple of DVDs nearby, borrowed from the public library. No library books. No daily papers.

Ellie moved on to the main bedroom. Hetty had few clothes, probably bought from charity shops. All were of reasonable quality and in good nick. Underwear was from Marks & Spencer's, shoes from Clarks. There were a few, very few, toiletries, all from Boots. On the bedside table was a small radio-cum-alarm, a box of tissues and a copy of that old time favourite, the *People's Friend*, whose readership was Middle England.

The second bedroom looked as if it had never been used. A squidgy cushion without a cover was on the bed. Presumably something had been spilled on the outer cover and that was now in the wash.

There was nothing on top of the wardrobes in either room, and nothing at the back of drawers. Ellie almost lost her balance again and put out a hand to steady herself. Whatever was the matter with her? Was she going down with something?

The bathroom was clean and sweet smelling.

Along the corridor was the store cupboard containing the usual cleaning materials, the Hoover, mop and pan, dusters etc. Plus one large and one small suitcase on wheels. They were unlocked and empty. Ellie hauled them out and felt around in all the corners. Nothing.

Hetty had looked after her rooms well.

Which left the kitchen. Not much cooking had been done here. A small collection of plates, mugs and a glass tumbler had been left to dry on the draining board, together with the odd knife, fork and spoon. The small dishwasher did not appear to have been used at all. The cupboards contained nothing which should not be there; staple foods only. The fridge contained some sliced bread, margarine, milk, cheese and a packet of ham. There were some onions and potatoes in a vegetable stand at the side. There was nothing which ought not to be there.

Ellie went back to the landing, and looked through the open doors into each room in turn. What had she missed?

Nothing.

But there must be something! She couldn't have been that wrong about Hetty, could she? Was the woman really nothing more than she claimed to be? Had she put the lock on the door out of an exaggerated sense of privacy and not because she had something to hide? If so, then Ellie had damaged the door for nothing.

Ellie looked at her watch. How long was Hetty going to be? Was Ellie wasting her time up here when there was so much else that she had planned to do that day? She shook her head to clear it.

There was only one item out of place. Just one. What about the cushion on the spare bedroom bed, the one which had no slip cover on it?

There were still two cushions on the settee, so why was there a spare sitting on the bed in the second bedroom, without an outer cover?

The three-piece suite had been bought for the flat within the last couple of years, which meant it was subject to flame retardant policies. The cushions were filled with non-flammable material, a spongy material which imitated the old-fashioned and now very expensive rubber shapes of old.

So, if there was a cushion without a cover in the spare bedroom, then what was inside the cover of one of the cushions in the sitting room?

Ellie investigated.

Yes, one felt different from the other. It felt lumpy. There was a zip down one side, hidden by a fold of fabric. Ellie ripped the slip cover open and eased out a second cushion which had been roughly tacked together out of a couple of tea towels. This improvised bag had been filled with objects of all shapes and sizes.

Ellie pulled the tea towels apart and out fell a collection of packets of pills which would do credit to any pharmacy. Ellie picked one up. It had been opened and a couple of pills removed.

She looked at the label. These were heavy painkillers, the sort you were advised not to take for more than a couple of days at a time. How on earth had Hetty come by them, why had she kept them, and what did she propose to do with them?

None of the possible answers to these questions made Ellie feel comfortable.

The next packet she picked up was almost empty. Ellie read the label and didn't recognize the medication. The next one . . . the drug company's leaflet advised these pills were sleeping tablets to be used under this and that circumstances only. Warnings about this and that were included. She stirred the heap. Some of the packets had the patients' names on. Some didn't.

A door banged shut below. Ellie started up. Was that the front door?

Hetty had returned? What would she do when she realized Ellie was in her rooms?

SIXTEEN

Saturday, noon

Ellie put a trembling hand to her head. She was not good at facing down angry people, especially today when she didn't seem to be firing on all cylinders. But perhaps there would be no need for it? Perhaps Hetty would be fine about Ellie breaking into her rooms?

A scream of rage from below told Ellie otherwise. Hetty had spotted the door hanging open. 'How dare you, Ellie Quicke! You come down here, this instant!'

Ellie called out, 'Hetty, is that you? I'm up here!' Knowing that she sounded ridiculous but not knowing in the least how to manage a scene with an angry woman. How could she diffuse the situation?

Perhaps the best thing to do was to pretend for now that all was well, and that she hadn't found the packets. She could hear

Hetty panting her way up the stairs, shouting, 'You come out
of my rooms! Now! This minute!'

Ellie shovelled the pills back into the cushion and zipped
it up. She pushed the cushion back into place and realized too
late that two packets had fallen to the floor. She scooped them
up. There wasn't time to put them back into the cushion. What
to do? Her skirt had no pockets in it. Why don't they put pockets
in skirts any longer? Where to hide the medication?

She did what women throughout the ages have done. She
popped them into the front of her bra and made it to the door
of the sitting room just as Hetty reached the head of the stairs.

Hetty was in no mood to play softly, softly. She was holding
the discarded chisel in her hand and looked as if she were
prepared to ram it into something, or someone. 'How dare you
enter my rooms without my consent?'

'You forget,' said Ellie, trying to keep calm, 'that this is my
house. You had no right to put a lock on that door, and I have
every right to walk around my own house. Suppose there'd been
a leak in the cistern, or the central heating man needed to get
at the tank? Of course I need access. I'm afraid you didn't think
about that.'

Hetty was not soothed. She advanced a step, holding the chisel
up and pointing at Ellie's throat. 'I told you I'd give you a key
but you wouldn't listen, would you? I had a right to a spot of
privacy and you had no business breaking my door down.'

Ellie wanted to say that it wasn't Hetty's door that had been
broken down, but didn't. She made a soothing motion with her
hands. 'Well, no harm done. There's no leak from the cistern
and I see you've looked after your rooms beautifully.'

Hetty's chin came forward. 'You deceived me. You invited
me into your house and pretended to be my friend and now
you've turned against me. You've been poking and prying in
my things which is against the law, and I'll have you for that,
I will! After all I've done for you and Thomas, I might have
known you'd turn on me in the end. You come across all high
and mighty but you're nothing but filth!'

Ellie held up her hands. The chisel was a formidable weapon
and Hetty looked as if she were fully prepared to use it. 'Look,
I'm sorry things haven't worked out for you, but—'

'But me no "buts".' Hetty gestured with the chisel. 'Come away from that door so that I can see what damage you've done to my things.'

Ellie stepped sideways into the landing and Hetty peered into the sitting room. And saw nothing amiss, except . . .

Midge the cat had been disturbed by the shouting, and now jumped down from his chair.

Hetty brandished the chisel. 'What's that mangy cat doing up here? I don't like cats. Nasty, smelly things. Shoo! Shoo! Out you go!'

Midge knew when he was being threatened. He wanted out of the situation, but his only way out and down the stairs was blocked by Hetty. He assessed the odds and streaked past her, ears flattened, tail bushing up . . . brushing past her . . .

Hetty screamed and lost her balance . . . and fell against the wall, threatening to topple back down the stairs.

Ellie leaped to Hetty's side to drag her upright and further into the landing away from danger. 'It's all right. You're quite safe!'

Hetty shoved Ellie away. 'You did that on purpose! You tried to push me down the stairs so that I'd be killed and you'd inherit my money! Murderess!'

What money?

'No, no! Hetty, please! Be calm! That's not how it happened!'

Hetty was not to be placated. 'I see what it is now. You were nice to me till you'd got me in your power, and all along you've been plotting my death. Well, two can play at that game! Back! Back, I say!'

She swung the chisel at Ellie, who cast a despairing eye in the direction of the stairs, realizing she couldn't get round Hetty to reach them.

Ellie retreated a step, calculating the odds.

Hetty was twenty years younger and a lot fitter. There was no way Ellie could win a bout of fisticuffs, even if Hetty were not waving a lethal weapon around.

'Back, back, I say! I'm going to put you in a safe place till I've packed my things and have well and truly gone. I'm not telling you where I'm going, and no, you'll never find me, not if you search for ever! But till I'm safely away, I'm not having you ring the police and making up stories about me being a bad girl. Into the spare bedroom with you! Go and sit on the naughty step, that's what they tell children who misbehave, isn't it? That's what you're going to do. Sit and think about all the bad things you've done to me. Someone will let you out eventually, I suppose. That is if Thomas is ever released from hospital – I'm hoping they'll keep him in because those pills can do you a whole lot of no good if they don't agree with you, right? If he never gets out, then that's going to be too bad for you, isn't it?'

With one smooth movement Hetty pushed Ellie into the spare bedroom and slammed the door on her. Ellie discovered she was trembling. She retreated to the bed and let herself down on to it, thinking that as soon as Hetty was occupied with her packing, she would creep out and down the stairs.

The key turned in the lock on the door, and Ellie's mouth shot open. She was locked in!

Well, it was no big deal. Hetty would let her out when she'd finished packing, wouldn't she?

The woman didn't mean to leave her there. No. Of course not.

Well, she might. But if not, it was no big deal.

For a start, Ellie could use her mobile phone to call for help . . . except that her phone was in her handbag somewhere on the ground floor, either in the kitchen or the sitting room. Ellie wasn't sure where she'd left it, but it would not be leaping into her hand to fetch help.

Ellie shook her head, trying to clear it. What was the matter with her? She couldn't think straight. All that morning, she'd been feeling . . .

She must be going down with a virus.

She glanced at the window, which did not look out on to the road but out over the back garden. It was still raining. The lawn was getting a good soaking. It wouldn't be possible to mow it until it had dried out a bit. The garden was bounded by a high brick wall and masked by trees. If she opened the window and yelled, no one would hear her. Except Hetty, who was unstable.

Ellie didn't like to think about how many people had tried to help Hetty and then found themselves facing not a pet lamb, but a rabid dog.

Ellie was so tired. She let herself lie down flat on the bed. Ah, that was better. Her eyes were closing on her. She could do with a spot of rest.

From the landing came the sound of luggage being bumped out of the cupboard along the landing. One of the wheels squeaked. More banging. Noisy. Wardrobe doors were flung wide. Drawers were pulled open.

Hetty was packing.

Faintly from the hall far below came the sound of the telephone. Hetty wasn't going to answer it, was she? Ellie hoped it wasn't Thomas asking to be collected from hospital. What would he think if he rang and she didn't pick up? Would he ring her mobile? But that wouldn't get answered either, would it?

The bumping and banging in the other rooms stopped. Hetty had worked her way along the landing, clearing out her possessions as she went. She would certainly take the contents of the cushion with her, and Ellie dreaded to think what use she might put them to.

Moreover, if Hetty left with them now, Ellie would have lost any chance of discovering what exactly Hetty might have been up to, and how she might or might not have been linked to the people who'd sent Thomas so much money. The police needed evidence, and Hetty was going to walk away with the only evidence Ellie had come across.

Oh, frustration! Oh well, what did it matter?

Nothing mattered, much. She yawned.

Finally, there came the sound of a large suitcase being bumped, step by step, down the stairs. A pause, the sound of someone climbing the stairs again, and then another piece of luggage was being bumped down to the first floor.

Hetty had had one large suitcase, and a smaller carry-on bag on wheels in the cupboard. Anything else could probably go in a plastic bag or two.

The phone rang again down below. Faintly. Ellie shrugged. She couldn't do anything about it. Then there was a lot more silence, which was rather comforting after the racket that had been going on.

Ellie told herself not to panic, though in fact she was feeling remarkably calm. Was Hetty really going to leave her in a locked room, alone in the house? No, surely not . . .

She was roused by footsteps climbing the stairs again. And a knock on the door.

Ellie tried to sit up. She was feeling decidedly groggy but happy that she was going to be let out. Of course Hetty wouldn't leave her!

The door didn't open. Instead, Hetty spoke. 'I'm leaving now. You've been such a bad girl, I think it's best for you to stay where you are for the time being and consider how naughty you've been. I suppose someone will come and let you out eventually, although I don't know who that might be. Thomas is still in hospital and, with what I put in his coffee, he's not likely to come out in a hurry, if at all. As for those fly-by-night people you let sleep here last night, they'll not think of looking up here for you. I'm using some heavy-duty tape to put the broken door back into place. No one will notice anything wrong, by the time I've finished with it.'

Ellie managed, 'Hetty, no . . .!'

Hetty puffed out a laugh. 'Are you on your knees, praying? Well, when I'm safely away I might feel like forgiving you and phone someone to let you out. Maybe. At the moment I feel you ought to suffer for what you've put me through. You're going to have plenty of time to think about your sins. Even without food and water you'll live for some days, maybe even a week.'

'Hetty, they're expecting me back at the hospital—'

'No, they're not.'

'Someone rang just now, and you answered it.'

'That was your fly-by-night friend Rafael and his bit of fluff. I told them you were very angry with them for leaving you alone and that if they came back here, you were not going to let them in again.'

Ellie gasped.

'And, I rang the hospital. I told them that you'd had a tumble and booked yourself into a nursing home for a fortnight, so if Thomas is ever going to be released, he'd better find himself somewhere else to go. They said they'd make sure he got the message.'

Ellie said nothing. She knew that neither Rafael nor Thomas would accept those messages as genuine, but she could also see that under certain circumstances they might think there was enough truth in what Hetty said to leave Ellie alone for a while, locked up in the house.

'As for your horrible cat,' said Hetty, 'if I can catch him before I go, I'll wring his neck.'

Ellie leaned back and closed her eyes. *Midge, run for your life!*

Hetty banged on the door. 'Are you still there? Answer me!'

Ellie thought that if she didn't reply, perhaps Hetty would open the door to see what was happening . . .

'Be like that, then!' A grating sound as the key was withdrawn from the lock, and Hetty's footsteps retreated. Ellie could hear the woman descending the stairs . . . and thumping the ruined door into position. Presumably she was taping over the damage, so that at a casual glance, no one would see there was anything wrong.

Again the phone rang down below.

Hetty let it go to voicemail.

A lengthy pause. Far away and down below, the front door slammed shut.

Ellie prised open her eyes and looked over to the window. It was still raining.

This wasn't happening. It was all a dream.

She thought of various ways in which people had escaped locked rooms in the past. They pushed a piece of paper under the door, knocked the key out so that it fell on the paper, and drew it back into the room so that they could let themselves out. Hetty had taken the precaution of removing the key from the lock. Anyway, the door fitted neatly and there was no room to pass a key or even a piece of paper beneath it.

She was drifting away on a slow boat to China. Drifting into the Land of Nod.

She could hang something out of the window. But there was no way anyone would see it, in the rain and across the width of the garden, the trees and the wall beyond. There were a couple of small windows in the hotel which looked this way, but at such a distance they might as well have been on Mars.

She could flash a Morse code SOS with a mirror . . . but there was no one who would see it.

She could tie the bedding together and let herself down from the window . . . except that there was no bedding on the unmade bed, and if there was one certain way to break your leg, it would be for an unfit sixtyish woman to try to climb down two storeys on a rope made of non-existent sheets. Ellie believed that this was how the Empress Matilda had once escaped from durance vile, but Matilda had been much younger and used to riding horses and hunting and so on.

She could break a window. Fine. Who would notice it?

She settled herself more comfortably on the bed.

She could pray.

Yes, she could do that. In fact, it was probably the most sensible thing to do. Some ideas might pop into her head if she did that. She was sure – well, she was pretty sure – that neither Thomas nor Rafael nor Susan would believe what Hetty had told them, but . . . well, it was good to take precautions.

She told herself to breathe deep and quietly. And pray.

Our father and all that . . . oh dear, I'm not making any sense at all. Dear Lord, I'm in trouble again. I don't like to bother you when you must be busy looking after people in pain and danger . . . not that I'm not in danger, I don't mean that, but . . .

I'm not making much sense, am I? Sorry about that. To be absolutely frank, I'm in something of a pickle. I know you like us to help ourselves out of trouble, and I'm all for that but just at the moment, I'm out of ideas.

And look after Thomas, won't you? Just in case . . .

No, I'm not going to think bad thoughts. He is not going to die. He is NOT going to die.

And Midge. Though I think I can trust Midge to look after himself.

Rafael and Susan, too. And I'm sure the hospital will help Thomas . . . what did that woman say? That she'd fed him something . . . it was the coffee, wasn't it? Remind me to throw away the rest of his jar of coffee. No point in risking . . .

What time is it?

It must be nearly lunchtime. I must admit, I could do with something to eat . . . and some water. I'm thirsty.

Don't think about it.

Dear Lord, in your mercy . . .

A feeling of general wellbeing stole through her. Incredibly, she relaxed, nerve by nerve. Her legs and then her arms. And finally her breathing. It was going to be all right. She didn't know how. But it would be.

She woke, thinking someone had called her name. She sat up, dazedly wondering where she was . . . and heard a door shut somewhere. She couldn't think straight. She was in Hetty's rooms. Why? Oh, she put a hand to her head. She remembered now. Thomas. Midge. Rafael and Susan. Where were they?

Was that a door shutting down below?

With an effort, Ellie pushed herself to her feet and, holding on to furniture, she made her way slowly to the window. It had stopped raining. The light looked different. She looked at her watch. Could that possibly be the time? Nearly four o'clock? What had happened to the day? And where was everybody?

She decided she must still be asleep. And dreaming.

She tried the door. It was still locked. She put her ear to it. Was that someone moving about downstairs? She banged on the door. 'Is anyone there?'

Yes, there were muted voices down below. Rafael and Susan, with any luck.

She hammered on the door again. 'Rafael? Susan? I'm up here!'

Doors slamming. Voices raised. All in the distance. They hadn't heard her.

She raised her voice another notch. 'Help!'

At this rate, she'd have a sore throat in no time at all. The best thing to do was to go back to sleep. Yes, sleep it off . . .

She leaned against the door, fighting sleep.

And tried to work it out. If this wasn't just a bad dream then it was real. And if the door on the landing had been put back into place, Rafael and Susan would never think of exploring further. They might search the rest of the house, but that would be that.

If she were going to get out of here, if she were going to break her dream, then it was up to her to do something. But what?

She picked up the bedroom chair, which was heavy and unwieldy but with an effort she managed to swing it at the door.

Boom!

And again.

Boom!

Her arms were aching. She was going to drop the chair. She couldn't hold on to it any longer. If only she were twenty or thirty years younger and an Olympic athlete . . . But she wasn't. One more try. *BOOM!*

There were some nice dents in the door, but it was too solid to break open. A pity she'd asked for good quality doors up here.

She paused, panting. Letting the chair slip to the floor. It would be a lot easier to go back to sleep. Could she make it to the bed before falling over?

There were more raised voices downstairs.

'Up here!' she cried.

A silence, followed by muted, questioning voices. Had they heard her?

Yes, she could hear halting steps making their way up to the attic floor.

She yelled, 'I'm here! Locked in!'

A muffled voice shouted, 'What? Ellie? Are you up there? But why . . .?'

Ellie tried to shout but it came out almost as a whisper. 'The second bedroom. I'm locked in!'

'Where's the keys, Susan?' Yes, that was definitely Rafael.

Susan, panting a bit, 'In the locks, of course.' She was so heavily pregnant, it must have taken it out of her to climb up to the top of the house.

'No keys,' said Rafael. His voice came closer. 'Ellie, you in there? Are you all right?'

'Sort of, yes,' said Ellie. She found she was sitting on the floor. How did she get there? She said, 'Hetty wanted to leave me to starve to death.' And suddenly the thought was so funny that she had an impulse to laugh. And had to quell it. With an effort. Hysteria, of course.

Susan's voice came through, nice and clear. 'The locks up here are all the same. I never needed to use them, but there were spare keys somewhere. I kept them in the kitchen . . .'

Her voice faded, and then returned. 'Here. They were hanging on the back of the cupboard door. Try it.'

It worked. Rafael turned the key in the lock and threw open the door.

Ellie said, 'Thank you.' She tried to get up off the floor. And failed.

Rafael picked her up and deposited her on the bed.

Susan put her arms around Ellie. 'What a fright you gave us! Are you all right? We couldn't think what was happening. We got this strange message from Hetty. She said not to come back here, but we couldn't believe that you'd asked her to phone us, especially since we'd left our overnight things here. So we decided to see what was happening for ourselves. We got back as quickly as we could. We found the front door had been bolted from the inside which was stranger still. I knew you always kept a kitchen door key in the shed out back, so we got in all right, only to find . . . but we never thought of looking up here.'

'No, indeed,' said Rafael. 'Ellie, are you all right? You look half asleep.'

She blinked. His face was going in and out of focus. He looked worried. About her?

She said, 'I'll be all right in a minute. Is Thomas with you?'

'He left us a message, said he couldn't get through to you so thought we'd check up for him. They're keeping him in for the weekend but he's beginning to feel a lot better. We said we'd ring him back when we'd made contact with you.'

'Thank God he's better,' said Ellie, trying to make sense of a world that seemed to keep slipping out of focus. 'So why your long faces?'

Susan said to Rafael, 'She'll have to see for herself.' And to Ellie, 'There's nothing seriously wrong.'

With Rafael's help, Ellie managed to get to her feet. 'I'm all right, really.' Though she wasn't. She was good at pretending, wasn't she?

Rafael gave Ellie his arm. 'Take it easy.'

Ellie tried to stand, and her legs gave way. A second try, and she managed to balance on her feet. She thought, *Thomas is all right, and coming home soon. Nothing else matters.*

Rafael steered her across the landing to the top of the stairs, where Ellie pulled away to look into Hetty's sitting room. There was something she had to check up on. Wavering on her feet, she said, 'Ah, she's taken the whole cushion. I thought she might have left the cover, but she probably didn't bother.'

'She stole one of your cushions?' Susan was almost amused.

Ellie tried to explain. Why was it so difficult to concentrate? 'It contained a cache of drugs. She wouldn't want to leave that behind. I'll tell you all about it in a minute.'

Down the stairs they went. Slowly. Ellie wasn't up to moving fast, and neither was Susan.

Midge was in the hall, waiting for them. Ellie's legs nearly gave way again when she saw him. She'd been hoping he'd be all right, but it was a relief to see him alive and kicking, so to speak. At least Hetty had failed to carry out one of her threats.

Ellie dabbed at her throat. 'Rather warm, isn't it?' she said.

'Yes,' said Rafael. 'The central heating had been cranked up to maximum. I've turned it off. Now, brace yourself.'

The kitchen was a disaster area. The door to the fridge had been left open, and the contents spilled on the floor. Ditto the door to the freezer. Everything inside both was ruined. In pools of water.

'Oh!' cried Ellie, subsiding into a chair. 'All that lovely food spoilt!'

Susan sighed. She'd cooked a lot of the stuff that had been in the freezer. 'Yes, but what I'm more worried about is that she's cut the wire to your landline in the hall. And what about your handbag?'

It lay open on the table, its contents exposed. Ellie could see at a glance that her wallet, containing some notes and her credit cards, was missing. So was her mobile phone. At least Hetty hadn't taken Ellie's keys, although she'd probably retained her own set.

Ellie rubbed her forehead. Why couldn't she think straight? She wanted to lie down and die, but couldn't allow herself to do so, yet. Hetty must be traced. Arrested. Questioned.

The credit cards must be reported stolen. The mobile phone must be replaced. The landline fault reported. Thomas would be trying to contact her.

She couldn't decide which to do first.

Rafael said, 'Have you got insurance? Which is your bank? Shall I phone them?'

Her mind cleared. She unzipped the inside pocket of her handbag and produced a card from the insurance people. 'Ring that number. They'll cancel the cards and get me new ones. Oh, and I had about fifty pounds in notes, which may be covered by them. Try it, anyway. That's the first thing to do. Next, Susan, can you ring the police for me? Try to get Lesley if you can. Tell her what's happened and say they must try to find Hetty, because she's a killer on the loose.'

SEVENTEEN

Saturday afternoon

Susan gaped. 'Hetty's murdered someone? I know she locked you in, but . . . really a murderer?'

Ellie struggled to think clearly. 'I can't be sure and I have no proof, but I'm very much afraid that she has been up to no good. I found a whole stack of pills inside one of the cushions on the settee. All sorts and sizes. And colours. And . . .' She swallowed hard. 'Will you phone the police now for me, Susan? I'll make myself a cup of tea, and then I'll be perfectly all right.'

'If you say so.' Susan used her phone, while Ellie considered the number of steps she'd have to take to get to the kettle. She'd have to go right across the kitchen. Three steps, possibly four. She could manage that, if she put her mind to it. She told her legs to go into action, and they refused. She could imagine her knees saying, *She can tell us what to do till the kingdom comes, but the poor old thing doesn't realize we're knackered.*

Rafael returned, smiling. 'An efficient company. Cards cancelled, money loss reported, replacement cards on their way.'

Ellie said, 'Thomas lost his keys once when we were on holiday. Someone found them and popped them in the nearest postbox. When we got back, his keys were sitting in the letterbox here, waiting for us. He hadn't even known he'd lost them.'

Susan handed the phone to Ellie. 'Lesley's on the line. You explain.'

Ellie looked longingly at the kettle. 'You couldn't make me a cuppa, could you?'

And to Lesley, she said, 'Sorry to trouble you, but there's been a nasty development and I think . . . oh dear, I'm going to cry! So sorry! I'm being such an idiot, what with Thomas being so sick and in hospital and all. I'll be all right in a minute.' She gulped.

Lesley sounded anxious. 'What is it, Ellie? Susan said you've been assaulted? Are you all right?'

'I'm very far from all right at the moment, but I'll bounce back. Of course I will. The thing is that I gave Hetty a cheque to help her find somewhere else to go to and while she was out I discovered she'd been hoarding a whole lot of pills, all sorts, from different pharmacies, issued to different people. I'm wondering if she's been giving them to the people she's been in contact with, and if so, do you think she might have been responsible for some of the deaths we've heard about recently? Ones where people have left money to Thomas?'

'Why would she do that?'

'I'm not sure. Perhaps she got them to leave her some money as well? I don't *know* that this is what she's been doing, but perhaps you can check? Anyway, she admitted that she'd made Thomas ill by giving him Ibuprofen, which he can't tolerate. The thing is that I challenged her about it, and now she's run off and I don't know where she is. She's taken her hoard of pills with her.'

'Have you any proof of what you say?'

'Well, I suppose I could press charges for locking me into one of the top rooms. When she left me there, she said she hoped I'd starve. I didn't, because Rafael and Susan didn't believe the nasty message she'd sent them, but she's cut the landline wires and spoiled all the food in the fridge and freezer and I think we'll probably have to throw everything edible away because I know she put Ibuprofen into Thomas's coffee and she might well have tampered with the rest of our food, too.'

Lesley was shocked. 'But she's your housekeeper!'

'No, she isn't. That was her idea, not mine. We gave her somewhere to live till she got back on her feet but it was never supposed to become a permanent arrangement. Midge didn't like her. Took against her from the beginning. Midge always knows, doesn't he? Sorry, Lesley, I'm afraid I'm all of a heap at the moment. Oh yes, and she stole my cards and my mobile phone and some money as well, but Rafael's dealt with that.'

Rafael took the phone from Ellie and spoke into it. 'Rafael here. Ellie's very shaken. It's all true. We got a message supposedly from Ellie, saying she didn't want to see us again. We thought it odd to say the least, and so we came anyway and found Ellie, locked in a room at the top of the house. She's dehydrated and in shock, but I don't think she needs to go to hospital. The rest is as Ellie has said. Money, cards and phone gone; landline cut. All the food in the fridge and freezer spoilt. And Hetty seems to have kept her keys to this house.'

'I'll be round in a trice,' said Lesley, and clicked off the phone.

Susan put a big mug of tea in front of Ellie. 'Drink up. I've smelled and tasted the milk and it seems all right. You like Breakfast Tea, don't you? I thought of putting some sugar into the tea for shock, but you don't like sugar in your tea, so I didn't. The thing is you're not quite yourself. Would you prefer coffee?'

Hetty had given Ellie a mug of coffee with too much sugar in it that morning.

Hetty admitted she'd put Ibuprofen in Thomas's jar of coffee.

Thomas had ended up in hospital.

Ellie had slept most of the day and still felt peculiar. She sipped the tea. It was just how she liked it. 'Bless you, my dear. This is made with a tea bag so it must be all right. Can you find my jar of instant coffee, and Thomas's, too? I think Hetty adulterated both. We must set them aside for the police to see.'

Susan opened the jar which contained the special coffee Thomas liked. 'It smells all right, but it's a very strong blend, isn't it? There's some whitish flecks mixed in with it. Did you have some of this at breakfast time?'

'No, she made me a cup of my own instant coffee, rather stronger than usual, and she put a lot of sugar in it. It was too strong and sweet for me but I was in such a state that I didn't think anything of it at the time. I think she may have put sleeping tablets in my coffee this morning because I've been out of it since breakfast time and still feel woozy.'

Rafael got some tissues and put the two jars of instant coffee on to the windowsill. 'We'll give them to the police.'

Susan found the biscuit tin and inspected the contents. She said, 'I think these last few biscuits are all right. Rafael, can you get rid of all that melting food? Put the lot in a bin bag and shove it outside. You can't trust food that's been half thawed and then refrozen.'

Rafael reached for a bin bag and set about his task.

Ellie's mind cleared a little. She drank the water, nibbled a biscuit, got the tea down her and held out her mug for a refill. Carbohydrates always helped. 'Rafael, the phone in my study is an extension of the one in the hall, but the one in Thomas's study is on a different line. Maybe that's still all right?'

'I'll check.' Rafael set off down the corridor. Susan hesitated for a long moment before drawing up a chair to finish fishing food out of the freezer.

Ellie put two and two together. She said, 'Braxton Hicks? You had contractions in the night? Rafael didn't want to worry me, but he didn't have a meeting today. Instead, he took you to the hospital for a check-up? You're still having contractions? How often are they coming?'

'Now and then. Another five days to go, they say. I must admit it's tiresome.'

'First babies are usually late, they say. But who believes anything people say any longer?'

Susan grinned. 'Fake news of the week. "Susan's baby is on its way."'

Ellie felt very relaxed. She yawned and said, 'I love you both. You know that, don't you?'

Susan's smile turned into a broad grin. 'Ditto.'

Ellie played back what she'd just said and was slightly perturbed. 'Susan, I'm not functioning correctly, am I? I mean, I meant that about loving you, I really did, but it's not like me to come out with it just like that, is it?'

'I like it.' Susan tied the top of a second bag holding spoilt food.

They both heard it and turned their heads to the corridor. A thump or a bump? Ellie said, 'What was that?'

'Rafael?'

They started for the corridor, Susan ahead, holding on to the small of her back and saying, 'Ouch!'

Midge met them in the hall, streaking out of the corridor which led to the library.

Rafael wasn't in the hall. He'd gone to Ellie's study to check if the landline worked there, hadn't he? And then to Thomas's study at the end?

He was lying on the floor just inside the door to the library, surrounded by books and an overturned chair. Blood pooled on the floor by his head.

Susan cried out, 'Rafael!' and went down on her knees with a flump.

He stirred. He wasn't dead. He exclaimed some words in Italian which didn't need translation. He tried to push himself up off the floor and failed.

Ellie joined Susan on the floor, somehow preventing herself from lying down beside him which is what she wanted to do. She jerked herself awake.

She didn't think Rafael had broken anything, but he'd taken a right old battering. There was a fine cord under Rafael leading from the door knob to the back of the fallen chair.

Ellie worked it out. It had been a booby trap. Rafael had opened the door and pulled a chair into his path which had caused him to take a tumble. In his fall he'd hit his head against something . . . the chair? Yes, there was a glistening patch of blood on the chair leg. The books had been on the chair and added a nice touch to the scene.

Ellie said, 'Hetty did this.' Had the woman hoped Ellie would fall for the trap, or Thomas? Perhaps she hadn't cared who might be hurt.

Susan was white with shock. 'Rafael!'

He put both hands to his head and winced. Blood ran down from his temple, but he said, 'I'm all right!' He was very, very angry. 'That woman! When I get hold of her . . .! What else . . .!' He held on to his head tightly. 'Ouch! My shoulder! And my ankle!'

Susan sat back on her heels, with an expression of mingled astonishment and alarm on her face. 'Oh, oh! What's happening! I think . . . Oh, no! Not now!'

Ellie's head was swimming but when she realized what had happened she forced herself to take control of the situation. 'Your waters have broken. No problem. Let's get you into a chair.' She tried to stand and failed.

Rafael also tried to stand and failed. He was as pale as his wife. 'Susan! Are you all right? I mean, does it hurt? Bloody hell, I'm bleeding all over the place.'

Susan closed her eyes and gasped. 'The pain goes right round to my back!'

Someone pounded on the front door.

'Lesley? Or Diana?' Ellie managed to pull and push herself to her feet. 'I'll go.'

Susan opened her mouth and screamed. She had a good pair of lungs on her.

Ellie, on her way down the corridor, tried to look at her watch, thinking she ought to time Susan's contractions. Only, when you're banging off this wall here and that wall there, you can't see your watch properly.

The pounding on the front door didn't stop. Well, it wouldn't, would it? Lesley knew there was a problem. Thank God for Lesley. She'd know exactly what to do next. Call an ambulance. Call two. They were going to need two at least, weren't they?

Ellie got to the front door and concentrated. She knew how to open it, didn't she? Why couldn't she remember what to do? Ah, perhaps you pulled this bit here . . .

She managed to wrestle the door open. She was cross with herself. Everything took so much of an effort!

It wasn't Lesley standing in the porch.

It was Diana. 'Mother, I had the most extraordinary phone call from your housekeeper, saying you'd booked yourself into a nursing home and forbidden me to contact you. When I tried your phone it went to voice message. You didn't expect me to believe such a ridiculous excuse, did you? We need to talk about the house and—!'

Ellie put a hand on Diana's shoulder to steady herself. She was swaying on her feet. 'Diana, I need your help. Susan's started in labour, Rafael's been in an accident and I'm not drunk, but have taken some sleeping pills by mistake. What's more, the phone line's been cut and all the food in the kitchen must be thrown away. Can you take over, please?'

'What? You're not making sense!'

Ellie felt she'd had enough of making decisions for the time being. It was all too, too tiring. She sank to the floor, saying, 'And, could you feed Midge before you go?'

She let sleep take her away into La-La Land.

Sunday morning

She woke slowly. Lazily.

And yawned.

She couldn't remember when she'd last slept so long and so deeply.

A memory of some unpleasantness nudged her mind, and she pushed it away.

She was all right now. Well, a bit sore as to throat, but . . . she'd been going down with the cold, hadn't she? No . . . it wasn't that.

She shifted in the bed. Something wasn't quite right. The sounds coming to her ears were not from her usual early morning routine, and neither were the scents. Muffled voices. Squeak of wheels on composite floor. Clopping shoes. And her bed was not cradling her in its usual comfortable manner.

She opened her eyes to find herself looking at a strange woman, who said, 'Sleeping Beauty wakes up? Had a nice rest, have you?'

Ellie blinked.

The nurse took Ellie's blood pressure and temperature.

Ellie said, 'What . . .?'

'You're in hospital, dear. You took some sleeping tablets, didn't you? They brought you in and washed you out and left you to sleep it off.'

Ellie pressed a hand to her forehead. And remembered.

Hetty. That oversweet cuppa at breakfast time. No wonder I couldn't function properly.

She struggled to sit upright. 'My husband? Thomas? He's in

the hospital here, with stomach pains. And oh, my goodness, what about Rafael and Susan? Has she had her baby? Are they all right?'

In her agitation, she tried to get off the bed. The nurse pressed her back and pulled the sides of the bed up so that Ellie couldn't leave. 'Now, now. You just lie back and rest. I'm sure everything's all right with your friends. Breakfast will be up in a minute.' She left.

Ellie looked around her. She was in a four-bed ward. Two other women were taking their time to open their eyes and welcome the day. One looked as if she were never going to do so. One of the ones who was awake flipped herself off her bed – no side gates for her – and trundled off to the loo.

Ellie looked down. She was wearing her undies under a hospital gown. No shoes. Where were her outer clothes? She must get out of here! She must find Thomas. And Rafael. And poor Susan. Would Susan be in this hospital or another?

She spotted her handbag on the bedside table and dragged it on to the bed. There was no phone in it. No, of course not. Hetty had taken it, hadn't she? How was she to find out what had happened to the others?

The last thing she remembered was Diana – Diana, of all people! – standing over her, phoning for an ambulance. For once, Diana had been helpful. Wonders would never cease.

Ellie fell back on the pillows and closed her eyes. She told herself to breathe deeply. Softly. And, relax. When the nurse came back, Ellie would get her to ring round and find out what was happening.

Ellie woke again when breakfast arrived. It wasn't a nurse who brought it but a carer of some kind. No use asking her for a phone. Ellie ate and drank without interest in what she was given. And incredibly, dozed off again . . .

Only to be woken by someone calling her name.

Rafael stood over her. One eye was swollen and closed, he had strips of plaster holding the cut on his forehead in place, and all that side of his face was yellow and black. One of his arms was in a sling, and he was leaning on a stick. 'Ellie, wake up!'

'I am awake,' she said, struggling to sit upright. 'What's the news? Are you all right? Is Susan?'

His rather harsh features lit up with a grin. 'It's a girl, born at midnight. I can't make out if her birthday will be today or yesterday. My darling Susan says she's worn out, but she looks wonderful, like a glorious, opulent rose in full bloom. Motherhood suits her. As for our little girl, she's perfect in every way with a head of black hair and . . . ah, she's exquisite! I was there when she was born. The moment they put her in my arms, I said, "Hello, Fifi!" and I swear she knew me, though the midwives said that that wasn't possible. We don't plan to call her Fifi, of course . . .'

He went on about how wonderful the baby was, and how Susan had had an easy time of it . . . at least that was what the midwives had said, though Susan thought otherwise.

Ellie knew that whatever name the baby was given at her christening, she would always be known as Fifi. Which was all very right and proper.

'And so,' said Rafael, 'they said that I could take Susan home if there were someone to look after her, and I tried to explain that we're in a flat on the second floor with no lift and that I'm pretty well useless at the moment. However, I said I did know someone who might, in the goodness of her heart, take us in and look after us.' He gave Ellie his best imitation of a poor, wounded soldier looking for someone to soothe his fevered brow.

Ellie was not in the least taken in. 'What you mean is that you told them I'd do it, right? Can you drop the sides of this bed for me? I want to get dressed.'

Rafael's grin widened. 'I told the nurses I was your son-in-law, which is sort of true because you've always been better than a mother to Susan. The nurse here told me you had slept off the effects of whatever you'd taken and might well be discharged when the doctor's been round but—'

Ellie moved to the edge of her bed and dangled her legs over. The room went round a bit, and then settled. 'How about Thomas? How is he?'

'It's a Sunday morning and nothing much is happening so I blagged my way up to see him, too. He's in a ward on the next floor up. Looking a lot better, because whatever they've got him on seems to be working. He's champing at the bit to get out of here, says he's occupying a bed under false pretences.'

'Are my clothes in my locker? Pass them to me, will you?'

Rafael opened the locker, one-handed, and passed over her outer clothing and shoes. 'They X-rayed my shoulder and my ankle and say both are sprained. I have to take it easy for a while. No heavy lifting, and I'm to keep my leg elevated.'

Ellie grunted, trying to get her shoes on. Her balance still wasn't perfect. 'How are we going to get home if you can't drive?'

'I've ordered a cab. Thomas said he'd meet us down at the front entrance in forty-five minutes and' – Rafael consulted his watch – 'that's thirty minutes to go. Which gives us plenty of time to browbeat the nurses here into discharging you. We'll pick up Thomas first and then collect Susan and Fifi. Susan can't wait to get away from here and look after Fifi herself, but she's been told to take things easy and I can't really do anything for her with my arm in a sling, can I?'

Ellie stamped her feet into her shoes and eyed him up and down. Innocence radiated from every pore but his mouth had curved into a smile, indicating how much he was enjoying his little game.

She said, 'You and Susan want to move in and live with us and you've arranged matters so that I can't possibly refuse. I doubt very much that you'll be keeping that arm in a sling once we get out of here, and I suppose you intend to lose the stick on the way home. You know what? You are a very naughty boy!'

At which they both laughed out loud, causing two of the other women in the ward to look shocked and the third to groan in her sleep.

Rafael hushed his voice and tried to look penitent. 'You're right, of course. The flat we've been living in is all right in its way, but it doesn't feel like home. Susan has never liked it, but she put up with it till we found somewhere we could settle in. She loved living with you, and I rather like it, too. Yes, if you can bear it, we'd love to stay with you for a while.'

'On the basis that "home is where the heart is"? What about your own mother and father?'

'They congratulated me on producing a child and said they'd "be over to inspect the baby when things are a little more settled".' His mimicry of two disinterested, unloving parents was uncanny.

Ellie knew he'd always had a distant relationship with them, and her heart went out to him. She also knew that Susan's mother had always preferred a pretty cousin to her own daughter, and that there was no father in the picture. Practically, they were both orphans. And Ellie and Thomas, for all that they had offspring of their own, would have no trouble in unofficially adopting the pair . . . plus Fifi, the very new baby.

She smoothed out a smile. 'Well, I suppose I could put up with having the three of you underfoot for a while, if Thomas agrees.'

'He suggested it. He said he liked having babies around the house. He said babies always take to him.'

It was true. They did. Ellie moved into housewifely mode. 'I don't suppose we've got a speck of food in the house, and the place is a mess. But we'll manage, somehow.'

'Well, Diana said—'

'You've been in touch with Diana?'

'Well, yes. You don't remember? No, you'd fallen asleep, hadn't you? While we waited for the ambulances which didn't come for a good half hour, with me dripping blood all over the place and rubbing Susan's back and Susan letting go with a good scream now and then, I told Diana what had been happening, and asked if she knew how to contact your cleaners and get them to come in and clean up. She said she would. She said she'd put out some food for Midge but that she couldn't stay the night because of her own young family. I thought that was very helpful of her.'

Ellie eyed him in disillusion. 'You didn't offer to buy their option for the land by the river off them, did you?'

Eyes, wide. All innocence. 'No, no. Of course not. I'm not made of money. I did mention that I knew someone who might be interested in buying them out.'

'What? How?'

'Well, you have to understand what makes some people tick. There are two other groups who had been thinking about taking on the site down by the river, only Evan got in first and bought the option to develop. I let my contact at one of these firms know that Evan might be willing to sell on his option at a reasonable price now, this minute. You see, if my contact waits till the option expires, there'd be a bidding war, and my contact would have to pay way over the odds for the site. But, if he bought the option off Evan, then he's got a clear run through to the title and can go ahead and develop at leisure. He's delighted by the idea of putting one over his rival.'

'Does he know he may not get permission to develop?'

He spread his hands. 'He's been informed that will not be a problem as the new developer has agreed to ensure the houses have flood defences.'

'Are you taking a cut yourself?'

Rafael shook his head. 'Susan would kill me if I did.'

'I suppose,' said Ellie, testing the waters, 'you'll want to stand for the council yourself one day?'

'Not me. There's no money in it.' A naughty grin.

'You,' said Ellie, 'don't fool me!'

He sighed. 'I know. I'm an unprincipled blackguard, but it might work.'

Ellie picked up her handbag and put it down again. Something wasn't quite right. She wriggled a bit. She drew a used hankie and two rather squashed packets of pills from her bra. Where had the pills come from? Ah, from Hetty's hoard. She put them in her handbag.

'Spoils of war, collected by Hetty, and found by me in her rooms. I'll hand them over to Lesley when I see her. Hospitals are wonderful places when you're poorly, and they've looked after us all splendidly, but we're ready to go and I'm sure they need the beds. Let's work out how to escape from Colditz.'

EIGHTEEN

Sunday onwards

They returned to find there were already a number of vehicles in the forecourt of the big house. A supermarket delivery van was the largest, followed in order of size by a British Telecom van and a large, very new, black saloon.

The saloon was a family car, fitted with seats for a toddler and a baby in the back.

Thomas was first out of the taxi as he'd been sitting in front beside the driver. He was looking a little pale, but otherwise himself. 'Ellie, did you place a supermarket order for food?'

'I didn't have time. That's Diana's car.'

Thomas looked at Diana's car. 'Oh, well. Once more into the fray, dear friends.' He opened the back passenger door. 'Susan, will you let me hold Fifi while you get out?'

On the other side of the car, Rafael hung his stick over his arm to help Ellie out, too.

Ellie wondered if it were her fancy, or could she really hear Diana's scolding voice through their very solid front door? She found her keys and let them into the hall, when the volume of her daughter's sharp voice expanded to fill the ears of everyone in the vicinity.

Diana was in full flow. 'Will you look at the dirt you've tracked through the hall!'

A supermarket delivery man bolted past Ellie, making a bid for the outside world and freedom.

'Typical!' Diana concluded. 'Without so much as a word of apology!' Hands on hips, she stood victorious over the battle-field or rather, over a hall full of people. Annie and Betty, two of the cleaners who usually looked after Ellie, were there, a-polishing of this and a-dusting of that, while a BT engineer fiddled with wires by the phone.

Diana's toddler son, little Evan, slowly but surely stomped his way up the stairs; two steps up and then two steps down, hampered by having a biscuit in either hand. Meanwhile, his little sister worked on undoing the straps which held her into her bouncy child seat.

Diana registered the appearance of her mother and friends long enough to say, 'Your cleaners could do with retraining, Mother. They don't seem to know how to put a good shine on the parquet floor.' Before Ellie could explain that she didn't want a floor to be so shiny that she'd slip on it, Diana had turned on Annie and Betty. 'Well, leave that, now! It's more important that you put the food away in the fridge and the freezer. And make sure you check the temperature!'

Annie and Betty synchronized an eyeroll in Ellie's direction and disappeared down the rabbit hole . . . or, rather, the corridor to the kitchen. Ellie resolved to give them both a bonus for coming in on a Sunday, and for putting up with Diana treating them like slaves.

Diana looked at her watch and tapped her foot. Mistress Impatience. She frowned and then, unexpectedly, smiled. 'Welcome home, Mother. I believe you will find everything in order. The beds have been made, the bedrooms vacuumed, the bathrooms and the kitchen cleaned. All the spoilt food has been removed and replacements delivered. I ordered a number of pre-cooked dishes for you to be getting on with, and trust that you will be able to cope with them until you are ready to cook again. I paid for everything on my credit card and will let you have the bill.'

Ellie pinched herself. Was Diana really thinking of someone other than herself for a change? She said, 'That's amazing. Thank you, Diana. I am most grateful.' And she really was.

Diana was ungracious as ever. 'Yes, well. It was the least I could do. Now, we must have a talk about the deeds to our house some time. I'm sure we can come to some arrangement whereby we can pay a peppercorn rent.'

'Perhaps so,' said Ellie, thinking they could deal with that another day.

Diana's eyes flickered over Thomas, who was carrying the baby, and Susan, whom she decided to ignore. She focused on Rafael. 'Your tip about the man who might be interested in discussing a certain project . . . Well, I'm meeting him later on today.' She looked at her watch again and raised her voice to her son. 'Evan, come down this minute, at once, do you hear? We're going out for lunch, remember?' She scooped up her daughter in her bouncy seat, grabbed her son's arm and nodded to Rafael to open the front door for her . . . and made her exit, head held high.

There was a general relaxation of tense muscles at her departure, though no one was prepared to comment on Diana's behaviour in front of Ellie. Ellie herself didn't know what to say. Diana had done a very good job of putting everything to rights, and so for once her bossy manners must be overlooked.

The telephone engineer stood up. 'All fixed. Sign here, please.'
Thomas signed and Susan began to fidget. 'I need to sit down.
Fifi's fussing to be fed.'

Ellie shepherded Susan into the sitting room. 'Make yourself
at home, my dear. Try the settee. Put a cushion under your arm
like this, which gives you support when you lay Fifi . . . yes,
that's it. Relax. Take your time. I'll bring you a cuppa in a minute.'

It was good to have a baby in the house. Ellie wondered
how many years it was since a baby had been suckled here.
Did you count Diana's two, who occasionally spent the night
in the house? Ellie decided that no, you didn't. In the first
place, Diana had never breastfed her children, and in the second,
Susan and Fifi were here to stay.

Fifi latched on to Susan with enthusiasm. No need to coax
her to do what came naturally. Ellie told herself that it was
only her imagination at work, but it did seem that the house
welcomed the new life.

Ellie, Thomas and Rafael watched the baby feed for a long
moment, and then Rafael abandoned his stick and his sling.
'If you don't object, Ellie, I'll get a cab to the flat and bring
some of the baby's stuff back here; Moses basket, buggy,
changing mat. Susan has it all piled up ready. Babies seem to
need a ton of belongings.'

Thomas hovered over Susan and Fifi like a rather large fairy
godfather. 'Put Fifi's stuff in the Quiet Room down the corridor.
That can be the downstairs nursery till we can sort out something
more permanent. Bring your stuff and Susan's over, too. Dump
everything in the spare bedroom and we'll sort it out later.'

Susan smiled up at Thomas. 'Bless you both.'

Thomas eased his back, fore and aft, and said, 'Ah, there's
no place like home.'

Once Rafael had departed, Thomas put his arm around Ellie
and drew her out into the hall.

'My dear, did I overstep the mark? It's all right with you that
they move in, isn't it? And how are you feeling, yourself?'

'It's very all right that they move in with us. I had a good
night's sleep and I'm fine. How about you?'

'I'm fine and dandy.' He patted his stomach. 'Do you think

I've lost some weight? The hospital gave me a list of what I should and shouldn't eat for a while. It sounds rather depressing. If Hetty's really gone, I'm sure my stomach will settle down soon. Your cooking's so good—'

'Oh, blame it all on me.'

He held her close and she leaned on him, holding him close, too. He kissed her ear. 'If anything had happened to you . . .'

'Ditto,' said Ellie. 'Double ditto.'

A thin wail rose from the sitting room and was quickly stilled as Susan changed the baby on to her other side.

Both Thomas and Ellie smiled. Thomas said, 'It's good to have a baby around the place.' He looked at his watch, remembering his workload. 'Ellie, I seem to have lost a couple of days' work. If it's all right with you, I'll just check on one or two things . . .' And off he went down the corridor to the library.

Ellie knew what was expected of her, which was to provide tea and coffee all round. She could do with a cup, herself. So she went along to the corridor to soothe her cleaners' wounded feelings, look over what Diana had ordered in the food department and turn herself back into the Universal Provider.

Oh yes, and she must ring Lesley to tell her about the pills which Hetty had inadvertently left behind.

Sunday afternoon

Ellie was smiling as she opened the door to let Lesley in. 'Come in, come in. Such a lot has been happening. We're all at sixes and sevens. Rafael and Susan have moved in to the big guest room at the end of the corridor upstairs, and Fifi – that's their baby – is supposed to be in the little bedroom opposite but at the moment she and Susan are both asleep on their big bed while Rafael moves in their bits and pieces around them.

'Thomas is back, too. He's asleep on his La-Z-boy in the sitting room. Yes, he's much better but you never sleep properly in hospital, do you? Oh, except for me, I had a really good night but that's due to the sleeping pills Hetty gave me. Me? I'm sorting out some food for supper. Join me in a cuppa in the kitchen?'

'Yes, but Ellie . . .!'

'All will be revealed. Or almost all. Some of it is guesswork. Let me tell you what I know and what I suspect. You can take it from there.'

'You want to prefer charges against your housekeeper?'

'Oh, that. Yes. She did drug me and lock me up. She did steal my money, my cards and my phone, and told lies to everyone so they wouldn't come looking for me. Only, of course they weren't fooled and Rafael stopped the cards for me so there's no great harm done. Yes, she did do Thomas a lot of no good by feeding him some pills which didn't agree with him, but hopefully he will recover from that all right. The most serious thing, I suppose, is that she set a booby trap which cost Rafael a couple of stitches in his forehead and a black eye, not to mention a sprained shoulder and ankle. I suppose you could put that down as misadventure. She couldn't have known he'd be really hurt. None of that is sufficient to charge her with murder.'

'Murder? You're joking! Who said anything about murder? What I'm interested in is the money that's been left to Thomas.'

'Ah, yes.' Ellie led the way down the corridor to the kitchen. 'Let's have a cuppa. Diana ordered some biscuits, not my usual ones, but they should do. I've never been fond of coconut. Do you like coconut?'

Lesley gave in. 'All right, I'll have a cuppa and listen to your story.'

'Oh, my!' Ellie gave a cry of joy. 'Look! Diana's ordered Jaffa cakes!'

Ellie never bought Jaffa cakes because she and Thomas were always trying to lose weight and once you opened a packet of those succulent delicacies, they had to be eaten straight away, before they went hard and became unpalatable. Well, that was the theory, anyway.

Ellie crammed one into her mouth and took another. Oh, bliss! Oh, rapture!

Lesley tried to look disapproving, but then took two herself. 'Begin at the beginning.'

'Background coming up. This is what I've gathered so far. Hetty was born in north London to a couple who split up soon

after. Her mother worked as a cleaner, changing jobs frequently
because she said she was always being cheated of her money
by her employers. They did eventually get a council flat but it
was badly maintained and gave her mother asthma because of
the mould on the bathroom wall. Hetty was bright enough to
get some O-levels and might have gone on to college education
if her mother hadn't been accidentally run over by a bus and
she herself had gone down with some sort of glandular problem,
which meant she couldn't work for a while. She had to go on
the social, who mismanaged her case so that when a neighbour
laid false accusations against her, Hetty lost the council flat
and had to move into a series of rented rooms.'

Lesley took a third Jaffa cake. 'I sense a pattern emerging.
Whatever bad luck she had, it was always someone else's fault?'

'Indeed. Hetty tried very hard to better herself. She took all
sorts of part-time jobs, as a cleaner, in a shop, looking after the
elderly, and she applied once more for council housing.'

'Council housing for single people is at a premium. What's
the waiting list? Ten years?'

'Very likely. Still living in rented accommodation, this time
in west London, she had an on-and-off relationship with a feck-
less man who drank her earnings and beat her up before disap-
pearing to jail because, in addition to his other gifts, he was a
career burglar. Refusing to be daunted, Hetty set about building
up her savings once again, hoping that eventually she'd have
enough to buy her own little flat in this neighbourhood.'

'Fat chance,' said Lesley, taking another Jaffa cake. 'On a
minimum wage.'

'Yes. Thomas visits an old people's home nearby. One day
he walked in on a full-scale riot with half the residents accusing
one of the cleaners of stealing from them, and the other half
in full-throated uproar, declaring it was the woman who worked
part-time in the office.'

'Hetty was the cleaner?'

'No, Hetty was the woman in the office. She was in tears,
swearing that she might have made a mistake but she would
never, ever . . . et cetera. The cleaner then came clean and
confessed to having taken some, though not all, of the missing
items. Long story short, both women got the sack. Thomas took

them to a cafe, fed them tea and cake and generally put them back on track, so to speak. Hetty continued to swear she hadn't stolen anything, ever, and I really don't think she had. I'm sure Thomas would have spotted it if she'd lied. Thomas was sorry for her.'

'Uh-oh!'

'Yes, it didn't take me long to work out that she was a passive-aggressive personality. You'd have thought Thomas would have got there before me, but he didn't. She said she was at her wits' end and going to be thrown out of her rented room if the old people's home didn't pay the wages due to her that week. He went back to the office and got them for her. She was ever so grateful. He kept in touch through her various ups and downs until one day she rang to say she'd had to leave her accommodation because the owner's dog had bitten her, and that's when he made his big mistake. Knowing that our upstairs flat was empty and being redecorated he asked me if I'd let her stay for a couple of weeks till she got back on her feet. I agreed. Hetty fell on his neck and thanked him.

'She's quite personable, you know, and a hard worker. She really does try. Within a week I knew it wasn't going to work out for all sorts of reasons. For one thing, she couldn't bear our cat, Midge, and he couldn't stand her. You may say that's a trivial reason, and if she'd kept to her own quarters it wouldn't have mattered, but she wasn't happy to do that. She wanted to be part of our family and started to edge her way into the kitchen down here. That's her side of the story. What I've told you so far, I've heard from her own lips, or from Thomas. Now for the bit I can't prove.'

Ellie reached for another Jaffa cake, only to find the packet empty. How had that happened? She was sure she hadn't had more than two or three. Maybe four.

Lesley had the last one in her hand. 'Are we coming to the money?'

'We are. In the course of her various jobs in the community, Hetty had access to elderly people's homes. I believe that when she cleaned for them, she did their shopping and she took them out for walks. If one of them died, she helped to clear out their belongings in the bathroom cabinets, on the bedside tables and in the kitchen cupboards. She found packets and bottles of all sorts of medicines prescribed by doctors for the ailments that afflict older people. She found strong painkillers, sleeping tablets, pills for angina, for high blood pressure and low, for diabetes, for cramp, for emphysema, for asthma, for different forms of cancer. You name it, it's hanging around after the person concerned has died. Someone is supposed to take the leftover pills to the pharmacist to be destroyed.

'I believe that Hetty put them in her bag to do just that but then the next old lady she visited was having trouble sleeping and told Hetty that the pills the doctor had been giving her didn't do any good. So Hetty topped up that person's sleeping tablets with ones that she had to hand. Now, Thomas was also visiting this old dear as part of his job. Hetty told the woman how good Thomas had been to her. Hetty was overflowing with gratitude to Thomas for taking her in. I think that, quite innocently, Hetty suggested to the old lady that she might leave a little something to Thomas in her will.'

'And something for Hetty as well?'

'It seems likely, doesn't it? And why ever not? A couple of hundred to Thomas, and perhaps the same to Hetty? Lesley, I suggest you might find it worthwhile to get copies of all the wills by which Thomas has benefited, to see if Hetty is also mentioned in them. It would take me for ever to get those copies, but you could do it overnight.'

Lesley pushed her mug forward for a refill. 'You think Hetty was feathering her own nest at the same time that she was encouraging people to give Thomas a hefty tip?'

'It makes sense.' Ellie refilled both their mugs. 'The old lady died, possibly without help from Hetty's cache of pills, possibly with their assistance. Thomas and, I think, Hetty were among those who'd been left some money. Fine. Hetty had lost that particular job so started to look for another. She was probably registered with an agency who passed her on to this person and that, taking her cache of pills with her . . . possibly with some additions from the cupboards of the recently deceased.'

Lesley made a note. 'Wills. Agency. The agency you use?'

'No. It wasn't. I checked. They'd never heard of her. But

there's several domestic agencies hereabouts, and she could be registered with any one of them.'

'Go on. You think that, having done it once, she went on to do it again and again, which is why Thomas has been inundated with cheques.'

'It's going to be difficult to prove but yes, that's what I think. Only, back at the ranch here, the situation had changed. Thomas had begun to realize he'd made a mistake in taking her in, and to worry about the origin of the money which was being showered on him from all directions. He couldn't understand it, and neither could I. At the same time, I made it clear to Hetty that we would like her to move on. So, far from being grateful to Thomas, she now began to wish him ill, to punish him for his change of heart. She put ground-up Ibuprofen in his jar of instant coffee. Most people find Ibuprofen helpful, but some end up with very nasty gastric problems. Thomas was made ill by them. The doctors say he should recover, but it will take time for his stomach to settle down.'

'Then she turned on you, too?'

'Well, I did break down the door to her flat. Admittedly, that was only after I discovered she'd put a lock on the door to her rooms without permission, and asked her repeatedly for the key. I think that as long as she had the flat here, she felt safe. When I asked her to go, it tipped her over into action. I don't think violence is her usual way of reacting. Yes, she did feed me sleeping pills and lock me in upstairs. And yes, she made a mess here in the kitchen, and set up a booby trap in the library . . . though that was probably aimed at Thomas and not Rafael.

'The booby trap did cause Rafael to have a nasty fall, but she didn't attack either of us physically. It's true that, after locking me into the spare room upstairs, she told everyone I'd booked myself into a nursing home for a while and not to contact me. That might have meant my starving to death, but that didn't work, either. There's nothing planned about the way she operates. I think she rationalizes everything to suit herself. If someone dies from her the pills she gives them, she tells herself that it's their fault for taking the stuff. She really believes she can't be held responsible. If people happen to die, then she inherits some cash. If they don't, well, there's always another day and another old person who needs help.'

Lesley leaned back in her chair. 'Do you really think she helped those who left money to Thomas to die?'

'I don't know. Some of them may have died of natural causes. Some have been dead and buried – or cremated – for six months at least.' Ellie produced the two rather squashed packets of pills which she'd managed to retain from Hetty's stash in the cushion. 'I found these two in her quarters. One lot of pills are for blood pressure, the others are strong painkillers. Both packets have had some pills removed already. They are from two different pharmacies, but neither gives the name of the person who was supposed to take this medication. My fingerprints will be all over them but I suppose Hetty's will be, too. She kept them for a purpose, didn't she?'

Lesley shook her head, slowly. 'I see what you mean. You have no proof that she misused the medication. I agree that in theory we could exhume the bodies which were not cremated and test them for poison. No, not poison. If you're right, we'd have to test them for an overdose of painkillers, sleeping tablets or of some perfectly ordinary medicine for asthma or high blood pressure. Even if we found levels too high for normal administration, we couldn't prove that Hetty was responsible. We might charge her on imprisoning you, setting the booby trap and dosing Thomas with Ibuprofen . . . by the way, can you actually prove that she did that?'

'I have the half-empty pack of pills we found where she'd been sitting, and we kept the jar of Thomas's coffee and mine which we think she adulterated . . . except,' said Ellie, looking at the empty windowsill, 'the cleaners seem to have thrown them away when they were clearing everything up. Perhaps I could find it if I go through the rubbish bins . . .' Ellie grimaced. 'It's not enough, is it?'

Lesley said, 'If you could find the jar of coffee, and if it contained traces of Ibuprofen, it might help, but you can't prove that she was responsible. There's no proof that she ever administered medication to anyone, let alone with malicious intent. The only thing you have is the fact that she imprisoned you upstairs.'

'I can just see her front of the jury. She'd weep and say she didn't know what she had come over her but it was all my fault for turning her out into the cold, and the booby trap – which has all been cleared away by the cleaners, by the way – was a bit of a joke that had gone wrong, and that her silly messages to everyone were also a joke, and no harm had come to me. No jury would convict her.'

Lesley sighed. 'You're right. They wouldn't.'

Ellie said at last, 'The problem is that unless she's stopped, I think she's going to go on doing it. What's more, she's taken the keys to this house with her. It would be a nuisance to have to change the locks here, but I suppose I will have to do it. I won't have a minute's peace till she's been dealt with. So, Lesley, will you get hold of the wills and see if she's named in all of them? I know that, even if she did benefit that way, it doesn't prove that she had anything to do with the testators' deaths, but if she realized we were on to her, it might make her think twice about doing it again.'

Lesley made a note. 'Yes, I'll check the wills to see if she's mentioned. If her name comes up more than twice, I'll have a quiet word with her sometime. That should do the trick.'

With that Ellie told herself she must be content.

NINETEEN

Monday morning

Some Monday mornings are easier to cope with than others. Ellie began hers by making notes about what she needed to do that week. First, she must tell the trust about Monique's money and, following from that, find out the exact position with regard to Evan and Diana's house.

Then, was it appropriate to mention Rafael and Susan's weird suggestion of dividing the house into two? Rafael's offer to serve on the trust must certainly go on the agenda.

Ellie gazed out of the window. If so much more money was going to be at the trust's disposal, did they need to take on extra staff to cope with the work involved? And in what direction should the trust go? Buy to let? Student accommodation? A hostel for single people?

The phone rang. She considered letting it go to voicemail but did eventually pick it up.

'Mrs Quicke?' A harsh voice. A man's. 'I've been waiting all weekend for you to call. What you up to, eh? Promising us you'd help, leading us on, and then letting us down. It's people like you that stand in the way of people like us getting their rights and as for—'

Ellie broke in. 'Who *is* this?'

'As if you didn't know! You said, you promised us faithfully, and it's not as if you didn't do it before witnesses, because my sister was stood right beside me, and she'll back me up if it comes to a tribunal—'

'What are you talking about? Are you sure you have the right number?' And yet, there was something knocking at the back of her mind. The caller's heavy breathing reminded her of someone.

'As if you didn't know! I get your sort! You make promises and then pretend you never did anything of the—'

Ellie got it. 'Mr Pullin? Is that Bob Pullin?' She'd gone to see the daughter . . . no, it was the stepdaughter, what had her first name been? . . . Of someone who'd left Thomas money.

The memory trickled back in pieces. A neglected house, filled with old-fashioned furniture and littered with the rubbish left by a younger family member who'd been living there rent free. There'd been a downtrodden daughter, Dawn, who'd been trying to clean the Aegean stables – a task far too big for her to undertake – and yes, a bullying brother.

Ellie remembered that she'd made an offer to help. She'd promised to give them a contract to sign in which she'd lend them some money to get professional cleaners in.

Immediately after that, Ellie's personal life had gone haywire: her daughter had tried blackmail; Monique's funeral had been held; Thomas had been admitted to hospital; and she herself had been imprisoned at the top of the house.

Bob Pullin was still talking, so Ellie overrode his complaint. 'I'm so sorry. Yes, I should have got back to you. We had a death in the family and my husband was taken to hospital, but I ought to have let you know what was happening.'

'Indeed you should! Here we've been all weekend, worrying ourselves sick, with my wife developing nervous spasms which meant she couldn't go in to work and I had to take time off to look after her, and I tell you, I'm adding that on to the bill for you to pay.'

'I'm truly sorry, Mr Pullin, but I am not responsible for your wife's nerves. Now, this is my first day back at work. I'll get on to my solicitor without delay and ask him to draw up a contract on the terms we agreed.'

For the moment she couldn't remember what terms they had agreed, but she was sure it would come back to her in a minute. 'So, are you at work today? Give me a phone number where I can reach you when I've got the contract in my hand—'

'You can't expect me to work today, with my wife having panic attacks and our Bryony moving back in with her boyfriend. I'm telling you for nothing, my wife's going to kill that boyfriend if he doesn't keep his feet off our sofa that she's just had recovered—'

'I understand,' said Ellie. As indeed, she did. How awful it would have been if Susan and Rafael had been such slobs!

She remembered that she'd had some vague ideas about what the trust might do with the Pullin house when it came on to the market. Though it was not looking its best at present, it might be something the trust might buy, renovate and let out for student digs? Yes, that was it. The house was not far from the university and such accommodation was always in demand. Or yes, it could be turned into three flats if an extension were built on to the back to provide a kitchen and bathroom on each floor. She would have their surveyor visit and he could recommend which option they might take.

Monique had left all that money to the trust, and surely this was the sort of proposition which she would have liked?

'Mr Pullin, it is just possible I might know of a possible buyer for the property as it stands but—'

'You think I'm such a fool as to fall for that? You'd buy it cheap at the poor price they put on it for probate, do it up and sell it for double the amount.'

'No, no. The trust would give you a fair price. The benefit from your point of view is that you'd get your money more quickly than if you have to put the house in order before placing it on the open market. Also, you wouldn't have to pay commission to an estate agent. Now, have you had a valuer round yet to look at the furniture? There are some decent bits which might fetch a bob or two for you in an auction.'

'You think I'm made of money that I can spend money on a valuer? As for the probate value, everyone knows they undervalue, and we can get more than that on the open market.'

Ellie tried not to grind her teeth. Was the man really so ignorant of what happened in such situations? 'On the open market you would have to wait for a buyer to surface, preferably one without a chain. Now, I'm prepared to advance you the thousand pounds which your mother left to my husband, in order to clean up the house. If you don't want to keep any of the furniture, you should get the house clearance people to take everything away. After that I suggest we get at least two valuations from local estate agents; one of your choice, one of mine, and we see if we can agree on a price. I suspect the place needs rewiring and replumbing, which will have to be taken into consideration. Now, you will want to consult your sister about this before—'

'No need for that. I make all the decisions about whether or not to sell.'

Ellie suspected that if Bully Bob were given half a chance, Dawn would see very little of the money from the house. 'I have her phone number somewhere. I'll ring her in a minute and put my proposition to her. If she says we should go ahead, we will have everything put in writing so that there will be no misunderstandings. Do you agree?'

Well, of course he did. He had to, didn't he?

Ellie ended the call and crossed her fingers in the hope that the trust would in fact agree to buy. They'd never objected to any of her suggestions before, but there was always a first time.

Someone loomed in the doorway. Rafael. He said, 'Can you spare a minute? Thomas and I were going to see what it would look like if we moved his two desks from the library into the dining room, but we can't see how to fit them in round the big dining table there.'

Off the top of her head, Ellie said, 'Take two of the leaves out of the table. That would make it small enough for you and Susan to use in the library.'

'Of course!' Rafael vanished, and soon Ellie heard laughter and humping sounds as the two men set about swapping furniture around.

Ellie clutched her desk. Did she really want to lose her dining room? Fond memories surfaced of the early meetings of the trust, when they'd all been rather overwhelmed by the task of dealing with so much money. There'd been some heated discussions at times, much laughter, some triumphs and a few failures.

If the big table went, then Ellie would have to find another space in which to hold the meetings of the trust. Perhaps not at home any more, but at the trust's offices? In which case, someone would have to ferry her around. Or she could take a taxi.

Everything was happening too quickly. She told herself that she had only to raise an objection and there would be no changes. Things would go on as before.

At the same time, she knew very well that however much you might like to hold the clock back, you couldn't really do so. She looked around at her study and realized that Rafael would need a study in the future and that this would be the best place for it.

Another thing: theirs was a growing family and they were going to need three bedrooms in the future, whereas Ellie and Thomas would only need two. Which meant that the nice guest room must be included in their side of the house.

Ah, but Ellie and Thomas could always use the one on the other side of the landing, which was en suite and had once been occupied by their old housekeeper, years ago.

For a moment she felt quite dizzy.

Then she told herself that she could easily move her bits and pieces from her present study into the room off the kitchen, which had once been used as a sitting room by their old house-keeper. That room was slightly bigger than her existing study, which would be a plus factor.

Oh, but the window looked on to the drive, and not the garden!

Well, yes. But she would be nearer the kitchen and it would be easier to make herself a cuppa and dip into the biscuit tin.

Ellie looked out on to the garden – it was raining again and the grass was growing shaggy – and accepted the necessity for change.

She listened to the sounds of people going about their business in the house. Thomas and Rafael, laughing as they humped furniture, Susan singing to Fifi in the sitting room, Midge giving himself a good wash on top of her filing cabinet.

And it was good.

Over the next few days, the old library was transformed into a pleasant living room for the young family with the addition of: a three-piece suite, the reduced version of the dining table plus chairs, a coffee table, pictures and a gilt-framed mirror. Oh, and a huge television set. Some of the existing shelves received Rafael's somewhat eclectic collection of books, and Susan placed family photographs in frames around, plus some odd bits and pieces of porcelain, a couple of not-too-modern landscapes and a large porcelain pot holding a fern . . . which Ellie warned them would die in the centrally heated room.

The fern took no notice of what she'd said and thrived.

Meanwhile the old dining room adjusted to becoming Thomas's study and Quiet Room with some of the old library's bookcases re-erected there. The room immediately resumed the air of slight disorder which characterized Thomas's habitat wherever he went.

Monday to Friday morning

Ellie gradually worked through a long list of phone calls to make. First she contacted her solicitor about the Pullin house, which took some time. Then she phoned a locksmith to replace all the locks to which Hetty had retained the keys.

She organized cleaners and a plumber to start on the Pullin house when the contract was signed, and made an appointment to visit Monique's solicitor the following week. She spent time on the phone to the other members of the trust, updating them on what was going on.

She put off phoning Lesley for some time, but eventually did so. 'Is there any news on Hetty?'

Lesley said she'd checked the wills of the people who had left Thomas money, and found that in four of those cases, Hetty had also been left some money. As far as the police were concerned, this meant that Thomas could rest easy and accept the monies he'd been given.

Lesley added that they'd located the employment agency Hetty had been using, only to discover she'd left them without giving any notice. The police had tried the other local agencies, but there'd been no trace of the woman. No one seemed to know where she'd gone. It looked as if she'd left the area.

Lesley said that, in view of the cuts to public services, et cetera, the file on Hetty would not be closed, but the police would not actively seek to find her.

Ellie told herself that everything had worked out for the best, and that she should stop worrying. As a born worrier, she also knew that telling yourself not to worry never worked.

She worried about Thomas, who managed to get the magazine

off to the printers but wasn't picking up as quickly as she felt he ought to have done. He hadn't had a proper holiday for a couple of years and, although he talked about taking things more easily in future, he hadn't done anything about it.

Ellie also worried about Diana, who was being very quiet. Suspiciously so. There were no last-minute demands for Ellie to look after the children or to come up with money to support some new plan or other.

She worried about how long Rafael and Susan would put up with the present makeshift situation. They had fitted into the household remarkably well. Thomas taught Rafael how to change nappies! Rafael himself was out and about most days, Susan helped Ellie run the house and did most of the cooking while little Fifi thrived. She was happy whoever she was with, provided she could see what was going on. Put her in a room by herself, and she wailed till rescued.

Surely this state of affairs couldn't last? Surely Susan needed a kitchen of her own? And Rafael and Thomas needed their own separate telephone lines? And at some point the boiler needed to be changed, which meant more upset and anyway, they would need two boilers in future, wouldn't they?

Worse was the fact that every now and then Ellie had flashbacks to the time she found herself locked in a room at the top of the house, when no one knew where she might be.

She busied herself with work. Bob Pullin did actually bestir himself enough to get a valuer to look at the furniture in the house. This firm removed the few bits and pieces which were saleable and the house clearance people went in to deal with the rest.

On Wednesday night Ellie, Susan and their two husbands had a long discussion about dividing the house into two separate residences. They sketched this proposal and debated that. Gradually, the beginnings of a plan emerged as to what needed to be done. The next thing was to take their tentative ideas to an architect.

On Thursday the directors of the trust met in Ellie's sitting room, trying to make room for papers and people around the gateleg table. It was agreed that in future meetings would be held at the trust's offices, which might well need to expand to accommodate the extra work required in managing Monique's money.

It was also agreed that Rafael should be invited to join the board of trustees. Various other interesting matters were discussed, such as taking on the Pullin house and what the future might hold for Ellie's big house in the years to come.

Diana's demand that she be a director of the trust was mentioned and dismissed without discussion.

On Friday morning Ellie took her general manager and the trust's surveyor to meet Bob and Dawn Pullin at their stepmother's old house. First they needed to get the loan contract signed, and then Ellie and her staff had to consider whether or not the house might be a suitable project for the trust to take on. Agreement was quickly reached that the house appeared to be structurally sound, though in dire need of replumbing and rewiring.

It was agreed that the trust would now commission an architect to produce plans for the place to be turned into three self-contained flats. Tentatively, agreement was reached with the Pullins on a possible price.

Ellie left them to argue about details. She'd had enough of being businesslike and having to watch her words so that she didn't offend Bob Pullin.

She stepped out into the road. What next? Paperwork was piling up at home, and there was Diana's problem still to be addressed, but it was a fine day for once, and she wanted to be out in the sunshine.

She remembered Dawn Pullin saying that her stepmother had been at odds with an elderly neighbour. It would be only polite for Ellie to warn Her Next Door of the building work which was going to be necessary soon.

A sprightly little lady of some eighty years or so answered the door. Ellie said, 'I represent a trust fund which is proposing to buy the house next door and turn it into three flats. I'd like to apologize. I'm afraid there's bound to be more disruption and noise before the house can be occupied again.'

'Come in, come in. My name's Jermyn, by the way. Not that you need to know, but that's what it is. I find builders are always very helpful when I need a curtain rail put up that has come down, though my lodgers are good for changing light bulbs. I'm all alone today as they're off on holiday; Ibiza is it, or Lanzarote? One or the other. I was just about to have a cuppa. You'll join me, won't you?'

Mrs Jermyn' s house was a twin of the one next door, but better maintained and furnished. Ellie was taken down a cream-painted hall to a kitchen full of sunlight and modern equipment. Mrs Jermyn made Ellie a cup of instant coffee and switched off a radio which had been burbling away on a shelf on the wall.

Ellie said, 'I believe you used to get a lot of noise through that wall. I hope the new people will be quieter, for your sake.'

'These old houses. Well-built, but with odd spots where you can hear everything. Same as the bathroom upstairs. I sit there in the mornings thinking about things and everything's quiet as a mouse and then, just as I reach for the toilet roll, I hear her next door unrolling hers. The front rooms are all right. We've got the two halls between. It's just the kitchen and the bathroom upstairs. Mrs Pullin knew about it. Put her radio on that wall just to rile me. Turned the sound up. I used to go round and tell her at first but she didn't take no notice, so I put my own radio on the shelf this side of the wall, and found a cassette I could start with the volume turned up high, and there was a battle between us sometimes, I can tell you.'

Ellie had to laugh. 'You came off best, I assume?'

Mrs Jermyn beamed. 'Some rock and roll used to do it nicely. Took me back to me dancing days.'

'Her cats were a problem, too, I gather.'

'I quite like cats, but they used to do their business wherever I planted anything out, and they killed a whole nest full of baby robins last year. Broke my heart, that did.' Mrs Jermyn proffered a tin full of biscuits, most of them chocolate covered. Ellie accepted one with pleasure.

Mrs Jermyn said, 'I was sorry for her at the end, though. All that shouting. I thought she was having a row with someone in the family but apparently they all had alibis that night. The police thought I'd heard a soap opera on her radio instead. I said I knew the difference but they thought I was daft. It happens, when you get older. They think you've lost your hearing or your wits and shouldn't be sitting in a big house like this but be tucked away in a home for the elderly and incontinent.'

Ellie nodded. Yes, she knew that some people did think like that. She also recognized that Mrs Jermyn was nowhere near that state. 'Tell me about it.'

Mrs Jermyn sipped her coffee, which she took black without sugar or milk. Her eyes were on the wall behind her radio. 'When you're renovating next door, you might like to put some soundproofing material on that wall, upstairs and down.'

Ellie said, 'That's a good idea. I'll tell them.'

Mrs Jermyn's eyes lost their focus. 'You can tell the soaps by the accents, whether it's on the telly or the radio. There's always a mix of old and young, men and women, and you can hear the difference. Mrs Pullin was addicted to *The Archers*. Seven p.m. to seven fifteen. You could set your clock by it. I have my tea about half six, so that I can watch the cookery programmes on the telly later. When I've finished, I take my tray back into the kitchen and set the dirty dishes in a bowl of water in the sink, ready to wash up in the morning after breakfast. Then I make myself a nice pot of tea, and I'll be brewing up when *The Archers* started. Sometimes I'd bang on the wall when I heard that dratted music come on and she'd bang back, just for the hell of it. Not meaning anything serious. Then I'd take my tea into the front room, put the telly on, and that would be that for the evening.'

Mrs Jermyn sipped more coffee. 'You don't expect *The Archers* to come on at half past nine at night when you're filling your hot water bottle ready to take up to bed with you. I've got an electric blanket, but the switch is fiddly and I can put a hot water bottle just where it does most good under my bad leg, and that sees me through the night. I can't be doing with those switches that you turn this and you press that and I can never find the instructions. Plus, the hot water bottle is better for the environment, isn't it?'

Ellie picked up on the important point. 'The night she died, you heard *The Archers* come on at half past nine? No, that's not what you said. You heard shouting from her kitchen at half past nine?'

'Might have started earlier, but I heard it when I went out

to the kitchen to put the kettle on. It might have been going on for a while before. It wasn't *The Archers*, like those numb-skulls from the police said it was. It wasn't the radio. It was two women screaming at one another. Or rather, her, Mrs Pullin, shouting. I know her shout. Been living with it for years. The other one screamed, and it was a woman, yes. High-pitched. Screeching, rather than screaming. It went right through me. I nearly dropped the kettle. Then I banged on the wall. You can see the dent where I've been banging for years.'

They both looked at the wall, and yes, there was a dent in the plaster next to where the radio stood.

Mrs Jermyn said, 'I banged and I shouted, but they were going at it too hard to hear me. I thought that she was having a row with someone in her family so I didn't do nothing about it. I feel guilty about that. Someone stuck a knife in her that night. Or maybe it was an accident and she did it to herself, like the police said. I don't know which it was. But if I had gone round, I could have got help for her and she might not have bled out.'

'Did you have a key?'

'No, but you can't help thinking what if, can you? Anyway, while I was stood there, with the kettle in one hand and the hot water bottle in the other, wondering if I ought to do something or not, the screaming stopped and her wireless was switched on. So I thought, well, her visitor's gone and she didn't yell for help, so that's all right. I went up to bed and didn't think anything of it till the next morning when I came down and her wireless was still on, which it didn't ought to have been as she never got up as early as me. So I went round there and rang the bell and couldn't get no answer. I came back in and the radio was still playing. That's when I called the police. I've never had to call the police before. I kept thinking I was doing the wrong thing, that there'd be some mistake and Mrs Pullin would be annoyed with me for bringing the police in when there was nothing the matter with her. Only, there was. She was dead. Bled to death, they said. If I'd only gone round there.' Mrs Jermyn finished off her coffee and put the mug down on the table. 'But I didn't.'

'If you had gone round and she'd been stabbed by someone else, you might have been killed, too.'

'I know, I know. Nor I didn't have keys.'

'Who did have keys?'

'Her stepson and stepdaughter, though they didn't come round often. The cleaner must have had a set because I've seen her coming out and locking up behind her when she leaves. And there was some woman come from the social, or the church, was it? I think they used to let themselves in when they came. I've been thinking about it a lot. If I ever get so's I can't get to the front door to let someone in, then I'll have one of those boxes for keys put in the porch that you can only open if you have the combination.'

'Good idea,' said Ellie. 'It was definitely a woman you heard screeching?'

'It's that high, hysterical note you can't mistake. Not the radio.'

'The police didn't believe you heard people. They thought you heard the radio, right?'

'It was easier for them not to believe me, wasn't it? They said Mrs Pullin must have been listening to the radio and cutting something up for the cats when the knife slipped and she couldn't stop the bleeding. End of story. They looked at me and thought I was some old dear who'd slipped her cogs and mistook the time that *The Archers* come on. I told them and told them: the radio come on *after* the screeching stopped.'

Ellie tried to think it through. 'They proved it wasn't a member of the family with Mrs Pullin that night. They all had alibis. Who else would she have let in at that hour? Surely a cleaner wouldn't have called at that time, would she?'

'The cleaner could be on her way back from some other job, calling in to collect her wages, or dropping back some stuff that Mrs Pullin wanted from the supermarket. That's more likely than it being someone from the social because they don't work that late, do they?'

'Did the police talk to her cleaner, or enquire about someone visiting from the social?'

'If so, they didn't tell me. I got back to them a couple of times, and they said enquires were proceeding but that the family were out of it, and would I please shove off and plant some daisies. Or words to that effect.'

There was a tingle starting at the back of Ellie's neck. 'You think that she had a visitor who got into a fight and stabbed her? Or that Mrs Pullin stabbed herself by accident while her visitor was there? You think that when the visitor saw what had happened she panicked and, instead of calling for help, made herself scarce?'

'Mrs Pullin wouldn't have opened the door to anyone who didn't have a key after dark, unless she knew them. I asked the police if there was a bunch of keys missing, but they said they had everything in hand and I should have a sit down with a cup of tea.'

Ellie inched forward in her chair. 'The cleaner. What did she look like?'

A shrug. 'I only saw her once or twice, coming or going. She had keys. She was fiftyish maybe, all pepper and salt, fuzzy hair, dress and shoes. Not dirty, but not good clothing. Handbag by charity shop. Large shopping bag from the Co-op.' She inhaled sharply. 'You know her?'

Ellie rubbed her eyes. 'I might do. I knew someone like that once, and yes, I do think that person might well have got into a fight about something and lashed out, but I might be quite wrong. Did you hear her name, by any chance?'

'No. I weren't on visiting terms with Mrs Pullin, so she never told me, neither. You'll tell the police?'

'I would do if I were sure of the facts. I did tell the police that someone who answers to your description and whom I know as Hetty, played some tricks on me and my husband, and they've made enquiries, but she's moved on somewhere, no one seems to know where. The police have given up looking for her. She didn't actually murder anyone . . .' Ellie's voice died away. 'Or . . . you think she killed Mrs Pullin? Your neighbour might have cut herself after her visitor had gone.'

'I thought of that. I thought of a dozen different ways it could have happened. That she cut or stabbed herself, that this woman – whoever she was – and Mrs Pullin had a struggle over the knife for some reason and Mrs Pullin stabbed herself by accident. All I know is that they were both shouting at one another.

Then the shouting stopped and the radio came on. Nothing more till I heard the front door shut with a bang as the visitor left. I've told myself a dozen times that if you're alone and you hurt yourself badly, you do something about it. You scream. You reach for the phone. You bang on the party wall and yell for your neighbour to help you.'

'Unless you lose consciousness too quickly to do anything. It depends if you've cut an artery or not. Could you make out the words they were shouting at one another?'

'No. But if someone shouts "Help!" that's different from shouting in anger, isn't it? What I heard was anger. The thing is, if Mrs Pullin cut herself by accident, why didn't her visitor call for an ambulance?'

Ellie said, 'You've described the woman I know as Hetty to a T. If it is her, then that isn't the only time she's been faced with a dying person and then run away. She's never been caught, never been interviewed by the police. If only we had some idea where she went when she left me!'

TWENTY

Friday, noon, continued

M rs Jermyn looked at her fingers. 'My cleaner said . . . but she might be quite wrong. She's a dreadful gossip.'

'Your cleaner knows Mrs Pullin's cleaner?'

'Not to speak to, but she noticed her coming and going. She says, but she may be mistaken, she says that she thought she saw Mrs Pullin's cleaner go into the care home on the main road. The Cedars, it's called, though there's not a tree in sight. It's like my calling this house Oak Place, or Mansion or whatever. Someone had a flight of fancy, calling it that.'

'When was that?'

'Yesterday. I've been thinking about it, not sure what to do since the police took no notice of what I said. Now you turn up looking for her, and it looks like it was meant.'

'The Cedars,' said Ellie. 'Got it. You want me to go and have a look? And then what? Make a citizen's arrest?'

A grin. 'I've always wanted to do that, but I'm too old, now. I can't go chasing criminals down the road, yelling "Stop, Thief!" I don't own a pepper spray or a car so that I can tail villains to their lair like the detectives on the telly. I can only sit in my chair and think what I might have done if I were twenty years younger. I'll see you to the door, shall I? And you'll let me know what happens? I hate to miss the end of a good story.'

Ellie got to her feet and reached for her handbag. 'Life's not as tidy as that, but I promise to let you know if I find her.'

Ellie set off down the road, keeping her eyes open for Hetty. The houses in this street were all like Mrs Jermyn's and Mrs Pullin's. Each had its own small but usually well-tended front garden. It was a neighbourhood in which the occupants took pride in their property, had their weekly food shopping delivered from Waitrose or Tesco, sent their smallest children to nurseries, saw that their primary school offspring did their homework more or less, and considered recycling to be important.

Following Mrs Jermyn's instructions, Ellie came to a main road which boasted a small parade of shops. There was a deli, a Co-op, a dry cleaners, a hairdressers and a coffee shop. The Cedars stood some way along on the opposite side of the road. It was a modern, three-storey, purpose-built affair, with ample parking space in front. This would be a privately-run property and the residents would expect a sherry with their evening meal. It was exactly the sort of place in which Ellie might have expected Hetty to work. Wealthy people would pay to live there, ending their days in comfort.

Hetty was attracted to wealthy old people, wasn't she?

Could she have passed herself off as a qualified carer? No. She would be there as a cleaner, perhaps? Or as a cook on a minimum wage?

Ellie crossed the busy road and approached The Cedars. The front door was locked. Of course. Ellie tried the intercom and a disembodied voice asked who she wished to speak to.

Ellie said, 'I'm trying to track down my old housekeeper,

Hetty, who left without her last week's pay. Someone said they thought she was now working here.'

'Oh. Hetty. Yes. Well. She's cleaning on the top floor at the moment but will be free in half an hour at the end of her shift. Who shall I say wants to speak to her?'

Bingo! Hetty was still using her own name.

Ellie thought it wouldn't do any good to identify herself as Mrs Quicke, considering the circumstances under which Hetty had left. Well, why not say she was the widow of a man who had died under slightly suspect circumstances? Why not give Ellie's old friend Gwen Harris's name? Ellie didn't think Gwen would mind. An added benefit was that Gwen had said Hetty had only been employed after she, Gwen, had left the house, so Hetty would not know what Mrs Harris looked like.

Ellie bent closer to the intercom. 'Harris. Hetty looked after my husband, Harold, that was. I don't think Hetty was given her last week's wages. Also, I believe he meant to leave her something in his will. I'd like to check up that she got the money all right.'

'I'll tell her to ring you when she comes off duty, shall I?'

'I'm in the neighbourhood at the moment and I did rather want to see her. There's a coffee shop just down the road. Perhaps she'd like to join me for a cuppa when she comes off work?'

'I'll tell her.' The intercom clicked off. Ellie found her way to the coffee shop and took a seat at the back of the cafe so that Hetty wouldn't spot her immediately when she came in.

Ellie treated herself to a latte and a big wodge of Victoria sponge, home-made and beautifully light as well as tasty.

The main road was busy. Ellie amused herself by noting how busy it was. Two different bus services used the route. The pavements were thronged with shoppers. The cafe was popular with a mix of young mums and older, retired men and women. A nice little earner, clean and quiet. The musak wasn't intrusive, either.

Ellie pulled out her mobile phone and after a struggle with the technology – why did they have to keep 'improving' these gadgets? – managed to get through to her old friend, Gwen Harris.

'Gwen, it's Ellie. How are you doing?'

'A bit better, I suppose. I make myself walk around the block twice a day. Are you coming round for a cuppa this afternoon?'

'Can't today. I'll ring you tomorrow. Just one quick question. What's the name of your cleaner, the one who looked after Harold while you were away?'

'Um, dunno. Never met her. Hang on a mo. It was Henry. At least, I think that's what Harold called her. No, that's not right, is it? He got her from an agency, don't know which one. He said she had some poncey name that he couldn't pronounce, so he called her Henry.'

'Henrietta? Hetty for short?'

'Mm. Yes. That sounds about right. He said she cleaned better than me, and it's true the house was spotless when I got back. You know what he was like, had to have things just so. Did you want to contact her? I'm afraid I don't have the address. I gave all the bills to the solicitor and he dealt with them for me. I suppose I could ask him for her details, if it's important.'

'You don't remember whether or not Harold left Hetty some money in his will?'

'I didn't pay much attention. I remember there were lots of small legacies to charities and such. Surprising, really, as he never had much time for them in his life. Salvation Army, Cancer Research. You know the sort of thing.'

'Thanks, Gwen. It was just a thought. I'll be in touch tomorrow.'

Ellie considered a possible scenario. Hetty gets job with an elderly gent – Harold Harris – through an agency. Elderly gent complains that his wife, Gwen, has deserted him. He makes a will.

Why does he make a will? Because he realizes he's not immortal? Perhaps he's been prompted to do it by a friend . . . or by his cleaner?

Harold mentions he's making a will to Hetty, who suggests he might leave a little something to Thomas and herself along with other worthy causes. Harold is in a lot of pain, feeling sorry for himself. Hetty offers him some of her stash of tablets to ease his suffering. Elderly gent dies. Hetty loses her job but gets a windfall from his estate.

In this scenario, Hetty is not guilty of anything except passing on some medication which she had acquired legally.

The same might well have applied to other cases in which

she'd been involved. It wasn't a criminal offence to get herself and Thomas mentioned in various people's wills. True, she ought not to have passed on tablets prescribed for someone else and yes, she ought not to have kept tablets which she'd been asked to dispose of. But none of that amounted to murder.

Ellie wondered if Hetty had ever done anything which could be classed as murder.

Well, she'd fed tablets to Thomas which had put him in hospital. That was a criminal offence, surely . . . although a clever person could argue that Hetty had had no idea that Thomas had a susceptibility for the tablets he'd been given, and that they wouldn't have affected anyone else so badly.

Yes, Hetty had drugged Ellie and locked her in. That had been naughty but there had been no ill effects. Yes, Hetty might get a slap on the wrist for that if taken to court, but . . . murder? No.

Mrs Pullin? What had happened there? What had all the shouting been about? A knife had ended Mrs Pullin's life, but there was no proof that Hetty had been within five miles of the woman at the time. It had probably just been an accident.

Yet Ellie had a horrid feeling that Hetty and murder went together like sage and onion, or Darby and Joan. Only, there was no proof.

Ellie thought she might as well abandon her projected meeting with Hetty and go home, where there was plenty to do.

But here came Hetty, peering into the window of the cafe to see if she could spot Mrs Gwen Harris, whom she'd never met. There was no other older woman in the cafe sitting by herself, so with any luck Hetty would assume that Ellie was the unknown Mrs Harris. Ellie held the menu up before her face, so that Hetty couldn't immediately identify her.

Hetty fell for it. She picked her way through the tables to sit down opposite Ellie.

Ellie lowered the menu.

Hetty started to her feet, alarmed at facing someone whom she'd left, drugged and locked into an attic room.

Ellie said, 'Yes, it's me, and I'm here on behalf of Mrs Harris. Now, what would you like to eat, Hetty? They do an all-day breakfast here which looks good.' Ellie was counting on the fact that Hetty was always hungry, had just come off her shift at The Cedars and wouldn't yet have had time to eat lunch.

Sure enough, Hetty relaxed enough to resume her seat, though she looked ready to fly at the slightest threat. 'I meant no harm when I locked the door on you. I knew someone would let you out eventually.'

Liar, liar! Your pants are on fire!

Ellie signalled to the waitress. 'The all-day breakfast do you? With coffee or tea?'

'No, I don't want to . . . Perhaps an egg and cress sandwich and a coffee to take away?' She looked at her watch. A ruse? 'I don't have much time before my next job.'

The waitress took the order and Hetty relaxed another notch. 'How is Thomas? Still in hospital? I was sorry to leave you in that great big house without notice. Are you managing all right? Are you ready for me to come back?'

'Thomas spent some time in hospital and still has to be careful of his diet, but he's getting on all right.'

'Yes. Well.' Hetty glanced at her watch again. She was still very much on edge, but the twin lures of food and money kept her on her seat. 'Was it you who left a message for me at The Cedars? Some money I'm owed?'

'I've checked with Mrs Harris. She believes the agency would have paid you all the hours you worked, but she wants to be sure you received a legacy from her husband.'

Hetty held on to her large handbag with both hands but relaxed half a notch more. 'Well, yes. I was surprised, naturally. Good of him.'

'How much?' Ellie tried to speak casually, as if the answer didn't matter much.

'Oh, not as much as he gave Thomas.' Resentment made Hetty's mouth tighten. 'I thought Thomas deserved something, then. I didn't realize at the time what a horrible person he was.'

'It's good that Mr Harris remembered worthy causes at the end. Salvation Army, Cancer Research, Cats' Protection League—'

'Oh, he wasn't interested in cats. Nor dogs, come to think of it. He gave some money to refugees and clean water in Africa. Stuff like that.'

'And to you.'

Hetty bridled. 'Didn't I look after him when his wife had deserted him in his hour of need? Mary Poppins, everyone's favourite nurse, that's what he called me.'

'Because you were able to top up his pills so that he got a good night's sleep?'

'What if I did? That's what he wanted.'

Ellie felt very tired. 'Yes, I expect it was. You like to help other people when they're in pain, don't you, Hetty? How long have you been doing this?'

'Dunno. Some time. It started with Elsie and Lily.'

Ah-ha! Ellie concentrated. Elsie and Lily. They were the first people to leave Thomas something in their wills. 'They lived locally and he used to visit them, right? Did you look after them as well?'

'Of course. What silly sausages they were, fluttering around about how much they loved having dear Thomas visit them. They'd ring one another up and say how long Thomas had spent with them each time, as if it were a competition! So I said, one day, not really meaning it, that they should leave him something in their wills, and that's what they did!' She exuded satisfaction, which morphed into discontent. 'They didn't think of leaving me anything, the mean old things.'

'Did you help them to go to sleep?'

A shrug. 'What if I did? They were well past their sell-by dates, and always complaining about their aches and pains. They couldn't get a good night's sleep on what the doctor gave them, and I had these pills by me from when another of my ladies died. It's good to help people.'

'You do it whenever you see someone in pain? Like Councillor Thornwell. I understand he was in a bad way before he died. Drink, wasn't it?'

Hetty sighed. 'Poor man. The agency said he was difficult, but I never found him so. He had so many things wrong with him, diabetes, heart, liver, you name it. He'd divorced his wife when she took up with another man, and he drank so that he could forget his troubles. Then his dog had to be put down, poor thing. I told him, he should get another from the rescue place, but he didn't feel up to it.'

'Yes, someone told me he was fond of dogs.'

'He had this Labrador, a beautiful dog but smelly, some stomach problem, and it was getting on, nearly eighteen, was it? Something like that. Councillor Thornwell seemed to lose the will to live after the dog died. I found him slipping into a coma twice and managed to bring him round, but I couldn't watch him twenty-four hours a day, no one could. What with the whisky and the insulin and him getting muddled about which he'd taken . . .! He wasn't in his right mind at the end, you know. That last day he asked me to bring him in a bottle of whisky, and as I came through the door he grabbed it from me and poured some out. I said it was a bit early for a drink, wasn't it, and he said that was no business of mine and I was to get out and leave him in peace. So what was I supposed to do, eh? I left him. Of course I did. You'd have done the same. It was no skin off my nose if he tipped over into another coma and died. I never got paid for that whisky, neither.'

'Didn't you keep the receipt from the shop, and present it to the executors?'

'Well, no. He'd left me a bit in his will, you see. Not a fortune, but enough to cover the cost of the drink. Remembering that, I didn't feel I could ask for more. A sad day. Poor Councillor Thornwell. He had a nice house and all. His wife took a lot of the ornaments when they divorced and left it a bit bare, but that made it a pleasure to clean.'

'A tragedy,' said Ellie. 'One you couldn't have prevented.'

'I defy anyone to say I could. They simply don't know what they're talking about.'

'*Who* doesn't know what they're talking about? Someone you know?'

Hetty said, 'One of his old cronies. Stupid woman! Didn't know beans! How long had I been cleaning for her? Nigh on three years. She grudged every penny she gave me. She was like that man as turned everything to gold, never getting anything new, refusing to spend any money to keep the house nice, that damp patch on the landing was a disgrace, and as for her cats, the hairs were everywhere.'

'Do you mean Mrs Pullin? Was it she who accused you of helping Councillor Thornwell to an early death?'

'She did so! Rang me out of the blue and said as his solicitor had asked to see her because he'd done her will only that week and he'd noticed she'd left the same amounts to Thomas and to me as Councillor Thornwell, and he wanted to be sure she knew what she was doing.'

Ellie leaned back in her chair. So that was it! Mrs Pullin's solicitor had compared the wording of the two wills, found identical bequests and queried it with his client.

Hetty said, 'I couldn't understand what Mrs Pullin was making all that fuss about. Yes, I'd known she and Councillor Thornwell were both going to make their wills, and we'd talked about it a bit, which charities to give to, and all that. They'd both got plenty of money to give away and why shouldn't I come in for a bit, seeing as I'd worked for them for so long? And yes, I did suggest they leave a bit to Thomas, because in those days I was completely deceived as to his character and thought he deserved a bit of good luck. More fool me! If I'd known then what I know now, I'd never had suggested he get any money from anyone. But there, that's what happens when you're trying to do the right thing by people.'

Ellie felt slightly unwell. 'Mrs Pullin asked you to call in that evening? She wanted to know why you'd suggested Thomas's name to Councillor Thornwell and persuaded her to include both yourself and him in her will? Why did you go at that time of night? Why not wait till morning?'

'I was passing her house on my way home from the church hall where I'd been helping to clean up after a children's party. She didn't want to wait till morning. She was that mad! Round the bend! Called me all names under the sun, saying I'd been plotting with Thomas to fleece older people and that I was a money-grubbing slut and other words which I won't sully my mouth with repeating. She said she wanted me to know, then and there, that she was going to cancel that bit of her will the next day!'

Ellie was surprised into a laugh. 'She thought you and Thomas were in a plot together to . . .? No! Words fail me.'

'Stupid cow!' Hetty reddened. 'I could have had her up for libel—'

'Slander, not libel. Libel is written.'

'But would she listen? She was screaming at me, saying I was a wicked woman! She was holding this knife because she was cutting something up for the cats, and she poked it at me, and I grabbed her arm and took it off her in self-defence, of course I did. What else was I supposed to do! The stupid creature! But that didn't stop her! She swung her arms at me like a windmill. Then one of her dratted cats got between her feet and she fell forward on to the knife that I'd taken off her and was still holding. And that was that. It wasn't my fault.'

Silence. It never was Hetty's fault, was it?

Ellie said, 'Was there a lot of blood?'

Hetty nodded. 'Some. I had to step back sharpish not to get it on me. I stood there, waiting for her to get up and apologize for the awful things she'd been saying to me, but she didn't. She just sat there with the knife stuck in her and her holding on to it. I told her, I said that if she ever repeated that about Thomas and me again, I'd have her up in court. Then I walked out and went home. The nerve of the woman!'

Ellie ventured. 'You put the radio on before you left?'

Another nod. 'She was making silly noises, like, "Ugh, ugh!" So I said, "It serves you right," and I put the radio on so that her next door wouldn't hear Madam going, "Ugh, Ugh!"'

'Mrs Pullin bled to death.'

'Not my fault. Nothing to do with me.'

'You might have saved her, if you'd got an ambulance.'

'She attacked me. I didn't know she was going to die. It was all her own fault if she did.'

'I don't get why you turned the radio on.'

'I wasn't having her repeat those sinful words of hers to her next-door neighbour. Talking about me and Thomas like that! Anyway, she usually had the radio on when she was working in the kitchen.'

'The people around you are accident prone, aren't they? Mr Harris, overdosing on painkillers, left to die in his bed. Councillor Thornwell, fuddled with lack of insulin and provided with enough whisky to see him off. Mrs Pullin, mortally wounded after a tussle with you, left to bleed to death.'

'They chose their own deaths. I can't be responsible for how they chose to die.'

Ellie felt a surge of rage. 'You persuaded them to leave you some money in their wills. You fed them pills they ought not to have had—'

'I didn't force them to take anything, did I?'

'You knew you shouldn't hand out pills like that! You had a tussle with Mrs Pullin which caused her to stab herself! The crux of the matter is that you left those three people to die, knowing you were going to profit by their deaths. That's murder!'

'How dare you take that tone with me!' Hetty reddened. 'Old people die every day. That's what they do.'

'Deaths seem to follow you around. How many more people have you conned into leaving you money, and how much have you made out of them so far?'

'No business of yours!' Hetty struggled to her feet. 'I'll thank you to keep your evil words to yourself, or I'll see you in court for slander and libel or whatever it is.'

Ellie lost it. 'You can't walk away from this. You've as good as murdered at least three people!'

Hetty got a grip on the table and thrust up and forwards over Ellie's lap. Crockery and cutlery crashed to the floor. Fortunately Ellie had finished her cup of coffee, but she was pinned to her chair. Helpless.

Hetty screamed. 'You . . . you filth!' She thrust her way through the startled customers and dashed out into the street.

Head down, almost running.

The girl behind the counter shouted, 'Stop! What about your takeaway?'

A woman on the pavement side-stepped out of Hetty's way. 'Watch it!'

Hetty darted into the road.

There was a scream of brakes. A bus shuddered to a halt.

Someone shouted, 'No!'

Ellie tried and failed to push the table off her. She began to shake.

Voices, shouting. A child screamed.

Someone wailed, 'Oh, oh!'

A passer-by in the street took out his phone to call for an ambulance.

The traffic slowed to a halt, causing a honking of horns.

Ellie closed her eyes and told herself to breathe deeply. In. Out. In and out. She didn't know whether she hoped Hetty had survived her fall under the wheels of the double decker bus . . . or not. Possibly not if you judged by what people were screaming outside in the street.

An untidy end. If it were an end.

She wondered, if Hetty were indeed dead, who would inherit the money she'd so carefully managed to acquire.

The verdict for Hetty would be accidental death. She'd stepped in front of the bus, without looking. The verdict would be the same for everyone else she'd helped to die. For all the people who'd left Thomas money, as well.

Sanity would return to life. Soon.

TWENTY-ONE

Saturday morning

Ellie was about to make a sandwich for lunch when the newly repaired doorbell rang. It was a subdued but lengthy ring. Almost tentative.

Ellie had been expecting – or rather, dreading – to hear from Diana for some days. Usually Diana rang or descended on Ellie several times a week with demands for her to babysit or, worse, to help with her money situation, but there'd been neither sight nor sound of her.

Diana usually rang with a strong, long push. A demanding, strident push, announcing that she was a busy woman and ought not to be kept waiting. So this couldn't be her, could it?

But it was. Diana was wearing black, as usual, but she did not look quite her normal polished self. She didn't have either of the children with her, either. So this visit must be money matters again. Oh dear.

Ellie said, 'I was about to have some lunch. Would you—?'

'This won't take long.' Diana usually stalked everywhere but this time she walked at a reasonable pace into the sitting room and stood looking out on to the garden. It was raining, but not hard. The lawn still hadn't been mown.

'Coffee?'

A slight shrug. 'Don't bother. I wanted you to know. I got Evan to the doctor's in the end. There were tests, and more tests. The upshot of it is that he's been diagnosed with the onset of Alzheimer's. He's furious . . .!' She laughed, a harsh sound, and put her hands over her mouth to stifle the sound.

'I'm sorry.'

Diana stiffened her shoulders. 'I should have guessed. I did wonder, but . . . Anyway, it's confirmed. There's nothing much they can do.'

'And you with two young children.'

'They'll be all right.' A note of impatience. 'I'm working on Evan to give me power of attorney. He tried at first to put me off, but he's seen sense at last. We're getting everything signed tomorrow. He's making over the business to me, of course. I insisted on that. He hardly ever goes in nowadays, anyway. And, thanks to that odd friend of yours, Raffy or whatever he calls himself, I've managed to offload our option on the development down by the river, so we're clear of debt. We'll manage.'

Ellie withheld a sigh. Diana had a history of making bad business decisions but she did seem to be doing the best for the family in the present circumstances.

Ellie said, 'I am so very sorry.'

Diana said, 'I've made my bed and must lie on it. Isn't that what you're always telling me? You warned me about marrying Evan but I went ahead and did it, anyway. You thought I was marrying him just for his money and there was that, of course. But also, I'm fond of him, and respect him . . . Or rather, I used to, but now . . . He has temper tantrums, like a two-year-old. I do worry about him. It hurts to see him fumbling for words and forgetting . . .' She stopped and put her hand over her eyes for a moment. 'Go on. Laugh, why don't you? Me, the Iron Maiden, weeping over a man.'

Ellie marvelled. Was Diana really crying for her husband?

Ellie lifted her hand to place it on her daughter's shoulder, and then let it drop. Diana did not like to be touched.

Diana rolled her shoulders to release tension. 'They say it can take years to develop or take you over like a galloping horse. This is the galloping kind. I will *not* shove him into a home. I will *not* have the children distressed. I'm thinking of employing a couple to live in and look after him when I'm at work, because I will have to continue working.'

Ellie was cautiously approving. 'That seems like an excellent idea.'

'But expensive. Which is why I came. The trust owns the house, right? I've been looking into the accounts and I can't see that Evan has been paying rent for the last couple of years, even though he's supposed to have done so. You may say I should downsize, but if I do, I wouldn't be able to offer free accommodation to the carers whom we are going to need and I would have to stay at home to look after him and the children, which means there'd be no money coming in.'

Monique had known Evan hadn't been paying rent, and she hadn't left instructions to sell the house over his head. So Monique had still had a soft spot for her ex-husband? Which meant that Ellie had some leeway in this matter?

Diana said, 'Do you think you could see your way to cancelling the arrears? If so, I am hopeful I can manage the rent in future.'

'Let me have a copy of the doctors' report to take to the trust and I will see what can be done. No promises, mind. There's always some maintenance work to be done on houses new and old, and that has to be paid for somehow.'

Diana nodded. She didn't say 'thank you'. As far as she was concerned, she had made a sensible proposal and Ellie had agreed to it. 'I'm afraid I won't have time to join the trust.'

Ellie said, 'You have two beautiful children, a lovely house and plenty of work to do. You'll manage.'

'You'll help me out if I get into difficulties? Not that I expect to do so, of course.'

Silence. Ellie didn't know how to answer that.

Diana flushed. 'Oh, isn't that typical of you? Just when I could do with some support.'

'I think,' said Ellie, feeling her way towards the truth, 'that you are a remarkable woman with many talents. You have proved your worth as a wife and as a mother. You are courageous. You are making the right decisions for the future. You have made mistakes in the past but you have learned from them, which a lot of people never do. I don't think you need me or the trust to fall back on. Realistically it's not going to be helpful for you to think you can always call on me to help you out of trouble. You have to accept that the trust has been set up in such a way that that is not possible. You can ask us for advice, but don't ask us to bail you out if you make another misjudgement. In my opinion, you have reached a point where you are ready to fly all by yourself.'

Diana almost spat the words, 'Some mother you are!'

'Yes,' said Ellie. 'I am the mother hen who is pushing her daughter out of the nest, as you will have to do for your own children eventually.'

Diana wept, open-mouthed and ugly. 'Everything is so . . .!'

Again Ellie lifted her arm to give Diana a hug and dropped it, knowing Diana would not welcome the caress.

Diana sniffed. She used her handkerchief and said, 'Well, time and tide wait for no one. I must go. Busy, busy. People to see. Children to collect from this place and that.'

She made for the door only to be met in the hall by Susan with Fifi in her arms.

Diana said, 'What! What is she doing here?'

Ellie said, 'Living here. Thomas is finding someone to take over the magazine. He and I are retiring, going on a long visit to Canada. I'm making the house over to the trust, though Thomas and I have the right to live here or elsewhere rent-free for the rest of our lives. The trust will pay for builders to divide the house into two, with separate plumbing and wiring. Architects have been contacted and are working on the plans as we speak. There'll be a new entrance and stairs for next door, our old Quiet Room will become Susan's kitchen, and the top flat will be let out separately, with its own new outside stair and entrance.'

Diana gasped. 'You'd never get planning permission for all that.'

'As the pressure on the housing list increases, so permission is easier to get. Legitimately with no hidden fees. You, of all people, should know that.'

Mm, that was a blow below the belt, wasn't it? But well deserved.

Diana clutched at her head. 'But . . . what happens to the other half? Can I have an option on that? It ought to come to me, anyway.'

'Rafael and Susan will be paying rent and living there for as long as they wish.'

Diana froze, her gaze fixed on Susan and the baby in her arms. Finally, she said, 'You're Susie, yes? With a baby, too. And you have a husband who is able to support you? I suppose I should offer my congratulations. You've managed to worm your way in here where I have failed.'

Diana let herself out of the house, closing the door quietly behind her.

Susan said, 'Ellie, are you all right? Here, hold Fifi for a moment while I put the kettle on.'

Ellie took the warm little bundle and began to sway from one foot to the other. It was very calming, nursing the baby.

Fifi opened her eyes and yawned. Her tiny fingers clutched the air. She smiled up at Ellie . . . or perhaps it was just wind.

Ellie began to sing, 'Rock a bye, baby . . .'

Fifi loved to be sung to. She didn't care whose voice it was. It could be Ellie's soprano, Susan's alto, Rafael's tenor or Thomas's bass. If she had a preference, it might be for Thomas's double bass. Rafael said he'd heard there was an opera singer in his family somewhere along the line, a great aunt or something like that. Perhaps Fifi had a musical bent.

Ellie recalled that Diana had never wanted anyone to sing to her. What a shame. But that was all in the past. Of course Ellie would keep in touch with Diana and all her beloved grandchildren, but the future was Thomas in a more manageable house. The future included more people to love and worry about: Rafael, Susan and Fifi. It was looking bright.

Susan called out, 'I'm making egg and cress sandwiches for lunch with some of my home-made leek soup. Also, I think we've still got some chocolate cake left over. You'd like some?'

Silly question. Of course she would.